Alistair MacLean's UNACO series

By John Denis
Hostage Tower
Air Force One is Down

By Alastair MacNeill
Death Train
Night Watch
Red Alert
Time of the Assassins
Dead Halt
Code Breaker

By Hugh Miller
Prime Target
Borrowed Time

Alistair MacLean was the bestselling author
of thirty books including the world-famous
The Guns of Navarone and *Force 10 from Navarone.*

Alistair MacLean's UNACO

BORROWED TIME

HUGH MILLER

Alistair MacLean's UNACO

Borrowed Time

HarperCollins*Publishers*

HarperCollins*Publishers*
77–85 Fulham Palace Road,
Hammersmith, London W6 8JB

Published by HarperCollins*Publishers* 1997
1 3 5 7 9 8 6 4 2

A catalogue record for this book is
available from the British Library

ISBN 0 00 225549 9

Set in Meridien by
Rowland Phototypesetting Ltd,
Bury St Edmunds, Suffolk

Printed and bound in Great Britain
by Caledonian International
Book Manufacturing Ltd, Glasgow

To Nettie,
and to both generations of the kids

Acknowledgements

I am grateful to Hasan Mantu and Desmond Hare for all the dope on Kashmir, to Reg Godwin who demystified digital cameras, and to Tamara Drake for explaining covert image transmission.

My thanks also to Sarah Leigh, who worked hard on my behalf and was always kinder than she had to be.

ONE

═══════════════

Malcolm Philpott's attention was fixed on the television screen. He stared, unblinking, as the CNN camera panned across a pocket of hand-to-hand fighting and showed a mercenary sticking a knife in the chest of a Bosnian rebel. Over by the door behind Philpott, Secretary Crane gasped.

'Brainless carnage,' he hissed.

They were in the semi-dark of Philpott's office, watching a video Philpott had switched on a moment before Crane entered. He had come in soundlessly, without knocking. He was known throughout the Secretariat building as Creeper Crane.

'The footage is sixteen hours old,' Philpott said. 'An orchestrated local outburst we'd been expecting.'

'Where?'

'South of Banja Luka. The men in grey battledress are our people, Task Force Four.'

Desmond Crane stood with his back almost touching the door. His sallow skin looked tanned in the half-light from the shaded window. He winced as a TF4 man side-stepped a rifle-swipe and spun sharply, kicking his attacker in the ribs. Behind them another UNACO operative head-butted a mercenary who fell in the churned mud of the roadway.

'Do you watch much of this stuff?' Crane said, his words clipped, conveying censure.

'Only what I have to. It pays to keep in touch. You weren't suggesting,' Philpott added coldly, 'that I would watch combat footage for recreation?'

'Heavens, no.' Crane smiled, but his eyes stayed reproachful.

Philpott tapped his handset and the screen went blank. He pointed the remote at the window and touched another button.

1

The vertical slats of the blind turned smoothly inward and the room brightened.

'So.' Philpott got behind his desk. 'How can I help Policy Control?'

Crane laid a photograph face up on the desk in front of Philpott. It was a snapshot, black and white, and it showed Philpott himself, walking on a Manhattan street.

'This must have been taken at least three years ago.' Philpott picked it up and studied it. 'That's the amount of hair I still had in 1994, and the chalkstripe suit went to the Salvation Army shop when I changed apartments a month before Christmas that year.' He looked up at Crane. 'What's the significance?'

'The picture was found by an NYPD detective among the possessions of a man called Arno Skuttnik who died last night.'

'How did he die?'

'Of a heart attack, in his one-room apartment at Waverly Place in Greenwich Village. You knew him, perhaps?'

'The name isn't familiar.'

'Look at the writing on the back of the picture.'

Philpott turned it over. In smudged, pencilled longhand it said: *Malcolm Philpott, Director of the United Nations Anti-Crime Organization (UNACO)*.

'So he knew who I am.'

'Indeed.'

'Who was he?'

'A seventy-year-old porter at the Washington Square Hotel. An immigrant who came to New York in 1964. Nothing exceptional is known about him – then again, nothing much *at all* is known about him.'

Philpott nodded patiently. 'Do you think maybe he was engaged in espionage?'

'Not at all. We're pretty sure he never broke the law once in the thirty-three years he lived in New York.'

'So what's the problem?'

Crane stared. 'I should have thought that was obvious.'

Philpott stared back. Crane was a man of middle years, roughly the same age as himself, but he possessed none of Philpott's natural authority. Crane always had to reach for an effect. The reaching put him under strain, and it never failed to show.

'Don't you find it extraordinary, and a trifle alarming,' he said, 'that a porter in a Greenwich Village hotel had in his possession a photograph that identifies you as the Director of UNACO?'

'Well, no . . .'

Crane's mouth twisted. It was meant to be scornful, but again it was mainly strain that showed.

'UNACO is not a secret organization,' Philpott said. 'True, we don't advertise our existence. Our offices are unmarked, our phone numbers are not listed, and our agents and employees never acknowledge their affiliation. Our profile is minimal, but secret we are not.'

'Yet this man, this porter, found out who you are.'

Philpott shrugged. 'I have no theories about how he did that. But it wouldn't have been too difficult, if he was determined.'

'And why did he want to know about you?'

'I have no theories about that, either.'

'The department is very unhappy with this, Mr Philpott . . .'

'The department?'

'Policy Control. We can't accept a situation where a senior officer of a sensitive department in the United Nations is so . . . so careless in his conduct of his affairs that any riffraff can find out what his job is and even take pictures of him on the street.'

Philpott stood up and came around the desk. He was smiling one-sidedly, a clear sign of displeasure.

'I don't really care how Policy Control feels about the way I run my life. To be frank, in my day-to-day awareness of this vast environment we share, your department seems scarcely to exist.'

Crane looked as if he had been punched. 'I think it would be easy enough,' he blustered, 'to demonstrate Policy Control's existence, and the way in which it enforces revisions of departmental procedure within the UN structure. That includes

3

departments which grandly imagine themselves to be above any form of restraint or governance.'

'Mr Crane, I am accountable only to two people. They are the Head of the Security Council, and the Secretary General of the United Nations. That's it. I explain myself to no others. Now if you'll excuse me . . .' Philpott pointed to the door. 'I've got real work to do.'

Crane stumped to the door and jerked it open. 'I'll tell my director what you said, and that you show no willingness to co-operate.'

Philpott nodded, going back behind the desk. 'You can also tell your director that I made a suggestion.'

'Which is?' Crane demanded.

'That you whistle Dixie through any orifice of your choice.'

Crane jumped aside as C. W. Whitlock strode into the office.

'Morning, gentlemen,' he said breezily.

Crane went out and slammed the door.

Whitlock put a folder on Philpott's desk. 'What's wrong with The Creeper?'

'There's a leak in his self-importance. What have you got?'

'A heartfelt letter from a missionary in the Vale of Kashmir.' Whitlock flipped open the folder.

'Not another one of your cries for help?'

'Smart of you to guess, sir.'

Whitlock was an instantly likeable man, in nature and appearance. He was a native Kenyan whose white grandfather's genes had bestowed a light umber skin, a strong jaw and a firm mouth, which Whitlock softened with a moustache.

'The letter was sent to the Security Council, they passed it along to us. Do you want to read it?'

'Later, perhaps,' Philpott said. 'Summarize for me.'

Whitlock leafed down through the documents to find the letter and his notes. Philpott couldn't help watching him. He was incredibly fastidious in his movements, a man who had been described by a former Secretary General as fitting his role so well that it might have been moulded around him. He breathed aptitude.

4

'Here it is.' Whitlock put the letter on the desk with the notes alongside. 'It's from the Reverend Alex Young, a Church of England priest. He runs a medical and teaching mission at Shahdara, a village near the town of Tangmarg in the Vale of Kashmir.'

'What does he want?'

'He's asking the UN to do something to curb the growing violence of the Muslim separatists, and the increasing influence of drug peddlers in the region. In a recent flare-up a local doctor's gardener was killed. The doctor in question is Simon Arberry, an American, who's doing big things with his public medical centres.'

'There was something in *Scientific American* . . .'

'Currently the Arberry Foundation is setting up a free hospital for the people of the region,' Whitlock said. 'Anyway, among Reverend Young's other concerns, he seems worried that the unrest and physical danger might drive the good Dr Arberry out of the area, which would set the public care programmes back a long way.'

Philpott picked up the top page of the letter. '"This is one of the most serenely beautiful places in the world",' he read aloud. '"It is a perfect spot to live, but the increase in drug trafficking and the disruptive influence of the extremists, fomenting ill feeling between Indian and Pakistani elements, threaten to plunge the region into bloody war."'

He put the page back. 'That's hardly news to the UN,' he said. 'Most of our observers know the root of the trouble lies west of Kashmir.'

'Afghanistan.' Whitlock nodded. 'I gather it all started for real when the Russians left.'

'The last Soviet troops pulled out of Kabul in 1989, and since then Afghanistan's turned into a breeding ground for Islamic activist groups. Nobody's clear on the details of the various schisms and squabbles, but they do involve territorial ambition, much of it centring on Kashmir.'

Whitlock looked at his notes. 'A number of activist-terrorist groups are keen to extend the Pakistani-held Azad region of

Kashmir to absorb the Indian-held areas. Some of them even want to take away the north-eastern territory, which has been occupied by China since 1962.'

'Lord,' Philpott breathed. 'Can you imagine what that might lead to?'

Whitlock rummaged in his notes. 'I have a status bulletin filed with the Security Council in August 1996.'

There was a tap on the door. It opened and Mike Graham put his head round the side. He looked troubled.

'How's the report coming?' Philpott asked him.

'There's been a serious emergency,' Mike said.

Philpott and Whitlock stared at him, waiting. Mike came into the room and closed the door. He wore jeans, cowboy boots and a black cotton shirt. He pushed the fingers of both hands through his dark hair.

'My coffee machine broke down,' he said.

Philpott grunted and waved at his miniature Gaggia machine on the long sideboard. 'Help yourself.'

Whitlock found the Security Council status bulletin.

'The meat of it is, in the summer of '96 a number of Islamic extremists, trained in Afghan terrorist camps, were infiltrating the Pakistani and Indian regions of Kashmir, rousing the rabble, spreading the message that Kashmir is rightly the territory of Muslim Pakistan.'

He ran his finger down the sheet and read out a section. '"Also, by sporadic acts of assassination and sabotage, they cause civil unrest and increasing disquiet among beleaguered minorities. The authorities in India and China, meanwhile, fear the loss of control."'

Mike Graham came across with his cup of coffee. 'Do I smell work?'

'Too early to say.' Philpott looked at Whitlock again. 'Any conclusions in the bulletin?'

'They said the problem still wasn't serious, but events had to be watched closely. Any corrective steps taken by the Indian or Chinese authorities, or by both, could result in widespread conflict.'

'This is the Islamic campaign in Kashmir you're talking about?' Mike said.

'Well spotted, Michael,' Philpott said. 'So you don't just read motorbike magazines all the time.'

'Sure I do. But I have my radio on a lot and things filter through. What's the pitch?'

As group leader of UNACO Task Force Three, Mike was entitled to know. Whitlock told him about the letter from Reverend Young.

'Could I study a copy?'

'Oh, use the photocopier, too, while you're here,' Philpott said. 'And if you can spare the time, I've got a new shoe-polisher that might divert you for a while.'

'What do you think?' Mike said. 'Is this a case for us?'

Philpott wasn't sure. 'We are an anti-crime organization. The crimes cited here are big enough to be classified as aggressive political activity, and that's not our bag.'

Whitlock nodded. 'Pretty much what I thought.'

'But, as ever,' Philpott said, 'I'll consider the matter, I'll think long and hard about it, and I'll issue a decision before the end of the week.'

Mike brought back the letter from the photocopier and handed it to Whitlock.

'Have you any special interest in Kashmir?' Philpott asked.

'Not really.' Like Whitlock, Mike radiated an amiable charm which he often used to deflect other people's curiosity. He did that now. He smiled and shrugged. 'You know me, sir. I like to keep up to speed on what's being thrown our way.'

'Fine,' Philpott said, 'as long as it doesn't interfere with the speed of your report.'

As Mike left the office Philpott told Whitlock he had a favour to ask. 'I want a thorough, confidential investigation into the background of a man called Arno Skuttnik who died, apparently of natural causes, at his lodgings in the Village last night. Make use of any resources you need. Keep all the details of your enquiry strictly off-record.'

'Can I ask what it's about?'

7

Philpott frowned for a moment. 'Yes, all right.'

He told Whitlock about the snapshot, and how Secretary Crane was intent on using it as a lever to apply restrictive legislation against UNACO. 'It's a tiny problem at present, but soon enough we may need all the help we can get.'

Whitlock picked up his folder. 'I'll see what I can do, sir.'

TWO

Inside UNACO Mike Graham was known to be a fiercely practical operator, a man of action. A top-level UN communiqué of November 1996 described him as 'a swift, focused instrument of international law and order'. He was a man who would have attracted medals had he served in a conventional army. His superiors and his colleagues knew all that, but what they remembered most about Mike Graham was that, years ago, terrorists had murdered his wife and baby son.

The drawn-out agony of his loss damaged Mike brutally, and for months afterwards he was beyond consolation. When grief had finally run its course he moved from New York to Vermont and there he took up a solitary off-duty existence – tranquil, controlled, relatively happy. That outcome was achieved, in great part, by the patient friendship of Lenny Trent, an agent of Drugwatch International. Now, an hour after reading the letter from Reverend Young in Kashmir, Mike was suddenly reminded of his old friend.

The clergyman's letter had stirred a buried ache. On a computer in the Secure Communications Suite, Mike called up the UNACO records archive. A quick title-search produced a memo from the World Health Organization – known internally as WHO – which gave details of a haul of highly refined drugs taken from a farm worker travelling to south China from the Vale of Kashmir. The drug courier had killed himself before he could be interrogated.

Mike prompted the system for more details, and up popped the name of his buddy, Lenny Trent. It was at the top of a telex from Drugwatch International marked for the attention of the Secretary General, WHO:

Origination Date – 28 December 1996. Source – agent Lenny Trent. Message reads:

Two heroin mules arrested today at the border of Burma and Thailand were from the Vale of Kashmir. Both were first-time offenders, carrying *exceptionally* fine H. While detained pending interrogation both swallowed potassium cyanide. Trail now as dead as they are.

Mike checked with Drugwatch International, a UN affiliated body, and learned that Trent was currently in Seattle, preparing a case against a Chilean drug runner caught importing cocaine inside hundreds of fish destined for the Pike Place Market.

Mike called Seattle; Lenny's assistant got a message to her boss, who was interrogating a courier; Lenny sent back word that if Mike could get to Seattle for ten the next morning, he would have an hour free. A rendezvous was set up.

Next morning Mike boarded a Washington-bound heli-shuttle on the roof of the UN Secretariat building. He was in Seattle by 9:45, and at two minutes to ten a taxi delivered him to the Seattle Art Museum on University Street. He entered the building, made his way to the café, and found Lenny Trent waiting at a table on the far side of the room.

'I got you coffee,' Lenny said, standing, spreading his arms wide. 'Let people talk. Gimme a hug.'

They embraced, slapping each other on the back. 'You never write,' Lenny said as they sat down. 'You never phone . . .'

'I keep meaning to. And yesterday I did.'

'Because you need to know something, or you want a favour.'

'Yeah. Well.' Mike tasted his coffee and shrugged.

Lenny grinned. He was short, wiry, with big grey eyes behind Armani steel-framed glasses. His hair, exposed for most of each year to tropical and subtropical sun, was lighter on top than at the sides.

'One question before we hit business,' he said. 'Are you OK?'

'I'm fine.'

'Truly? Where it matters?'

'Truly. I miss my wife and my son every day of my life. They

10

are my last thought before I sleep, always. But that's as it should be. I'm OK. I function, I can entertain hope, and I've a strong impulse to survive.'

'Even though you're in a suicidal occupation.'

'Even though.'

'Good. I needed to know that.'

'And you?'

'Still divorced. Still drinking. Still hoping for a change, and still working too hard to do anything but go with the current.' Lenny slapped the table gently. 'To business. How can I help you?'

'I have to tell you a story first,' Mike said. 'I'll try and keep it interesting. It's about a bully-boy called Paul Seaton. You remember in 1984, when the US began to help the mujahedin to fight the Soviets in Afghanistan? One of the key figures in that operation was Paul Seaton, a New Yorker from the Lower East Side. A very, very tough character. He was dropped into Kandahar to train Afghan rebels in the use of advanced weapons.'

'I've a fuzzy recollection,' Lenny said, flapping his fingers at the side of his head. 'Was there a CIA connection somewhere?'

'I'll get to that. Paul Seaton was a hard instructor, even by mujahedin standards. To graduate from the first stage of his combat course you had to shoot down a Russian helicopter with a ground-to-air Stinger missile. If the pilot survived, you had to kill him with your bare hands.'

'I heard about that. The Reagan administration sat on the details, but George Bush's boys finally blew the whistle about what went on out there in the name of democracy.'

'Seaton was unquestionably a talent,' Mike said. 'He had a genius for subversion, but he had never been stable. In 1986 he was known to be turning to Islam, and in 1987 he went native. He vanished into the hills with his own murderous little group of fundamentalists. At that time he declared he was a sworn enemy of the government of Afghanistan *and* the mujahedin movement. And that was the last official news of him.'

Mike paused to take a mouthful of coffee.

'Two years ago, however, on a satellite picture taken on a routine pass over Amritsar in northern India, somebody looking a lot like Paul Seaton showed up at the head of a drug convoy travelling through the hills north of the city.'

'Well, well.' Lenny was suddenly more alert. He pushed his spectacles along his nose. 'For a long time our people in India and Pakistan have been catching rumours about an American who runs drug convoys. His main route, allegedly, is along the border with Pakistan and Kashmir, then down the western territories of India as far as Firozpur in the Punjab. Until now, I was inclined to dismiss the stories as myth.'

'Seaton's real, no mistake. And I've studied the satellite picture enough times to be sure it's him leading the horse convoy.'

'So,' Lenny said, 'apart from a professional curiosity about criminal developments, what's your special interest in Seaton?'

Mike made an effort to look blank. 'It's nothing I'd call special.'

'Aw, come on . . .' Lenny was openly sceptical. 'I know you, remember? I know your different kinds of intensity. And I could do a monograph on your grades of determination. Tell me straight – are you harbouring one of those fashionable private agendas? Or a plain old personal grudge?'

'I might be. Let's just say Paul Seaton is owed a comeuppance. It's been owed a long time, but certain recent events mean there's an outside chance I can maybe do something about it.'

'Even up the score?'

'Something like that.'

'What do you want me to do?'

'Find out all you can about Seaton. If he's in the drug trade, you're the man to find out more.'

'I'll do what I can. Leave it with me.' Lenny looked at his watch. 'Let's have some more coffee. Then we can swap gossip until it's time for me to go back and terrorize another dope courier.'

UNACO occupied an entire floor of the Secretariat building on the UN's East River site. Two hundred and sixty employees, eighty of them specialists, handled the daily administration of

12

the world's most efficient crime-fighting body. Thirty prime-rated field agents, recruited from international police and intelligence agencies, formed the core of the ten Strike Forces, and each Strike Force had its own suite of rooms within the network of UNACO departments. On his return from Seattle, Mike went directly to Strike Force Three's 'withdrawing rooms', as Philpott called them.

To get there he had to pass through General Communications, a big, buzzing room filled with computers, telex machines, printers and satellite TV receivers. The department was staffed by twenty multilingual operators and twenty-three communications technologists, all of them women.

As Mike passed through, nodding and smiling from one desk to another, he saw what he was used to seeing: polite curiosity behind the warm smiles, a subtle prying as one individual after another looked for signs of pain still burning in him.

Behind the mahogany door with TF3 lettered on it, Mike sat down at one of the computers. He took a Zip disk from his shirt pocket and inserted it into the drive slot. A copy of Reverend Alex Young's letter came up on the screen. Mike read it again, picturing the scenario, trying to view it from the standpoint of a priest dedicated to the nurture of a place and its people.

I risk repeating myself, Reverend Young wrote, *when I say the Vale of Kashmir is an area of exceptional beauty, both physical and ethereal, a centre of harmony and growth, and it breaks my heart to foresee what the signs make plain – this wonderful place being sundered and ultimately destroyed by the incursions of greed, corruption, and brute violence.*

Mike sat back. He pictured Paul Seaton somewhere near the centre of that avarice and graft and brutality. The picture was easy to conjure.

He took out the Zip disk and tapped a command key marked SECURE CONFERENCING. A box appeared onscreen and invited him to enter a telephone number; simultaneously a tiny red light mounted on the camera atop the screen lit up.

Mike entered the number of CIA Records at Langley, Virginia. After a moment a screen announcement told him he was connected; who did he wish to talk to? Mike entered the name Joshua Flynn. A pause, then a white square appeared onscreen, which turned quickly to a live colour picture of a thin-faced, exceptionally gloomy-looking man. The dolour vanished and he smiled widely as two-way visual contact was established.

'Mike!' The voice was alarmingly realistic over the computer's sound system. 'Where have you been? It's so long since we spoke, I thought you must have defected.'

'There's no place left to run, Josh. How're you doing?'

'In spite of the wishes of my contemporaries, I must say I've thrived.' Flynn waved an arm at the shelves and machinery ranged behind him. 'I'm in charge these days. I'm one of only three men at Langley with all-level access to the files. If you forget how many lumps of sugar you take in your coffee, give me a call, we'll have a record of it here somewhere.'

'I'm chasing a favour, Josh.'

'I can't imagine any other reason why you'd call.'

'A man by the name of Paul Seaton. He was –'

'An employee of this agency,' Josh cut in. 'I knew him reasonably well, for a time. What do you need to know?'

'Background stuff, leading up to the time he took off and became a bandit.'

'You on to him for something?'

'I could be, with luck. Just in case the luck holds, I'd like to know as much about him as I can.'

'I could tell you most of it from memory,' Flynn said, 'but let's be professional about this, right? I'll call up the file. One second, Mike.'

It took four seconds. Flynn studied the printout, nodding.

'OK. A summary of the known career of Paul Elliot Seaton, who will now be forty-three years old.' Flynn put down the summary and looked directly out of the screen at Mike. 'From the time Seaton left college he put himself at the disposal of people with power, the kind of power he knew he could never generate himself. He was open about his technique – he once told me his motto for getting on in life was "Find the engine you need and hitch a ride". Anyway, Paul was pre-eminently

14

physical, he wasn't hampered by a conscience. He worked as errand-boy and muscle for several small and medium-sized politicians until an opportunity came along to join the CIA.'

'Who gave him the opportunity?'

'It was a recommendation from a grateful relative of our first director, Allen Welsh Dulles.'

'He did somebody a big muscular favour.'

'I'd guess so,' Flynn said. 'The job he got here carried no guarantee or likelihood of promotion, but Paul Seaton got to do harm, and he got to carry a prestigious ID that showed he was a legitimate employee of the Agency. For three years he was a happy young man. Then in 1977 Jimmy Carter arrived, and he directed a fresh administration to put tight controls on the clandestine activities of the CIA. A month later Paul Seaton was out of a job.'

'How did he get involved with the mujahedin initiative in Afghanistan?'

'Well, he wasn't a lot more than a dogsbody around here,' Flynn said, 'but one or two people at the Pentagon kept records of those boys from Langley who'd distinguished themselves in situations calling for, quote, effective physical action, unquote. Seaton had drawn attention to himself for some of the things he got up to in Cuba and Chile, and so, within a month of getting his can kicked out of the CIA, the former gofer-bodyguard-enforcer-saboteur had himself a new job with the military.'

'Did you see him at that time?'

'Once. While he was doing his three-month training at a government facility in the Ozarks. I went there with a pair of our covert operations people for a briefing on Project Kandahar, as they called it. I spoke to Seaton for a couple of minutes. He was full of himself, full of the mission ahead. He was mustard-keen to get over there and start teaching bodily assault and slaughter.'

'He was the man for the job,' Mike said, then quickly added, 'or so I gather.'

'Yeah. When I asked the fellow in charge just what it was that Seaton and the others were training to do, he said, "They're

15

gonna teach one group of Neanderthals how to exterminate another group of Neanderthals, in the interest of maintaining a balance of power consonant with the needs and purposes of the United States."'

'But Seaton didn't shape up the way they imagined he would, right?'

'He'd been in Afghanistan only three or four months,' Flynn said, 'when he discovered an inborn leaning to fanaticism. He also found he had an aptitude for the life of a brigand. After the end of his tenth month in Kandahar, he severed all contact with the military.'

'And what do you know about his present activities?'

'Nothing. There have been rumours he's into drug running, hill banditry, kidnapping, all the usual stuff villains get up to in the stretch of territory from Kabul to Chittagong. Nothing has ever been substantiated, and frankly he doesn't fall within our sphere of interest.'

'Well, you've been a help, Josh. I owe you one.'

'Now I'm boss I can let you run it up to *three* you owe me. Then you have to pay it off in wine. Let me know if you get anything new on Seaton.'

Mike promised he would. He closed the conference connection. At the top of the notebook page he had filled while Flynn was talking he scribbled *P. Seaton – background*.

Soon, he thought, pocketing the notebook. Soon, you heap of garbage.

THREE

The following morning at 9:15 a message went out to all personnel of Task Force Three to attend a meeting in UNACO's briefing room. Mike Graham was in a diner with coffee and the *Washington Post* when the pager vibrated against his chest. C. W. Whitlock got the message as he sat in his car in a street off Times Square, talking to a private detective he occasionally employed. Sabrina Carver heard the buzz of the pager where she had left it, resting on the ledge above her bathroom washbasin. She abruptly ended her telephone conversation with her mother, ran to the bathroom and read the terse message.

'Bang goes the gym,' she said, shutting off the last word, realizing she had started to talk to herself again. She had always believed the habit was harmless enough when she was at home, but lately she worried that it could spread to other places, or go really malignant and turn into a compulsion. She feared ending up like people she sometimes saw on the street and in stores, in deep conversation with themselves, detached and strange.

Bang went the gym, anyway. She had planned to go there at ten, do an hour, come back, shower, spend plenty of time getting dressed and made up, then have a long gossipy lunch with a school friend who was in town.

She could always go to the gym in the afternoon or the evening, so it was no disruption of the day, except that on a day when she was lunching out she liked to visit the gym in the morning, for then it felt like less of a misdemeanour to have dessert with her meal.

She got ready quickly and checked herself in the mirror. The dark gold Joseph Janard jersey suit was an extravagance she had been saving for the spring; it was still only February, a grey

New York day, but she felt sunny enough to carry it. Her mother, born and raised in Paris, had told her never to forget that because she was blonde, relatively tall, and had a lot of French in her DNA, she could get away with clothes that would make most other New York women look downright silly.

A Cartier watch and a light brown Elégance wool coat across her shoulders completed the ensemble. She slipped her SIG P220 pistol into her purse and left for the UN.

As she came out of the elevator opposite the UNACO main entrance she saw Mike Graham ahead of her. She hurried and caught up.

'What's the meeting about?'

'No idea,' he told her. 'But I hope it isn't something that needs all of us.'

Sabrina waited for more, but that was all he said.

When they stepped into the briefing room Philpott and C. W. Whitlock were already there. Philpott was by the big ceiling-to-floor window that overlooked the East River. He was muttering testily to his mobile phone. Whitlock leaned patiently against the shiny panelled wall, arms folded.

''Morning, kids,' he muttered.

Whitlock was the most versatile of all the UNACO agents, and the one most readily consulted by Philpott. He was a graduate of Oxford and a one-time officer in the Kenya Intelligence Corps. Philpott had personally recruited him into UNACO. They were often to be found together, although their closeness created no jealousy. Everybody knew Philpott was too much of a loner to have favourites.

'You look stunning, Sabrina,' Whitlock observed as she hung up her coat.

'That's what I was aiming for. I'm going straight to lunch after the meeting.'

'You're kind of overdressed for McDonald's,' Mike said. He sat down at the long central table and stared pointedly at Philpott, who was trying to terminate his call.

'We're going to the Arcadia,' Sabrina said, sliding into the chair opposite Mike. 'Special occasion. Me and Tania, an old

18

friend from school. The last time we met she was very pretty, but I haven't seen her in ten years so I have to assume the worst – she could be stunning. The *haute couture* is my best defence.'

Philpott ended the phone call and slammed the mobile down on the table. 'That was the Secretary General's office,' he said. 'UNACO is to be the subject of a techniques-and-procedures review. I resisted, but it would seem that somebody in Policy Control has a persuasive turn of argument – either that, or they're blackmailing one of the under secretaries.'

'They want to change the way we do things?' Mike said.

'At the administrative level,' Philpott nodded. 'It's aimed at *me*. It's personal. Just because I won't play the good doggie every time Secretary Crane or one of his lesser vermin set foot in the place. However.'

Philpott sat down at the end of the table and opened his leather document case. 'I want to brief you on the ground tactics and preliminary arrangements for an upcoming assignment.'

Mike raised his hand. 'If I might say something, sir, before you start.'

Philpott sighed. 'Hurry up, then.'

'I want to take a couple of weeks of my outstanding leave to nose around the situation in the Vale of Kashmir. You know, the troubles the clergyman wrote to the Security Council about.'

'Why would you want to do that?'

Mike adjusted his body language to look candid and open. 'I thought that if a small fuse were stepped on now, it would prevent major explosions later.'

'No,' Philpott said. 'I can't agree. Out there, stepping on a small fuse could mean simultaneously putting your foot on a land mine. It's not a place for one-man campaigns.'

Mike stared at Philpott for a long moment. 'I'm disappointed you feel that way.'

'No need to be,' Philpott said. 'There is time we can borrow.'

'Huh?'

'The ballistics-update course that you and the other members of Task Force Three should be attending from Tuesday next – it's been put back two weeks.'

Mike looked at Whitlock, who was now sitting beside him. He looked back at Philpott. 'I don't understand.'

'As I promised I would, I gave extended consideration to Reverend Young's plea. I also spoke to Sufi Gopal in our Delhi office. He spoke without the clergyman's passion, but his calm words were a good deal more chilling. I've decided there is enough criminal rumbling in Kashmir to justify organized UNACO intrusion.'

Mike stared. 'Really?'

'It's what I called the three of you here to discuss. It's a genuinely worrying picture. There is escalating terrorism, there is drug running, there is the calculated disruption of peaceful development, and there's the possibility that even a small increase in friction could spark off fighting that would involve Afghanistan, Pakistan, India and China.'

Mike was still bewildered at the turn of events. He had been sure Philpott had thrown this one out. 'You're saying we can go in as a team?'

'Indeed,' Philpott said. 'I believe a little *collective* defusing would be in order.' He passed three clipped documents along the table. 'These are preliminary strategic manoeuvres worked out between Sufi Gopal and myself. Let me have your comments and any suggested revisions of strategy by this time tomorrow.'

Sabrina frowned. 'Is that it? Is the meeting over?'

Philpott nodded. They all stood.

'That means I've got to hang about in these clothes for another two hours and still turn up at the Arcadia looking glitzy and fresh.'

'Go home and take them off,' Whitlock said.

'I can't do that. I can't take clothes off, then put them on again in a couple of hours. I'd feel like I was wearing stuff that should be in the cleaner's. And if I feel that way, I'll *look* that way. In front of *her*.'

'Go shopping,' Mike said. 'That'll keep you on your feet for two hours without noticing it, and you won't get your duds creased.'

Sabrina beamed at him. 'Great idea,' she said.

20

Whitlock stayed behind when Sabrina and Mike had gone. 'I spoke to Carl Grubb earlier,' he told Philpott.

'The private investigator?'

'I asked him to keep a watch on the funeral home where they're holding Arno Skuttnik's body. Quite a few people have shown up to pay their respects. Other staff from the hotel where he worked, his neighbours . . .'

Philpott was drumming the table softly. 'C. W.,' he said, 'you wouldn't have volunteered this information if it had been devoid of relevance, am I correct?'

'I was working up to it, the relevant bit.'

'Just skip the presentation. What's the story?'

'Adam Korwin showed up.'

'What?' Philpott's eyes grew wide. 'To look at the body?'

'Grubb was watching from an adjoining room. He said the way Korwin looked at the corpse, he was there to satisfy himself it was who people said it was.'

Philpott shook his head slowly. 'Can we be sure it was Korwin?'

'I have the Polaroids. It was him, all right.'

'I don't know whether to feel good or bad about this.'

'It's intriguing,' Whitlock said. 'An old immigrant with no family, no skills, no interesting history, no status you could measure, dies suddenly, and who shows up to run an eye over the body?'

'Adam Korwin,' Philpott breathed. 'Surprise, surprise . . .'

Korwin was the doyen of US East Coast spymasters. During the cold war his name had been cited by three Kremlin defectors, and his status as a principal Russian spy-handler had been confirmed by highly-placed Eastern Bloc sources. But Korwin was so good at his job that he had worked for thirty years under the noses of the FBI and CIA without once doing anything even remotely suspicious. To all appearances he was a harmless self-employed upholsterer, and no one could muster enough on him to work up a believable extradition order.

'What the hell was his connection with Skuttnik?' Philpott said.

21

'That's my next avenue of enquiry. Assuming you want me to take this further.'

'I'll say I do.'

'It'll take time. What about Kashmir?'

'With a touch of re-jigging and enough local help, that's a job Mike and Sabrina can tackle. Don't worry about it. Concentrate on the link between the late Arno Skuttnik and the boys from Red Square.'

Lenny Trent called that afternoon while Mike was in the TF3 suite, boning up on the geography of northern India and Kashmir. Maps and books were spread across two tables and a gazetteer lay open on the carpet. When the phone rang he had to dig it out from under the concertina folds of a Delhi street directory.

'Mike. It's Lenny. You still interested in pinpointing the whereabouts of Paul Seaton?'

'It's only been one day, Lenny. Of course I'm still interested. I'm flying out to India before the end of the week, so you could say I'm really anxious to get a line on him.'

'I may have something for you.'

'So soon?'

'Idle conversation can be a golden shovel, Mike. You never know what it'll turn up.'

'I'll put that on the cork board.'

'At lunch today I talked to my colleagues in general terms about what you and I discussed yesterday – the Afghanistan initiative, the way terrorist groups and drug routes have blossomed since the Russkies moved out – and I asked if anybody had ever had confirmation of the alleged drug convoys running from Kashmir down the western territories into the Punjab. Louise, who is in liaison with our north-west Indian contacts all year round, said she'd heard the convoys had stopped. Pakistani Army hotshots on the border had made it too dangerous.'

'Oh, well . . .'

'Hang on,' Lenny said. 'Louise then told me she'd heard from a good source that the American guy who led the big convoy was running another one now.'

'Did she say where?'

'From up near the Wular Lake region in north-west Kashmir, down the western territories to a destination unknown. It could be Batala or Kangra – they're places where you'll find run-on links for any kind of contraband.'

'Fascinating, Lenny. But it still sounds like hearsay.'

'You're not letting me unfold this the way I want,' Lenny complained. 'Just listen. When Louise told us about the new convoy route, up pipes Jonathan, our satellite communications guy. He said he visited the Aerial Defence Department's tracking and reconnaissance centre at Arlington six weeks ago, and they showed him some high-definition photographs, computer enhanced, taken from three miles up. He was impressed, especially by one that showed a suspected bandit convoy in the Pirpanjal Mountains in western Kashmir.'

'That sounds more promising.'

'Let me finish. The faces of several of the men in the horse convoy were clearly visible, so Jonathan says. I asked him if the leader's face was showing but he wasn't sure, he just recalled they were great pictures.'

'Lenny, you just made my day. I'm really grateful.'

'What are you gonna do? Get hold of the pictures?'

'Not easy, but yes, that's what I plan to do,' Mike said.

'Don't mention me or my people, will you? Jonathan was shown the stuff as a favour, and because I suppose the Aerial Defence guys couldn't help showing off. It was classified material and Jonathan was warned not to talk about any of it outside his professional circle.'

'And he didn't.'

'But I did. So keep *shtum*, unless you want Customs at Delhi to find an embarrassment of heroin in your baggage.'

'Noted. Thanks again, Lenny. You're a sweetheart.'

It took twenty minutes to raise anyone at Aerial Defence in Arlington who would speak to Mike. When he finally located a USAF lieutenant attached to Satellite Reconnaissance, the man was not keen to route the call to anyone with more authority.

23

'Lieutenant Ross, I need to discuss access to possibly classified aerial photographs,' Mike said, setting out his case all over again. 'I have Level One security clearance, you can make an integrity check with your own central computer right now. My security rating, plus my connection with the UN Security Council, permits me access to individuals and to data at the most sensitive levels.'

'I daresay all that is correct, Mr Graham, but I have no authorization to connect you with any other person at this facility.'

'Then who *can* patch me through to where I need to go?'

'Certainly not me,' Ross said coldly. 'And even if I knew of such an individual, I haven't the authorization to connect you with him in order that he might help you.'

'This is crazy.'

'You're entitled to your interpretation, sir.'

Mike put down the phone to kill the connection, then picked it up again. He tapped in the number of C. W. Whitlock's mobile. When Whitlock answered, Mike explained the Catch-22 conversation he'd had with the man at Aerial Defence.

'You went by the wrong route,' Whitlock said. 'They don't talk to anybody they don't know. The officer who froze you out, he would have checked the list of known characters. The short of it is, unless you've first of all been on face-to-face terms with someone up there, they won't give you the time of day by phone or fax.'

'Do they know you?'

'Of course they do,' Whitlock said smoothly.

Mike explained what he was trying to get. He added that he would deem it a favour if Whitlock said nothing to Philpott about the matter.

'What have you got going there?' Whitlock demanded. 'A vendetta?'

'Something of the kind,' Mike said; he knew an outright lie wouldn't work. 'It's a long story.' He paused. 'Well, no, it isn't really, but this is not the time . . .'

'Tell you what,' Whitlock said. 'If I get hold of what you're after, you'll tell me what's behind it. Deal?'

24

'For Pete's sake, C. W . . .'
'Deal?'
Mike nodded at the receiver. 'Deal.'

FOUR

Next morning the plans for the Kashmir assignment were firmed up and finalized in the briefing suite. It was agreed that Mike would be flown directly to Delhi, then taken north by helicopter to the mountains north-west of the Vale of Kashmir. There he would receive an intensive introduction to the region from a Kashmiri Indian, Ram Jarwal, who was a UN Area Observer stationed near Srinagar, in the west of the Indian-administered territory of Kashmir.

Sabrina would spend a single day being briefed by a team of WHO specialists before she travelled to a US-operated commercial airfield at Dehra Dun, eighty kilometres north-west of Delhi. From there she would be spirited northward and would finally become fully visible driving a car into the town of Kulu, in the Pradesh region, 160 kilometres south of the Kashmir border.

'As ever with agents collecting peripheral intelligence,' Philpott said, 'we want Sabrina to appear to have been around for a while, without anyone being able to pinpoint the place or time she arrived. The rule here is always worth remembering – a reassuring presence and a hazy history make for convincing cover.'

On her journey northward, Sabrina would carry the credentials of a WHO Ecology Monitor.

'Since you will both arrive in the Vale of Kashmir by different means and at different rates of progress,' Philpott continued, 'it's to be hoped you'll pick up widely different intelligence in the early stages of your assignment. What we need to know, principally, is the severity of criminal activity – of *recent origin*, remember – in the target region. Long-standing problems are

26

already accommodated by a number of means; we need to know what's being added to make the pot boil over, as it were. The causes could be far more widespread than Reverend Young or our observers think. The short version is, we badly need hard intelligence.'

'Nothing to be taken for granted,' Sabrina murmured, scribbling.

'Quite so,' Philpott said. 'We need to know the nature of the beast, where it's from and how far it sprawls. In more realistic terms, we need to find out how best to counter and prevent a series of political reactions which could result in an Indo-Chinese bloodbath.'

Mike wanted to know if current intelligence still indicated that the main troubles were orchestrated by one or two terrorist groups.

'That is still the view of our best-informed observers,' Philpott said. 'You may find differently once you get past the various façades, of course. If you do discover you're up against something that calls for a small army rather than a couple of smart saboteurs, then don't indulge in heroics. Evaluate the position, report to me, then clear out.'

Before dismissing them Philpott issued a caution. 'At all times, remain aware that UNACO's function is to combat and neutralize crime without impinging on local politics or customs. In this case it won't be easy to avoid trespassing on sensitive ground, so damage-limitation must be a priority. Making matters worse will be a lot easier than making them better.'

In the corridor outside, Mike and Sabrina wished each other luck. Sabrina even put a peck on Mike's cheek before they parted.

'*My*, but that was cordial and civilized,' Whitlock observed, stepping out of the recessed doorway of the briefing room. 'Not like you two at all.'

'Truces come and go,' Mike said. 'For a while now it's been OK between us.'

'Because you haven't been working closely with one another.'

'Precisely, C. W. The peace can't hold. Sooner or later we'll find ourselves sharing a predicament, and then she'll try to assert what she feels is her natural authority –'

'Over what you *know* to be yours.' Whitlock held up his attaché case and tapped the side. 'I've got something for you. Let's go to Secure Comms.'

Mike had expected photographs, but what C. W. took out of the case was a mini CD.

'This was the only way to do it.' He powered up a graphics computer on a steel table in the middle of the floor. 'Photographic prints at Aerial Defence are numbered and accounted for. They are also magnetically tagged through a ferrous component in the paper emulsion, so there was no way anybody was going to get one out of there. However, I have a resourceful friend on the strength, and he knows the code that unlocks the negative disks.'

'Negative disks?'

'The negatives aren't on film. They're electronic and they're stored on hard disks. So my compadre unlocked the negs and transferred identical copies to this minidisk.'

Whitlock opened a zippered pouch and took out a Sony MZ-R3 minidisk recorder. He plugged one end of a transfer cord into the tiny silver machine and put the other end into a socket in the back of the computer. He put the CD into the Sony and a moment later a picture began to appear on the screen. It built slowly at first, then accelerated until the whole screen was filled with a sharp photographic image of eleven turbaned men on horses travelling through mountainous countryside. No faces were visible.

'That's no good,' Mike said. 'I was told they could be identified . . .'

'There are over twenty still to go,' Whitlock said. 'Be patient, can't you?'

He began tapping a button on top of the Sony. With each tap the picture on the screen changed.

'Stop!' Mike pointed as the eighth picture came up. 'Stop right there!'

The image was a closer view and a different angle from the ones before. The faces of three men were visible. One was the leader, but he had moved his head at the moment of exposure and the features were blurred.

'Damn!' Mike growled.

Whitlock brought up the next shot. The same three faces were visible, but this time the leader gazed straight ahead, caught full face and pin sharp.

'My God.'

Whitlock watched Mike. He had the look of a man who had been searching for something under a stone and had found it; fascinated repulsion was the description that came to mind.

'That's the man?'

'That's him.'

Mike took in the wide clear eyes, the firm arrogant set of the mouth; the nose, once straight, had gone through a few changes of shape since boyhood. It had even changed since Mike last saw it.

'Ugly, isn't he?'

Whitlock frowned at the picture. 'He looks normal to me. Quite handsome, even.'

'OK. I'm prejudiced.'

'Tell me about him.'

Mike made a face.

'You promised.'

Mike got two Styrofoam cups of coffee from the machine by the door and brought them to the table. They sat down in front of the big monitor.

'Lenny Trent asked me if I had a private agenda where this man is concerned,' Mike said. 'You asked me if it was a vendetta. Well, yes to both questions. The agenda is bedded in a time long ago, when I was a kid. When I was, to be precise, a rookie quarterback for the New York Giants.'

'If this is a football story I may fall asleep.'

'Stay with me, you'll be all right. During my second week with the team one of the star players, Lou Kelly, got his career ended abruptly in the parking lot behind the ball park. He was

29

beaten half to death. At that time I had never seen anyone injured so badly. He lost an eye and had his left arm broken in so many places it had to be amputated below the elbow.'

'How come?'

'I didn't get the full story until years later. A certain senator had offered Lou Kelly money to perform badly in a crucial game. He only had to play badly enough to give the other team the edge, that was all they needed. Lou Kelly refused and he was promptly offered twice as much money. He still refused. So a man was sent to punish him for being so intractable.'

'A contract beating.'

'Yeah. It turned out worse than a killing for Lou. I still remember seeing the man waiting for him outside the players' exit and thinking, that guy is bad news. It was a long time ago and everybody was much younger then, but I've got no doubts. The man who destroyed Lou Kelly's career that night was Paul Seaton.'

They were silent for a minute, drinking coffee, staring at the picture on the screen.

'According to my contact at Aerial Defence,' Whitlock said, 'Seaton and his bandits are a bunch of crazies. They don't limit their activities to running drugs. They're into fundamentalist agitation, sabotage, even random murder. They could be a part of Reverend Young's local problem.'

'How much intelligence does Aerial Defence have on the bandits?'

'I just gave you all of it. The one other thing they know for sure is that nobody offers the bandits any resistance. People are too scared. Look over your shoulder at these guys, you won't survive past sunset.'

Mike leaned forward and touched the PRINT button on the computer keyboard. When the menu came up he clicked the High Resolution option. The printer started up.

'I'll take copies to Kashmir with me.'

'Just don't say where you got them,' Whitlock said.

Mike crossed his heart and finished his coffee.

*   *   *

30

At one o'clock Whitlock took a cab to an address on West 3rd Street. He checked a name in his notebook, then descended carefully on narrow steps from street level to a shadowy basement door. A neon sign outside said TIME OFF in letters that alternated buzzily between green and red.

There was a weary woman at a desk by the door. 'Five bucks,' she announced.

Whitlock gave her a five. She dropped it in the drawer and stared glassily past him.

'I'm looking for a man called Clancy Spencer,' Whitlock said.

'He's working.'

On the platform at the far end of the club a grizzled black man was singing croakily into a microphone. He was accompanied on piano, sax and drums by men who looked nearly as old as he was. They were doing 'Malted Milk', after a fashion.

'How do I get to speak to him when he's done?'

The woman glanced at Whitlock for a split second. 'Just let him see you got a drink for him, he'll come soon enough.'

At the bar Whitlock got a Coke for himself and a large scotch for Spencer. He took the drinks to a table near the platform. As he sat down he held up the whisky in one hand and pointed to the singer with the other. Spencer caught on straight away and nodded, still croaking into the mike.

There were no more than twenty other customers in the place. Their applause when Spencer and the combo finished was a thin rattle around the smoky room, a sound like twigs snapping. A moment later Spencer sat down opposite Whitlock.

'Nice meetin' you.' He reached across and shook Whitlock's hand. 'Call me Spence. What's your handle?'

'People call me C. W.'

Spence had the worst-fitting set of dentures Whitlock had ever seen. They were loose and they moved when he spoke, giving the impression that his mouth was out of sync with his speech.

'Well then, C. W., this is mighty nice of you.' Spence picked up the glass with finger and thumb, toasted Whitlock with a little swing of the glass, then swallowed half the whisky in one go.

31

'How long have you been doing this, Spence?'

'Singing in jazz dives? Since I was a kid.'

'Never done anything else?'

'I'd three years off to go to the war. Then I got married for a while and tried to make a go of a regular job. But it didn't work out.' He laughed throatily, making the dentures click. 'Most of my life it's been the way it is. Of course I ain't what I was. Used to be a regular Eckstine. Now I'm just a broken singer of mostly broken songs.'

'I thought that was Randy Newman.'

'He stole the line off me.' Spence laughed again. He finished the scotch and put down the glass, stared at it pointedly.

Whitlock got him another. 'Do you mind if I ask you a couple of questions, Spence?'

'You a cop?'

'No. I'm not anyone who means you harm.'

'Easy to say.' Spence picked up the fresh glass and sipped this time. 'What kind of questions?'

'About your friend who passed away the other day.'

'Arno?' Spence put down the glass. 'You *sure* you ain't a cop?'

'I'm just a man who needs to know more than I do. Did the law give Arno any kind of trouble?'

'Couldn't say.' Spence made a vague shape in the air with his hands. 'Him and me, we got along because we didn't pry in each other's back yards. We could sit and drink ourselves motionless without having to *communicate*. But I knew Arno steered clear of policemen. He used to call them Cossacks. That's what he'd mutter when he'd see one – Cossacks!'

The private investigator, Grubb, had told Whitlock that Spence had wept when he went to the funeral home to view Arno Skuttnik's remains. He also said Spence told the duty undertaker that he and Arno had been friends for thirty years.

'So what was it that made you buddies?' Whitlock said. 'Was Arno a jazz fan?'

'Not that you'd notice. I think what it was, we were both the kind of loners that like to have a friend, y'know? You maybe think it's strange in a man that sings for his livin', but I ain't really an outgoin' fellow. I never in my life had more than two, three real friends at any one time. Arno was the same, and they were like him, they kept themselves in the shade.'

'Do you know who they were, the others?'

Spence took a long pull on the whisky, studying Whitlock over the rim of the glass. When he put it down he smacked his lips. Whitlock could see he was making up his mind.

'I'm no good with names, and far as I recall, Arno never gave any, anyway. But there's a picture . . .' Spence fished a plastic wallet from his inside jacket pocket and opened it on the table. He pulled out a coloured snapshot and handed it to Whitlock.

'That was taken in here on Arno's last birthday, six or seven months ago. Harry the barman took it. Those two people had dropped by to pass on their good wishes and leave a bottle of gin for Arno. He loved gin.'

The picture showed Spence and Arno side by side on the padded bench along the wall beside the bar. A man was leaning down, saying something to Arno; he was in profile and he wore a hat, but Whitlock could see it was Adam Korwin. The other person in the picture was a woman. She was turned away from the camera, her shoulder hunched defensively.

'The lady didn't want her picture took,' Spence said. 'She looked kind of mad that Harry did it.'

Whitlock could make out her left eye, the shape of her nose, the general style of her short hair, and he could see the rings on her left hand. She also wore a distinctive checked coat.

'May I borrow this?'

'If you promise I'll get it back.'

'You will.' Whitlock finished his Coke and pushed back his chair. He didn't want to pressure the old man any more than he had to. As he stood up he pointed to Spence's glass. 'I'll leave you one at the bar.' He put the picture in his pocket and turned to leave. Then he remembered something. 'Spence. Do you know if Arno kept a diary, a journal, any kind of record of events?'

Spence shook his head. 'It don't sound like him. Besides, if he kept a diary, we'd none of us be able to read it.'

'What do you mean?'

'Arno never learned to write English.'

'Not at all? How did he get by?'

'People helped him out, I guess. Arno spoke English real well, but the writing was something he never got around to. He regretted that.'

Whitlock nodded and walked away. At the bar he paid for another large scotch and went outside. Upstairs, waiting for a cab to appear, he took out his notebook and scribbled a reminder to get the picture electronically copied and enhanced.

At the bottom of the page he put another entry in capitals: WHOSE WRITING ON THE PICTURE OF M. PHILPOTT?

FIVE

Two days later Mike Graham landed in a Boeing 747 at Delhi and transferred at once to a black unmarked Sikorsky helicopter, the property of the New Delhi division of United Nations Information and Services. He was flown 500 kilometres north and set down on a patch of beaten earth in front of a large, shabby-looking cabin, set into a hillside above the northern boundary of Srinagar in north-western Kashmir.

It was almost dark when they landed. The setting sun was leaving streamers of red and purple above the mountains on the Pakistani border.

'This is where I abandon you,' the pilot called as Mike jumped out. '*Bonne chance!*'

As the helicopter took off again and Mike stood doubled over, his eyes shut tight against the dust storm, a tall Indian emerged from the cabin. He wore Levi's and a checked lumberjack shirt. He smiled and waved.

'Hi,' he shouted, coming across. 'I'm Ram Jarwal.'

He took one of Mike's bags and led the way up to the cabin. When they went in, Mike stood in the living-room doorway and whistled softly.

'The dilapidated exterior is designed to deflect envy and avarice,' Ram said. 'Inside, we UN hill-dwellers like to have our comforts.'

'It's beautiful.'

Mike stepped in and put down his bags. There was a big console television in the corner, showing CNN News with the sound turned down. In the middle of the floor was a deep beige Indian rug with a sinuous pattern worked in dark and light shades of green and gold. Packed bookshelves covered two walls

35

from the floor nearly to the ceiling, with bracketed sconces at intervals above them, giving the room an amber glow. A couple of shaded lamps, with bases made from many-coloured porcelain vases, stood on black tables at opposite corners, spilling light across the polished floorboards.

'Sit down.' Ram pointed to one of the three armchairs. 'I'll get us a drink. You like Jim Beam, right?'

'They sent my CV on ahead,' Mike said, smiling. 'How civilized. Jim Beam will be just fine, with a little water.'

Ram brought the drinks and sat down with his own. He had the look of a successful businessman who spent time in the gym. His dark hair was slicked back over his ears; his umber skin, incredibly smooth, was wrinkled around the eyes and at the corners of the mouth, the only signs that he might be capable of ageing. When he looked up he had the eyes, Mike thought, of an interrogator.

'I've got instructions to crash-course you on the layout and culture and customs of the Vale of Kashmir,' he said. 'I don't have long, even by crash-course standards, so if you don't mind we'll start early tomorrow.'

'Does it involve anything painful?'

'Walking, mainly. If you tread the territory and use your eyes, you'll catch the tone and temper of the place faster than any other way. After that, we can get down to particulars – like studying the dope trails, pinpointing fundamentalist hotspots and identifying known and probable villains in the region.'

'What can you tell me about Reverend Alex Young?'

'We've met several times,' Ram said. 'He's a sincere man, a shade humourless for somebody so young, but his heart's where it should be. He runs a good little medical centre for the poorer people and he has a three-Rs infants' school operating two hours a day, Monday to Thursday. I don't know anybody who doesn't like him.'

'I suppose he got in touch with the Security Council because he didn't know there's a UN man in the vicinity.'

'That's right. He doesn't know what my job is – nobody here

36

does. I function as regional eyes and ears for the UN, so I have to work behind a cover. Reverend Young, like everybody else, thinks I'm a civil servant. As far as they're concerned I'm beavering away in my scabby cabin, engaged on a long-term proposal for improving rice production in the Vale.'

'And I'm to be – what?'

'A UN fact-finder. Sent in response to local uneasiness about the banditry and political shenanigans.'

Mike nodded. 'What do you make of the troubles?'

'They're all rooted in greed.' Ram ticked off his fingers. 'Territorial greed, because this is a very lush and desirable place to live; commercial greed, since it would take a thousand years of pesticide spraying to choke the fertility of this region; raw financial greed, because some of the most cunningly developed, efficient and profitable drug routes in Asia pass through or near this area.'

'And what would you say are the chances of bringing the violence and unrest under control?'

'If what we guess is true,' Ram said, 'that only a few really bad guys are at the heart of it all, then I think a UNACO team could swing it and put things back the way they were ten years ago – still not perfect, but less likely to blow up into something international.'

'Your guess could be wrong.'

'Sure it could. People say there are unknown hands operating in the Vale, ruthless hands representing big national interests. And of course there's the question of time. Even small random fires can set off powder kegs by accident. If that happens, there'll be no low-key way to put things right.'

Mike finished his drink and stood up. 'If we've got a really tough day ahead of us,' he said, 'I think I'd like to shower and hit the sack. Before I do I have to touch base. Do we have a satellite window?'

Ram looked at the clock. 'Half an hour left.'

Mike went outside and stood for a minute, listening to the insect noises, gazing up at the canopy of stars. He took a deep breath and caught the fragrance of flowers and grass and warm tree bark. It was like being at home in Vermont in the summer, with all the sensations multiplied by ten.

He took out his mobile and flipped on the illuminator. An insect landed on the status window as soon as the light came on. Mike tapped three buttons and put the phone to his ear. The scrambler noises cut in and went away again. Philpott spoke.

'It's Mike, sir. I'm in position. After a scrub and a snooze I'll be ready to go.'

Philpott asked if he had heard anything from Sabrina.

'No, but I wasn't expecting to.'

Philpott said she had arrived at Dehra Dun and had been moved north from there as scheduled, but now he had lost touch with her. 'She should have called in more than two hours ago.'

'I'll keep my unit switched on all night,' Mike said.

'And I'll do the same with mine. Keep me posted, Michael.'

As Mike began to fall asleep in his room at the cabin an hour later, less than a kilometre away a man called Ahmed Faiz was running for his life.

Ahmed had run for more than twenty minutes, through woods and thickets, down a ravine and across a rocky outcrop that tore the skin on his knees and hands. He was young, but the running and the fear had drained him, making his heart pound and his limbs drag like lead. He longed to stop and catch his breath, but to stop was to die.

'Muhammad be praised,' he panted, 'Muhammad is good. Muhammad be praised, Muhammad is good. Muhammad be praised . . .'

Whenever he felt himself flagging, when his feet slowed and threatened to stumble to a stop, he thought of his wife and his three small children. He saw their faces and the image put strength in him.

'Muhammad is good . . .'

He had to get back to where he came from, to the safety and enclosing love of his family. He had no idea how far he must still run until he was safe, he only knew he ran in the right direction; long ago, his father had taught him to read the stars.

He drove himself to the west, the west and the border. Beyond the border lay Islamabad and the safety of his home.

'Well now, Ahmed!'

He stopped and felt himself falling, losing his balance. He tumbled into the coarse grass and felt twigs tear his face. How had this happened? How did Iqbal get in front of him?

'Up, little man! Up!'

He was hoisted like a doll and shoved against a tree. A torch came on, right in his eyes, the light painful as a knife. Ahmed shut his eyes, squirmed and felt another pair of hands take hold of him from behind the tree.

'You were told, were you not, that there were severe penalties for stealing? You were told, also, that to flee would be senseless. There is no escape.'

Ahmed was panting too hard to reply. A heavy fist slammed into his stomach. Now he couldn't inhale. The pain flared into his chest and he thought he would faint. Through the pounding in his ears he heard Iqbal, his mouth close, the breath warm on his ear.

'There are no exemptions, Ahmed. You were well paid to do your simple job. You were given money to support your family. Yet you abused your master's generosity. You stole.'

'Twenty rupees!' Ahmed gasped. 'It was only twenty rupees! And I found it!'

'You cannot find what is not lost, little man.'

'It was lying on a bench!'

'It was not yours. It was a simple test of your loyalty.'

Ahmed's arms were gripped tighter. The torch was held higher as Iqbal stepped back. Ahmed heard the knife slide from under Iqbal's sash.

'Please! Please, I beg you! My wife and my children need me! I gave back the money, there is no need for this!'

'There are rules, Ahmed. To break them is to commit a grave insult to your master. You knew that. You were not kept in ignorance of what would happen if you transgressed.'

'Iqbal! No! I beg you!'

The kukri made a swift arc from right to left, slicing through

Ahmed's throat as if it was not there. It swung again from left to right and severed his head clean from his body.

Ram Jarwal woke Mike at six o'clock with a cup of coffee and told him he should be ready to leave in twenty minutes. Mike drank the coffee while he dressed. By the time he was ready, Ram was outside, tightening the laces on his walking boots.

It was a glorious morning. The sun shimmered through a light high mist and the air was fragrant and moist. Mike watched Ram do up the bolts and double-lock the cabin door.

'It's hard to imagine anyone would take the trouble to come all the way up here to burgle a cabin,' Mike said. He had been gazing down the sides of the valley, which seemed incredibly steep. 'On the other hand, some people might see it as a challenge.'

'Some people might see it as an opportunity to get inside and wait for whoever lives here,' Ram said. 'Homicide robberies are not uncommon. The best you can do is make sure there's no place for someone to hide. Before I moved in, I had all the trees within fifty metres cut down.'

Mike stood for a moment looking down into the valley. He pointed to a dark cluster beside a green thicket a hundred metres below them. 'What's that – the black patch? It looks like it's moving.'

'Vultures,' Ram said. 'They're waiting for the police to leave.'

'Police?'

'There was a bulletin on VHF at five o'clock. A murder can't stay hidden here for long. Vultures were spotted on the hillside. The police came up and found the body of a young man, they think he might be a Pakistani. Decapitated.' Ram shrugged. 'Another sadly frequent event.'

They set off walking south-east. They crossed sloping farmland and dusty roads, cutting across the natural lines and divisions of the land, taking shortcuts through woods and across gullies to a stretch of natural road. It was solid rock, the blunt edge of a ridge from which they could see terraced rice fields laid out like patchwork, every shade of green and yellow. A looming

40

backdrop of dark hills to the north and east intensified the colours and provided a windbreak for hundreds of acres of cultivated land.

'The pictorial view of Kashmir,' Ram said. 'From a distance everything is so orderly.'

After an hour the mist cleared, and even though they were high in the hills Mike and Ram began to sweat. They stopped to take water.

'It's a beautiful place,' Mike said, wiping his mouth with the back of his hand. 'I didn't imagine it was anything like this.' He pointed ahead of them, to a cluster of houses with a larger building at their centre. 'Have we come to a community?'

'Bahadur. The white cube bigger than the others is Reverend Young's medical centre. The school is inside his mission, which is farther down the slope.'

'This is where I do my UN fact-finder bit, is it?'

'With a minimum of acting required,' Ram said. 'This morning we simply introduce you. Discussions can come later. Reverend Young is expecting us, so there should be something cool waiting – he makes an admirable lemonade.'

They walked down the slope to Bahadur. Ram led the way through narrow twisting streets to the mission. As they approached he looked puzzled.

'I've never seen the door shut before.'

He went up the two little steps and knocked on the door, waited, then pushed it. It opened. He went in, took three steps across the tiny entry hall and turned.

'Come in, quick,' he told Mike. 'Close the door.'

Mike pushed the door shut and caught the smell at once, heavy on the warm air. It was unmistakable, the odour of decomposing human flesh.

Ram went into the room beyond. Mike heard him groan.

'What is it?'

Mike went through. It was a bare white room with two small windows high on opposite walls. On a wheeled examination table in the centre of the room lay the body of a priest, stretched out, the arms tied together under the table. The black vestments

41

were covered with blood. The face had been beaten to a pulp. Shards of white skull bone stuck up from the scarlet mass, catching the light.

'Is it Reverend Young?'

'I assume it is,' Ram said. 'I recognize the ring on his hand.' He touched the mangled head with a fingertip and drew it back. 'Not more than a couple of hours dead. Another hour and the stench will be unbearable.'

They went outside. Ram fished out his mobile phone. 'I'll get the police down here. Nobody will have seen a thing, of course. There are never ever any witnesses. Not even if it was done in broad daylight in the middle of the street.'

Ram spoke for a minute to the phone, then switched it off and dropped it back in his rucksack. 'The police will take care of everything,' he said. 'We can go. And it's best we do, before the locals take it into their heads that you brought bad luck with you.'

As they walked back up the slope Mike felt they were being watched, but he saw no one. 'Have you any idea who could have done it?' he said.

'Plenty of cut-throats to choose from,' Ram said. 'But I couldn't narrow it down to one or even a dozen. As I said, I don't know anybody who didn't like Reverend Young.'

SIX

Sabrina arrived at Kulu on time, and the first stage of her planned transformation to a WHO official went to schedule. Wearing a *shalwar kameez* – traditional tunic and trousers – and a scarf over her head, she went directly to a lockup garage in an underpopulated suburb north of the town and let herself in with a key she had been given at Dehra Dun.

The car waiting for her was a ten-year-old two-door Peugeot 205, metallic blue with dabs of rust on the roof and the lower edges of the doors. The engine had been reconditioned and made reliable, there were new tyres and secure locks. A creative after-touch was the attachment of a loose aluminium plate to the underside of the engine mounting, which rattled and vibrated and made the car sound frail and barely roadworthy.

Sabrina's change of clothes was in a holdall in the boot of the car. Staying low-key was always difficult, given her height, her figure and her looks, but UNACO Kitting and Outfitting had made the best selection they could: billowy blouses, long flowing skirts and baggy trousers in brown and ochre shades, stout boots and a couple of shapeless canvas jackets.

She took only a minute to change. Looking every inch the overseas social worker in her flapping shirt and sturdy footwear, her long hair done up in a bun and tucked into the brim of a floppy sun hat, she opened the garage door, got behind the wheel of the Peugeot and drove out into the sunlight of Kulu.

What happened next, she later decided, was an unprofessional lapse of a kind she could never let happen again. She stopped the car a few metres along the dusty road from the garage, went back and locked the garage door. She came back to find that her shoulder bag had gone from the front passenger seat.

She stood for a moment and stared at the empty seat, forcing herself to be calm, trying to raise a clear memory of how things had looked before she turned away from the car and went back the few steps to lock the garage door.

Anger and anxiety obscured her memory. She was mad at herself for being so careless, and she was seriously worried because her documentation, her gun and her folding money were all in the vanished bag – to say nothing of her Swiss Army knife. She forced her mind away from consequences and told herself firmly to think only along positive lines. Even so, she couldn't help visualizing Philpott, seeing him turn puce as he learned that one of his so-called prime agents had behaved like the worst kind of amateur.

She leaned both hands on the bonnet of the car and closed her eyes. She could see herself driving out into the light, feeling sudden warmth through the windscreen. She had braked, put the engine in neutral and got out, leaving the door open. She had no recollection of anyone else being near.

She opened her eyes, starting to feel desperate. She recalled something Philpott had told her, something she had subsequently written down. It was one of the chunks of advice he only ever imparted when he had taken a drink:

If ever you find yourself in a position where it seems possible you will damage UNACO, remember that it is worth any amount of effort, any measure of pain, and all the resourcefulness you can marshal to make sure that you deflect the harm away from UNACO, or undo the source of harm entirely.

Black marks against an agent were seldom erased. Sabrina had so far collected none. She had no intention of starting.

She shut her eyes tightly and tried again. She thought back further, saw the approach to the garage, the key in her hand extending to open the padlock.

She experienced a jolt now, realizing there had been something peripheral, something at the edge of her vision that should now register. She tried to freeze the image of her hand going forward to the lock and saw it slow down. Simultaneously she was aware of movement in herself, in her neck, the beginning of a reflex action.

Of course!

She had looked over her shoulder. She shut her eyes tighter and concentrated, inching through the recollection, aware that she had missed something, or at least she had taken no account of it. She saw again the shrubs and stunted trees at the side of the garage, with the yellow clay of the road dusted halfway up their trunks and stems.

A woman!

She had seen a woman on the other side of the trees, looking through a gap, her face impassive. She had simply been watching, doing nothing to raise the kind of curiosity that would get her remembered.

'Yes, yes, *yesss*!'

Now that the image of the woman had been raised Sabrina could hold it and stare at it. In her early training with the FBI, she had learned that even if she did not consciously see something that appeared in her line of vision, it would be printed on her memory. Raising such memories was now something she could do five times out of ten. She put the image to the centre of her mind and worked at enhancing it.

The woman was young, perhaps twenty, with typically dark eyes and black hair; she wore a silver chain around her neck and she . . .

The recollection stalled there. Something needed to be noticed.

'Come on, *come on*!'

There was an irregularity about the neck. *A scar!* There was a vertical scar, running down the midline of the larynx. It was an operation scar, perhaps an old tracheotomy, the thickened tissue raised and almost white against the surrounding brown skin.

The effort of finding a telltale sign had been so extreme that Sabrina heard herself pant. She kept her eyes shut and pictured the face again, imprinting it, making it a clear feature of fresh memory: small chin, wide upper lip, prominent cheekbones, rounded and deep-set dark amber eyes, hair combed back behind the ears.

Sabrina opened her eyes. She felt as if she had done a day's work. She looked at the empty seat again. The thought of her bag being somewhere else right now, in other hands that might do unthinkable mischief, was like a goad behind her, prodding, shoving.

She jumped in behind the wheel, banged the door shut and threw the engine into gear. As she tore away along the road she had no idea where she was going, beyond knowing she had to start her search in the town.

People were staring. Women had their hands over their mouths, others drew their veils protectively across their eyes. The whole market had stopped to watch the commotion at the vegetable stall.

'I do not speak English!' the stallholder howled. He was an old man, and Sabrina had him by the front of his shirt. She held on with both hands and looked determined enough to pick him up and throw him across the market. 'No English! I speak no English!'

'You just spoke it!' Sabrina rasped, falling into the character imposed by her unflattering clothes. 'Now you're going to rack your brains and answer my question or I'm going to drag your spindly old carcass down to the local clink!'

She had started out her enquiry much more gently, stopping by the old man's stall, asking him if he knew of a young woman with a scar at her throat, a good-looking young woman that Sabrina was anxious to find. Then she noticed that the old trader had his hand in her jacket pocket. She caught him by the wrist, twisted his arm up his back and pushed his face into a pile of green chillies. She let him stay that way, howling, his mouth half stoppered with his produce, while she did a good enough impression of a crazy woman to keep the other traders at a respectful distance. When she finally released the man and grabbed him by the collar, she guessed he was scared enough to rat on his mother.

'Are you going to tell me?' she demanded. 'Huh? Or do I beat you up and haul you off to the police?'

'Please, no, do not hurt me, I beg you . . .'

'Talk, then.'

'You are looking for a woman called Phoolan Sena . . .'

'Where do I find her?'

'She lives with her son over there.' He pointed to a clutch of small houses beyond the perimeter of the market. 'Her house has a blue door.'

'And you'll have a black eye if I go over there and find out you're lying to me.'

Sabrina let the man go and marched away. She pushed her way through the narrow lanes between the rickety barrows, past staring stallholders and their cringing customers.

Out on the bare ground at the rear of the market she paused and looked back, just able to see her car at the top of the narrow street where she had parked it. If the locks were as good as she had been told, it should be all right, although the way today had gone, she could not invest much faith in anything.

She found the house with the blue door and rapped on it, seeing paint fly off in little flakes under the impact of her knuckles. Feet shuffled beyond the door, then it swung open. For a split second the woman with the scar on her neck just stared. Then her memory kicked in and she jumped back, half turning as she leapt, getting ready to run for the back door.

'Hold it!'

Sabrina caught her by the hair and tugged. The woman yelled. Pulled hair, like a kicked shin, can immobilize a person long enough for an attacker to get the upper hand. Sabrina swept her leg behind the woman's knees and put her flat on her back.

'You're Phoolan, right?' Sabrina knelt beside her. 'Where is my bag, Phoolan?'

The woman looked hurt and frightened and surprised all at once.

'I have a memory for faces,' Sabrina told her, 'even ones I haven't really seen. So don't give me any stories about you being the wrong woman. You *do* speak English, by the way?'

The woman's stare was too mystified, too blank. She didn't know what Sabrina was saying. She knew who she was, though. Sabrina stood up and pointed a warning finger. 'Stay.'

The room was sparsely furnished; Sabrina could see at a glance that her bag wasn't there. She went into the other room, much smaller, and found a little boy sitting on the side of a truckle bed. He was five or six years old and incredibly thin, with eyes that looked too big for his head. Sabrina's bag lay behind him on the bed.

'Hi, there,' Sabrina said, making her voice soft. 'How you doing?'

The boy looked wary but he stayed where he was. Sabrina ruffled his hair. She reached past him and picked up the bag. She pulled open the drawstring at the top and checked the wallet first. The cards were there, her WHO ID and papers of accreditation were there, but the money, five hundred dollars, was gone.

She looked at the thin little kid again and decided she wouldn't make a noise about the cash. She pulled back the tab on the false bottom and there was the pistol. All in all, she could say she was in luck.

'I hope your mom uses the cash to do you both some good.'

Sabrina turned away, running her fingers through the stuff in the bag, aware that something else was missing.

Then a terrible pain hit her. She dropped to her knees and rolled on her side, gasping. The boy was standing, one empty hand outstretched, staring down at her. As he turned and ran, Sabrina reached behind her, clenched her teeth and pulled the Swiss Army knife from the back of her thigh.

'Aah! God! Aaow!'

She pushed herself up and turned at a commotion in the other room. She saw the feet scamper out the front door, the boy and his mother. They were off like the wind, with enough money to stay away for a while, or to just go and live somewhere else for good.

Sabrina stood up, grunting, feeling the stiffness in her leg. She got a field dressing and an ampoule of wound wash from the zippered pocket in the bag.

'I used to call it my *lucky* Swiss Army knife,' she grunted.

The kid had used the longest, sharpest blade. Judging by the margin of blood on the polished steel, it had gone in three full centimetres. It felt like he had used a bayonet, but on the plus side there wasn't much bleeding. Sabrina pulled up her skirt and squirted the antibacterial on to the wound.

'Oh hell, hell, hell!' A fresh agony hit her. 'Son of a bitch!'

It burned like a blowtorch. She distracted herself by tearing open the dressing wrapper with her teeth, and as the pain diffused away and left behind only the nagging throb of punctured muscle, she tried once again to tell herself that, on balance, she had been pretty lucky.

Philpott picked up the red phone on the second ring and waited for the scrambler noise to subside.

'Sabrina? Where in God's name have you been?'

'There was a hitch, sir. I'm truly sorry, I would have been in touch sooner if it had been possible.'

'Something wrong with the phone, is there? We can always get a replacement to you if you think you need one.'

'The phone's fine, sir. I just encountered a little setback, and what with one thing and another, my call-in got delayed. I've already smacked my wrist on your behalf.'

'Quite right. Are your problems sorted out now? Can I rely on you sticking to our agreed schedule from here on?'

'Yes, sir, you can.'

'Fine. Be careful.'

He put down the phone and immediately the black one beside it warbled. He picked it up, glancing at the clock. He had planned to leave half an hour ago.

'Philpott.'

'Thomas Lubbock.'

Philpott's eyes narrowed. A call direct from the Director of Policy Control could only mean the pressure was being turned up.

'What can I do for you?'

49

'Pencil a date in your diary.' Lubbock's voice was cold and offhand, a model of rehearsed detachment. 'Wednesday, March twelfth. Techniques-and-procedures review.'

'I don't think I can manage that date,' Philpott said.

'I wasn't offering you an option.'

'Of course you weren't,' Philpott said smoothly. 'You haven't the authority to do anything like that.'

'I . . .' Philpott listened, relishing the break in Lubbock's flow, the crack in his composure. 'I would point out that the Secretary General has agreed the date –'

'You've spoken to him?' Philpott injected a note of surprise.

'I have spoken with one of his staff . . .'

'Ah.' Philpott let that hang in the air. 'Look here, this is what we'll do. I'll speak to the SG in person and let him know that I'd favour another date. He can then convey the message to his staff, one of whom will no doubt get back to you. If your revised date doesn't suit me either, maybe I should suggest to the SG that I decide on a date and time myself.'

Lubbock was silent for five seconds. When he finally spoke it was clear he had trouble controlling his voice. 'I'm sure you enjoy this, Philpott,' he said. 'I can tell you're the type that likes games. But I would suggest – and you'd do well to note – that you're about to discover that a frivolous administration cannot survive in this organization.'

'Good of you to call.' Philpott hung up. He picked up the receiver again and tapped in Whitlock's extension number. 'Come in, C. W. I need to have a word.'

Whitlock appeared at once.

'The Arno Skuttnik enquiry,' Philpott said. 'Is it a solid one, or are we chasing bubbles?'

'It has promise.' Whitlock updated Philpott on the photograph, the mysterious woman, the growing mystery of the dead porter's connection with Adam Korwin, and the question of the handwriting on the picture. 'It could work against us, of course,' he added. 'At this stage who can say?'

'You think, nevertheless, that it could be something of substance, either way?'

'Definitely.'

'Then follow it. But now I want you to make it a priority. Lubbock is starting to lean. Or he's trying to. Sooner or later I'll have to accede to a techniques-and-procedures review. When I do, I don't want to go in there on the defensive.'

Whitlock nodded. 'If there's ammunition to be found, I'll do all I can to find it. But . . .'

'What?'

'Fingers crossed I don't find a booby trap instead.'

SEVEN

It had been a long and eventful day, but not the kind Mike favoured. He had ended up tired, footsore and dejected, and he had gained nothing. He had come back to base with more questions than answers, and that was not the way things were supposed to work.

He sat swirling his drink, watching Ram Jarwal read the faxes that had accumulated while they were out.

'It's depressing to think,' Mike said, 'that the death of the man they found down the slope this morning, and the death of Reverend Young, are everyday statistics by now. Just records on paper, with nothing being done about them.'

'Containment is beyond the police now, never mind catching villains,' Ram said, turning from the fax machine. 'They tidy up the consequences of crime and administer the paperwork.'

'Reverend Young seemed to think this was still a pretty civilized and well ordered area.'

'He worried that the troubles in the region would soon make it as bad as the rest of Kashmir,' Ram said. 'The fact is, in the space of a year things deteriorated a lot more than he realized. The only difference here, right here on the west side of the Vale, is they have community spirit, and that gives them the backbone to maintain something like independence.'

'Independence is hard to lick.'

'Sure,' Ram said, 'but criminals and the political agitators are on the case. They're wearing away the stability, erasing the civilizing factors . . .'

'Factors like Reverend Young.' Mike shook his head. 'Philpott should be out here seeing the situation for himself. This stuff would chivvy him into action. He's all for pulling out major stops when he thinks civilization is under threat from the barbarians.'

'I've heard about Philpott.' Ram brought the bottle of Jim Beam and topped up Mike's glass. 'English, isn't he? Used to be at Scotland Yard.'

'Technically Scottish, I believe. He had several years as a Detective Chief Superintendent and Joint Chief of the Special Branch. That gave him a solid point of view on the subject of government security.'

'An old school disciplinarian?'

Mike shook his head. 'He's nothing you can hang a label on. He's a champion of democratic government, but he feels democracy hasn't been correctly defined or formulated. It needs to lean towards benign dictatorship.'

'So he's kind of right-wing.'

'Kind of,' Mike said. 'But like I told you, it's hard to label him. He's an individualist. He believes, for example, that a man or woman with a cop's background is better at gathering results and evaluating them than even the best government man.'

'I thought the training was much the same for police and government law enforcers.'

'Philpott believes people trained in government agencies lack the policeman's out-on-the-street understanding of criminals. Cops are also better at keeping in mind the requirements of the law, especially in the way evidence has to be gathered and how it's put before the courts.'

'You think he's right about that?'

'Essentially, yes. On the other hand, Philpott occasionally uses the kind of undisciplined guerrilla tactics that no cop or G-man would get away with.'

'So he's a walking set of contradictions.'

Mike nodded. 'That's one label you could pin on him.'

Ram had gone to the window. He stood there listening.

'What're you doing?'

'You'll find out in a minute.' He went back to the fax machine. 'Philpott's certainly got interesting impulses.' He held up a sheet of paper. 'This is a communiqué from UN Information and

Services in New Delhi. It tells me that as a result of a snap decision by Director Philpott of UNACO, followed by rapid inter-departmental negotiations earlier today, we are due to have another visit from the Sikorsky.'

'When?'

'Any minute now.'

'What's it about?'

Ram winked. 'I'm sure you'd prefer a surprise.'

Mike stood up and drained his glass. As he put it down Ram held up a finger. 'I hear it. Let's get outside and shut the door before the dust covers everything.'

It was a cold, starry night with a crescent moon almost directly overhead. Mike and Ram stood with their backs against the front wall of the cabin, hugging themselves against the icy breeze as the black helicopter descended, deafening them with its noise, throwing up a whirlwind as first one wheel touched down, then the other.

The door swung open and a bag was thrown out. Mike peered past his shielding hand to see who had arrived. He saw boots, a flapping black coat and the top of a man's head bent low as he stepped out and snatched up the bag.

The helicopter door closed and a second later it was rising again, powering away from them, turning in a wide arc south-ward. The new arrival walked right up to Mike, who still couldn't see him for the wind and the dust.

'This is getting monotonous, Michael.'

Mike blinked a couple of times and saw the grinning face of Lenny Trent.

'Lenny! What the –'

'Amazing, isn't it? For years I see nothing of you, then we start bumping into each other all over the place.'

As the dust settled Ram opened the cabin door and beckoned them in. Lenny stood in the living room, flushed, combing his fingers through his hair.

'Somebody tell me what's happening,' Mike said.

'Be glad to.' Lenny took off his coat and dropped it on the back of an easy chair. He removed his steel-framed glasses, wiped

54

them with his scarf, put them on again. 'Just as soon as there's a drink working itself into my bloodstream.'

Ram handed him a jigger glass half full of bourbon.

'You have a fine memory there, old buddy.'

'You two know each other?' Mike said.

'Ten years,' Ram said, 'give or take.'

'I *have* been know to wander these fragrant slopes,' Lenny said.

'So why are you here now?'

'Mr Philpott called me in Seattle with a couple of questions about the possible location of drug routes through the Vale of Kashmir. I accommodated him, and I added that you and I had just talked about the same thing. He was intrigued to learn how far back we went, and right there and then, while he was on the line, he did some out-loud thinking.'

'Another idiosyncrasy,' Mike told Ram.

'In a nutshell,' Lenny said, 'he explained that he needed police liaison on this job, and normally he would have sent out C. W. Whitlock as part of the team. But he's got C. W. on something important in New York, so he wondered if I would consider secondment – without loss of status, of course – to this here mission.'

'Did he give you time to think about it?' Mike said.

'Oh, sure. He gave me from then until he was ready to hang up. I told him I was almost through with the job in Seattle, which would now be handled through the courts by the police and the DA's office, but I added I would have to clear things with my own immediate superiors.'

Mike was nodding. 'He told you not to worry about that, he would fix it.'

'Right. And he did. And here I am. I've an appointment the day after tomorrow with the Chief of Police at Srinagar. He'll give me an overview of developments in local drug shipping, and I'll swap him a few names he could use, and we should get along just fine.'

'That's going to be your job here? Police liaison?'

'Among much else, Mike. I don't like staying too narrow.

Linking and co-ordination are the things I do best out here, so that's what I'll concentrate on.' Lenny took a gulp of bourbon. 'Is there a schedule of events I can fall in with between now and when I visit the police?'

'We've a dinner date,' Ram said, holding up another fax. 'Dr Arberry. He's an American who settled here a couple of years ago.'

'He's doing big things with his public medical centres,' Mike told Lenny. 'Right now his foundation is setting up a free hospital for the disadvantaged people of the region. Reverend Young thought highly of him.'

'They told me what happened to Alex Young,' Lenny said. 'I met him a time or two. Nice guy.' He turned to Ram. 'So why do you think Dr Arberry has sent out a dinner invite?'

'He heard about the arrival of a UN fact-finder,' Ram said.

'That would do it. If I were in his place I'd want all the UN and Interpol contacts I could make.'

'He wants us to join him tomorrow at eight. I'm sure he'd be happy to have another guest along. What's your cover, Lenny?'

'Intelligence co-ordinator to the Security Council.' Lenny smiled. 'Sounds glossy, huh? The Council approved it, too. What plans do you have for tomorrow daytime?'

'More damned walking, probably,' Mike said.

'We've been on recon,' Ram explained. 'Getting Mike *au fait* with the terrain.'

'And the patterns of casual murder,' Mike added.

'I can show you some probable drug routes, if you like,' Lenny offered.

'Would Paul Seaton be likely to use any of them?'

'Who can say? Maybe I'll know more about that when I've talked with the police.'

'Paul Seaton?' Ram said.

Lenny sighed. 'It's a long story. But I'm sure that won't stop Mike telling it.'

After an overnight stay in the town of Manali, at a boarding house run by a couple from Yorkshire, Sabrina drove directly north, through scrub land and flat farm country, along roads scarcely wider than the car's wheelbase. Sticking to her brief, she stopped wherever she saw a community and asked directions, all the time evaluating the people and the social divisions. It wasn't easy to distinguish signs of criminal infiltration and political coercion in territory where all of the people appeared equally poor, but Sabrina had her orders.

Late in the afternoon she arrived at Palanjal, fifteen kilometres south of the Kashmir border, and there she began to see a difference. Palanjal was a medium-sized town with a population of perhaps twenty thousand. The difference here was that social divisions were visible. Some people were better dressed than others; better nourished, too; and on the sidewalks there appeared to be a rule of precedence, the poorer, shabbier citizens automatically making way for the others.

Sabrina stopped for petrol at a wayside station. The attendant spoke English, but he was not keen to engage in conversation. Sabrina persevered. She explained that she was doing a survey in the area, estimating the cumulative effects of weather and pollution on the environment.

'I have to report back to my people, that's the World Health Organization, maybe you've heard of them? On the basis of my findings, as well as those of maybe a hundred other ecology monitors, revised cultivation and crop-planting regimes will be devised, and it's hoped that communities such as this one will see real benefits in the years to come.'

The man on the pumps nodded, took the money for the petrol and disappeared indoors.

Ten minutes later, as Sabrina walked through the local market and spoke to people, the same thing kept happening. She was not directly shunned, but people wanted no prolonged contact with her. It could have been a local trait, but she didn't believe that. Sabrina knew when people were scared of saying too much, or were frightened by the consequences of being seen in certain company. She had experienced identical behaviour in Sicily before the Mafia trials, she had seen it in Guatemala, too, and in Chile and Bosnia.

She tried to get lodgings for the night in Palanjal, but no one had rooms. There was a hotel, empty-looking, but the clerk said sorry, they had no accommodation available now, or for the foreseeable future.

'Maybe you could recommend some place else?'

The clerk shook his head. 'There is nowhere else, I assure you.'

'Then I guess I'll have to sleep in the car.'

'There is time to move on to another town,' the clerk said. 'It is not advisable to stay here without proper accommodation.'

'I see.'

She left the hotel and got in the car. It was four in the afternoon. She decided to head for the next town, which according to her map was Jullaspur. If she couldn't get to the bottom of what troubled the people in this town, at least she could make a comparison with the way visitors were treated at the next place.

As she drove to the end of the main street, following the sign pointing to Jullaspur, a man stepped out in front of the car. Sabrina had to brake hard to keep from hitting him. He stood in the roadway with his hands on his hips, staring at her through the windscreen, his bearded face expressionless.

Sabrina sat tight, waiting, avoiding conclusions. The man, she noticed, was wearing western clothes: leather trousers, a striped collarless shirt, shiny black leather boots. He also wore a gun and a bandolier of ammunition across his chest.

Sabrina's door jerked open. Another man was there. He was clean-shaven and looked more Arab than Indian. He wore one silver earring and had a deep scar from the side of his nose across his cheek to his left ear, from which the lobe was missing.

'Out, please,' he said.

'Get away from me,' Sabrina said.

He took hold of her arm and pulled sharply, jerking her out on to the road. She landed on her back. He put his foot firmly on her stomach and snapped his fingers at the man standing in front of the car. He came and between them they put Sabrina on her feet and frog-marched her across the road to a battered

Mitsubishi pickup. Sabrina made a show of squirming resistance, but she was careful to do nothing to show she could handle herself in a situation like this.

'You will lie still in the bottom,' the clean-shaven one said as they hoisted her into the back of the pickup. 'This man will sit near you. If you try to escape, he has orders to shoot you in the knees. Do you understand?'

Sabrina nodded, looking terrified, choking back a whimper. She was dumped without ceremony into the hard metal bottom of the pickup trailer. The hairy-faced man got in beside her. When the engine started she closed her eyes and curled over on her side.

'Listen!' the man said harshly. 'You listen and remember!'

She nodded, her lower lip between her teeth.

'You move and I shoot.'

No worries, she thought. Escape was the last thing she planned. This might be dangerous, it might be fatal, but it was progress. In her job progress was *always* the option of choice, wherever it led.

EIGHT

C. W. Whitlock stood in a small, tidy laboratory two doors away from the TF3 suite in the UN Secretariat building, listening to a recital of complaints from Luther Flint. Luther was head of Scientific Resources, a subdivision of UNACO Clandestine Enterprises. He was also, in the view of many, a borderline clinical paranoid.

Today he had chosen Whitlock as the target for what Philpott called a 'querimonius diatribe'.

'I don't know how you people expect us to function, C. W. Time and again – you'd think it was deliberate, a matter of policy – you give us the scantiest, lowest quality material to work with, and expect us to turn in results of shimmering, incandescent excellence. And if the results of our exertions are disappointing, if they're less than you wanted, you put the word about that we just aren't up to the job we were hired to do.'

'That just isn't true –'

'Now you're calling me a liar.'

'I'm saying you're mistaken when you say people criticize you or evaluate your work in a negative way.' Whitlock knew there was no way to placate Luther. The best he could do was get him on a low simmer. 'Speaking for myself, I've nothing but admiration for the job you do. I appreciate that your consistently splendid results are all the more impressive considered alongside the downright cruddy source materials you often have to work with.'

'Well,' Luther grunted, 'just so long as you know the conditions imposed on us aren't ideal. The fact is, they're not even reasonable.'

'Sure, sure.' Whitlock pointed to the coloured snapshot

mounted on a copy easel on the bench beside them. It was the picture he had borrowed from Clancy Spencer. 'I'm not asking you to do the impossible here, truly I'm not. I just want you to make the best copy and the best blow-up you can, then scan the blow-up into your computer, enhance it, print it out at roughly fifteen hundred dpi and do another blow-up from that.'

'And of course you wouldn't be trying to tell me how to do my job, would you?'

'What?'

All you have to do,' Luther said, 'is tell me you want the best quality-enhanced blow-up I can make. No need to tell me the way I should achieve that. I'm a professional, remember. It's part of my job to know how to do whatever you ask.'

Whitlock was tempted to pull the picture off the easel, march out of there and do the job himself. But he held on to his composure; Luther, after all, did the best job of anyone in his field.

'I didn't mean to offend you.'

'I accept it maybe wasn't intentional.' Luther shook back a strand of white hair and adjusted his horn-rims. 'How soon do you want the print?'

'Tomorrow?' Whitlock ventured.

'Sweet God.' Luther glared at him. 'This isn't the only work I have to do, you know.'

'I appreciate that, but this is kind of pressing . . .'

Luther sighed. 'I'll see what I can do.'

Whitlock left the laboratory without another word. He went straight to the Secure Communications Suite and sat down at one of the computers. For a few seconds he was motionless, letting the padded, dimly-lit interior of the room work its soothing effect on him. He closed his eyes and sat back in the chair, feeling the reassuring support on his shoulders.

It had been a bad twenty-four hours. The pressure for once had not been professional – although there was plenty of that – but domestic. His wife had finally moved out. She had gone because his work received more of him than she did, and because she had found another man who was keen to devote himself to

61

her and to the life they would build together. Instead of her absence creating a gap in Whitlock's life, he was finding that it was more like a disheartening presence, something solid, a wall perhaps, that separated him from the life he would have preferred. On the other hand, he could never have come up to his wife's expectations, so there was a measure of relief in his gloom.

He opened his eyes and shook himself. He had almost fallen asleep. He tapped a code on the keyboard and a moment later he was connected to the Kremlin Archive, the third biggest database in Europe. The archive, consisting of millions of items of classified matter hijacked by US agents from a KGB hideaway in 1993, was maintained by technical staff of the US Embassy in Rome. The embassy boasted a state-of-the-art computer-communications installation among its other attractions, and in recent months UNACO had been granted unrestricted access to the archive.

Whitlock entered a request to review the picture files, and was asked what kind of pictures. He ticked PERSONNEL: ESPIONAGE. He entered the name Adam Korwin. A pause, then three pictures came up on the screen side by side. The first showed Korwin as a young man, photographed with the onion-domes of St Basil's in the background. In the second his head had been shaved and he wore a moustache. The third picture showed him as he looked in Clancy Spencer's snapshot, although the date on this picture was 1989.

Whitlock downloaded the third picture to the printer, and requested that a summary of Korwin's KGB service record be attached. In a couple of minutes he had a twelve-page dossier, most of it in summary, but impressive enough to put before a techniques-and-procedures review.

Next Whitlock entered a search under the name of Arno Skuttnik. It was a long shot and, as he expected, the archive found no match for that name. One Skuttnik was listed, but his first name was Tibor. Whitlock called for a picture and up came a grainy shot of a young man in a flat cap. The caption said: *Tibor Skuttnik, discipline officer to Narodnyi Kommissariat Vnutrennykh Dyel (People's Commissariat for Internal Affairs) Moscow,*

1938: subsequently appointed to Stalin's private staff – See file under Skuttnik, T.

Whitlock was inclined to leave it there. This was not his man. On the other hand, a look at the file couldn't hurt. He called it up and a single page appeared onscreen. If non-military medals were any guide, Skuttnik had been a good and loyal servant to Stalin; he had worked in the capacity of an enforcer, personally dealing with people who tried to approach their leader at public gatherings, also inflicting summary punishment on any of the domestic staff who fell short of requirements.

Skuttnik had been rewarded in 1948 with an appointment to the Leningrad Intelligence School, a training centre for spies, where he taught unarmed combat.

In the final paragraph the report became vague. Skuttnik, it said, was believed to have been posted as a sleeper to the United States, but confirmation of this was not contained in the archive; it was only mentioned in letters between other Kremlin employees of the time.

Whitlock thought about that. The fact was, a lot of Russian agents were sent to the United States during the fifties and sixties. It would be unprofessional to read anything significant into the last paragraph of the report.

'We still don't know who you were, Arno . . .'

Then, for the first time, Whitlock looked at the caption at the top of the page. It said: *Kremlin Service Record – Tibor Arno Skuttnik.*

After a bumpy trip – Sabrina estimated it took twenty minutes – the pickup turned off the rough country track and into a wooded hollow between two hills. She was hoisted from the truck by her abductors and frog-marched again, this time into a building that looked like a miniature temple.

Inside someone had been cooking. Analytical as always, Sabrina identified the smells of boiled rice, overcooked green vegetables and dhal. She also identified the man sitting at the far end of the tall central room. It was something of a shock, but she didn't let the recognition show. Instead, she went on looking scared.

Her captors marched her up to the throne-like chair where the man sat with one leg slung over the arm rest. He had a coarse, once-handsome face, with pads of fat at the temples and under the chin. His hair had receded until the hairline was halfway across the top of his scalp; to compensate, the remaining hair was long and tied back in a ponytail. He wore western clothes like the other two, although his looked much finer.

'I am Hafi,' he announced in English.

Hafi Bal Mardekhar, Sabrina recalled, leader of the Khalq faction. He was known to UNACO as a murdering Pakistani bandit with Afghan affiliations, who randomly terrorized towns and villages in northern India and south Kashmir. Like many self-styled warlords he had long ago swallowed his own propaganda and believed himself to be supremely charismatic and a politically important figure.

'Do you have a name?' he demanded.

'I'm – yes – I'm Susan,' Sabrina faltered. 'Susan Duke.'

'Oh.' Hafi's stiff face tried to look mocking. 'Not Nikita, then? Or Petrushka?'

'I don't follow you.'

'You are a Russian infiltrator!' Hafi shouted. 'You were trying to mislead us by taking the long route to Pakistan!'

Sabrina fished in her jacket pocket and produced her WHO identification. 'I work for the World Health Organization. I'm an American.'

'Paper will take on anything,' Hafi waved the document away. 'Besides, I know an infiltrator when I see one.'

'I promise you, I'm not a Russian,' Sabrina said, simultaneously thinking what an idiot he was. 'And anyway,' she added, 'what possible reason could Russia have for wanting to infiltrate or invade Pakistan now?'

'Russia has old scores to settle. Old ambitions to fulfil. Many times they have sent minions to mingle with the people and spread propaganda.' Hafi leaned forward. 'They try to establish a base of operations by cunning.'

'You've got me completely wrong, I assure you –'

'If I thought your masters would listen,' Hafi interrupted, 'I

64

would let you go and you could tell them they are wasting their time.' He smiled in a way that suggested he was trying to look evil. 'Of course, they wouldn't listen.'

'I am a citizen of the United States,' Sabrina said. 'I am in India under the terms of an international agreement that protects me from being impeded or molested. I –'

'You speak good English for a Russian,' Hafi said. He waved his arm. 'Take her away.'

She was marched to the back of the tall room, along a short passage and through a narrow doorway to a smaller room, much darker than the other. In the gloom she was aware of other people. There was an unmistakable smell of blood, musty and dried, and an overall odour of decay.

The men pushed her into a corner and went out. The door slammed shut and she heard the key turn.

'Are you English?' A woman's voice whispered.

Sabrina said nothing for the moment. She shut her eyes and counted to a hundred, letting her retinas sensitize and her pupils dilate.

She opened her eyes. The room looked brighter now. There were three other people. One was a man, young and very thin, asleep in a corner. An old woman was huddled on a stained mattress in the opposite corner, her head down and resting on her knees. The third person, a young woman in a blue sari, sat close to Sabrina.

'Are you?' she said. 'English?'

'American. How long have you been here? What's going on?'

'They brought me here yesterday. I am called Deena. I was at work in Chaudhuri, two hours' travelling from here. I work in a laundry. I was wheeling a basket of sheets across the yard at the back of the laundry when two men came in, grabbed me and put me in a truck. I was brought here and told nothing. But I know who they are. I know it is Hafi and the Khalq.'

'You speak very good English,' Sabrina said.

'I worked in London for three years. Battersea. My visa was withdrawn when my cousin, who sponsored me, was arrested and convicted of selling cannabis.'

'You seem very calm about all this, Deena. Aren't you scared?'

'I was when they brought me here. Then they put this bowl in the room.'

Sabrina looked. It was a willow pattern soup bowl, half full of chopped leaves. 'Bhang?'

'I chew enough to keep from being afraid.'

Sabrina had heard of that. There were people in Latin America who did it all the time, they chewed tiny pieces of marijuana leaf, and left just enough time between chews to maintain a near-normal existence, minus the anxieties.

'The old woman and the boy took so much they have been asleep all day,' Deena said.

'How long have they been here?'

'Since the day before yesterday, both of them. Hafi brought them when he took over this place. The boy was taken from the place where he worked, a field ten kilometres from here. The woman was asleep on a back porch in Jallapur when they snatched her. They brought her here and for several hours she was kept out in the main part of the building. This is a temple, very special, a private family place of worship.'

'And the bandits just took it over?'

'They killed the family, the old woman said. They were out there worshipping, men, women and children, and Hafi simply walked in and shot them. The bodies were kept in this room until it was dark.'

That explained the stink of blood and corruption, Sabrina thought.

'Then they were taken away and the old woman and the boy were thrown in here.' Deena leaned closer to Sabrina. 'Don't you wonder what they plan to do with us?'

'I was getting up the courage to ask. Hafi thinks I'm a spy, or he says he does. Does that mean I get treated any worse than anybody else?'

'Hafi treats all his captives the same,' Deena said. 'Everyone in this part of the country knows what to expect when they see him draw up in town in his big red jeep. He wants money. All the money a town can raise.'

'How are they persuaded to hand it over?'

'He brings persuasion with him. Always it is one of his captives, and always a person who does not come from the town Hafi wishes to rob. Hafi tells the people, "Look, nobody in your town has been hurt. Not yet. But see what will happen if I do not have the money I demand in one hour's time." And he puts the captive in the middle of the road and shoots him or her through the head.'

Sabrina was already framing plans to get out of there. Scope was limited by the certainty that she couldn't leave these others behind.

'Do you want a piece of bhang?' Deena said.

'No, thanks. What I need is a cup of coffee. I always think better with a cappuccino beside me.'

Two-thirds of the complication was removed an hour later, when the henchmen who abducted Sabrina came into the room and took away the old woman and the young man.

'They will be robbing two towns,' Deena said, chewing slowly on a chunk of leaf.

For a time Sabrina was shocked and distracted by the heartlessness of it, the shameful squandering of life. After a while her sense of self-preservation reasserted itself.

'Deena, do you know how many men are here with Hafi?'

'Only those two. His gang is very big, so big he calls it a movement. But when he's out raising money, it is just him and those two.'

'So you and I are here alone.'

'Yes, I suppose so.'

'Right. Do me a favour.'

'Mm?'

'Lay off the leaf. We'll have work to do.'

NINE

Dr Arberry sent a Land-Rover to pick up Mike, Ram and Lenny. The driver was Nisar, an old man with thick-lensed spectacles who drove with his face pushed over the wheel, as if he needed to be as close to the windscreen as possible. Nisar drove erratically but he appeared to be comfortable with the narrow, twisting roads. He swung the vehicle around blind bends with the certainty of a man who knew exactly what to expect.

'Back to first things,' Lenny said in the rumbling darkness, watching the cones of the headlights cut into the night. He was squeezed between Mike and Ram, holding on to the back of the front seats for support. 'This was my life at the start of my career.'

'Who with?' Ram said.

'The DEA. Riding around Colombia in jeeps and jalopies at dead of night, watching out for bad guys.'

'Except you didn't use headlights,' Mike said.

'Right. We had night-vision helmets. Blanketed engines, too. The element of surprise. We ran over more druggies than we arrested.'

'Around here,' Ram said, 'the bandits operating the drug convoys are the people with the hi-tech. The police caught a straggler off the end of a convoy last month and when they searched his saddlebags he had a night scope, laser-sighted pistol, secure-band radio and a Walkman.'

Nisar turned sharply down a gravelled road flanked by tall mature trees draped with moss. A hundred metres along there was an ornamental iron fence with a cultivated lawn behind it. In the distance they could see the house, a replica of a Southern plantation mansion, pure white, with a tall pillared porch and curved wings on either side.

68

'I get the impression Dr Arberry is made of money,' Lenny said. 'Do you know him, Ram?'

'We're acquainted. He's loaned me books from time to time. He's direct, balanced, incredibly focused on his work. He even looks right for the part, like Gregory Peck maybe thirty years ago.'

They passed through tall electrically-operated gates and the driver accelerated up the wide, red-chip drive to the front of the floodlit house. He braked as if it was an emergency, throwing his passengers forward. As they scrambled out, a deep, Boston-tinted voice greeted them.

'Gentlemen. You survived the journey. Magnificent.'

Simon Arberry stepped to the front of the porch. He was tall and lean, with clipped sandy hair that looked nearly blond against his tan. The impression of healthy middle age was enhanced by his white linen suit and pale blue open-necked shirt. Ram was dead right, Mike thought. It was like meeting a fiftyish Gregory Peck.

Ram made the introductions and Arberry led them inside. The hallway resembled the foyer of a good hotel: small black and white chequerboard tiles on the floor, dark green silk and hessian drapes, oak-panelled doors with brass fittings. There was even an ebony reproduction of Praxiteles' *Wrestlers*, mounted on a plinth by the door to the drawing room.

'This is where I fire up my enthusiasms,' Arberry said, showing them in. 'It's also my communications centre.'

The room was big enough to accommodate an ordinary bungalow, chimneys and all. One wall was fitted from floor to ceiling with bookshelves; on the opposite side of the room, on either side of the Adam-style fireplace, fine rosewood tables and cedar shelves held a range of electronic equipment – radio transmitters, receivers, DAT and reel-to-reel recorders and twin CD burners – all apparently on standby. There were also two satellite-tuned TV sets with the sound turned down.

With glasses of dry sherry, poured by an Indian in immaculate English butler's livery, the visitors listened as Simon Arberry bemoaned the death of his friend, Reverend Alex Young.

'He called me a visionary,' Arberry said, 'but I'll tell you something, I never had a tenth his insight or his dedication to these people. With anything he could scrape together, any meagre sums of money or threadbare resources, he would conjure a way of benefiting his flock. Time and again I watched him put together improvements to existing resources with his bare hands. And he was eternally involved, he never stood back.'

'Your own commitment to community health and welfare can't be played down,' Ram said. 'Reverend Young talked a great deal about your schemes, the facilities you've set in place, the plans you have . . .'

'My own dedication is to meeting God-awful challenges,' Arberry said. 'I am to an extent a humanitarian. My need to achieve things lies in the general direction of downtrodden and disadvantaged people. But first and foremost, what I relish is the provocation of an obstacle.'

When the butler announced that dinner was served they crossed the hall to the dining room. It was long and deep-carpeted, with a French crystal chandelier, gold silk window drapes and a table capable of seating thirty. For this occasion the large table had been put against the wall and another, two metres square, was set up in the centre of the room.

'You'll have noticed,' Arberry said as they sat down, 'that there are few if any Indian touches about my home. That's because I find it pretentious for a man of an entirely different culture to pretend he's at home with the styles and traditional trappings of a place he never saw until he was thirty. It's one thing to love the country, quite another to absorb its natives' cultural instincts.'

'Like a guy from California trying to feel at ease in a New York apartment,' Lenny said.

Arberry laughed. 'Something like that happened to me, come to think of it. I grew up in Boston, went to Harvard, did most of the Boston things right through my formative years. Then when I graduated med school I got an internship in a San Francisco hospital. The different way of life nearly finished me.'

The food was wheeled in on two trolleys by the butler and an Indian maid in a blue and silver sari.

'The point I was going to make,' Arberry said as the dishes were lined up on the sideboard, 'is that there may be none of the local cultural or decorative touches in the house, but the odour of Indian cooking sure as hell permeates the corridors. I adore the stuff.'

Mike had been warned that the food served in Kashmir was usually disappointing to anyone who had eaten Indian cuisine in the West. That may have been the case in the restaurants of Srinagar and Pahalgam, but not in Simon Arberry's house.

'This is the best Indian cooking I ever ate,' Mike declared.

Lenny nodded. So did Ram, both their mouths too full to speak. They were served dishes that even Ram had never seen or heard of before – sada pilau, kutchi biriani, aaloo tariwale – with a superb, bewildering selection of sauces and side dishes, and carafes of red, white, and rosé wine. Throughout the meal, Arberry managed to eat as fast as anyone, at the same delivering a monologue about his plans for the region.

'In eighteen months' time I'll open a treatment centre, right at the heart of the Vale, staffed by doctors and nurses specializing in tropical medicine. I have two district outpatient clinics already open, a regional surgical centre just up the hill from here, and the new nurses' school will train girls from the local towns and villages and qualify them to a standard acceptable anywhere in the world.'

'I can see that your motivation and belief in your work could get some amazing things done,' Mike said. 'But where does the money come from?'

'I'm kept afloat by two things,' Arberry said. 'One is the approval of the authorities, the other is cash from large organizations throughout the world.'

'How do you get them to part with it?'

'I'm good at badgering.'

Over brandy and coffee Arberry tried to correct the one-sided bias he had imposed on the conversation. He asked Ram how his research into agricultural practices was going.

71

Ram improvised smoothly, turning the topic around and making it an overview of the Vale of Kashmir through the eyes of one whose job it was to study the territory.

'Everything about this region is romantic. Did you know, Doctor, that the Vale is an ancient lake basin?'

Arberry shook his head.

'For hundreds of years it was full of water.'

'How long is the Vale?' Lenny asked.

'A hundred and forty kilometres,' Ram said. 'That's eighty-five miles. It's twenty miles wide. The mountains around the Vale are between twelve and sixteen thousand feet high. They shelter the area from the south-west monsoon. It's as if . . .' Ram held his hands out, palms vertical, facing each other; 'as if somebody had designed it all, laid it out and said, well now, it needs to be fertile, and because it's to be a centre for population, it has to be beautiful and also sheltered from the worst of the elements in the surrounding country.'

'And of course, any good Hindu will tell you it *was* designed,' Arberry said. 'By the god Brahma. Ask anybody at all, they'll tell you.'

'And the next peasant is likely to tell you it was Vishnu,' said Ram, 'and the one after him will swear it was Siva.'

'You lost me,' Mike said.

'Think of the Hindu gods this way,' Ram said. 'There is only one omnipresent god, but he has three physical forms to match his principal facets – he is Brahma, the creator, Vishnu, the preserver, and Siva, the destroyer and reproducer. In a way they all share characteristics of each other, which is because they're all really the same being.'

'The theology's all very well,' Lenny said, red-faced from the spices and the wine, 'but what I want to know is, why do official sources always call the country Kashmir-and-Jammu?' He knew the answer, but it did no harm to stick to his cover in a positive way, now and again.

'That's the official name,' Ram said. 'If you need the full historical and political picture, I'll lend you a book. It's enough to know, for now, that half the population of the state of Jammu and Kashmir lives here in the Vale, and we have two capitals – Srinagar in summer, Jammu in winter.'

'And it's as well to bear in mind the message of my dear dead friend Alex Young,' Arberry said. 'In a state troubled with conflicts of a dozen kinds, we in the Vale have the best of it. We are the stable centre.'

'But enough unrest here could plunge the whole of Kashmir into terrible, bloody war,' Ram said.

'Do you think that's a danger, Doctor?' Mike said.

'I certainly do. And I know how it is most likely to come about. If our society here ever breaks apart, it will be because of the bandits. The bandits, more than anyone else, are the ones dedicated to overthrowing the stability and the way of life we enjoy here. If something isn't done to stop them, soon, they will hack apart the unity of the region, they will lay waste to it, and they will spread such fear, such corruption, that nothing will stop them turning the Vale into a smoking wilderness.'

'And then the land grabbing will start,' Ram said.

Lenny nodded. 'And the empire building.'

'But with the right help none of it need happen.' Arberry held up his glass. 'A toast. To the Vale of Kashmir, and to its continued existence as one of the most beautiful, most magical places on earth.'

Later, Arberry led his guests up the hill to his new surgical centre, a long concrete building housing three operating theatres and two recovery wards. He took them through the anaesthetic preparation rooms, showed them a roving head scanner, the latest mobile X-ray machines, and a battery of examination instruments linked to a central computer equipped with a diag-nostic database.

'A surgical unit any community could be proud of,' Ram said.

'But so small,' Arberry pointed out. 'We have an enormous waiting list. To double the size of this place wouldn't cut the problem in half, it doesn't work that way. But two more of these units, equally spaced from this one in a two-hundred-square-mile area, would cut the challenge to a third.' He smiled. 'You can see why Alex Young's little medical facility was so valuable, and why it'll be such a loss until somebody gets it up and running again. Our people need all the help they can get.'

Before Mike, Ram and Lenny got back in the Land-Rover with old Nisar, Arberry led them down a steep stairway at the foot of the lawn behind the house. It took them a hundred metres underground. At the pitch-dark bottom of the stairs Arberry told them to stop, then he threw a switch.

'My God,' Mike breathed. 'That's amazing.'

They were in a natural subterranean cave lit by dozens of concealed spots and floodlamps.

'I call it the Golden Cavern,' Arberry said. 'That isn't very imaginative of me, but I think you'll agree the name fits.'

'It's like a dream,' Lenny said.

The craggy walls and high ceiling were covered in gold. The light thrown back was so bright, so sparkling, that Ram had to shield his eyes.

'It's actually not gold at all,' Arberry said. 'It's iron pyrites, but in this setting it's as beautiful as any real gold. And nature put it there all by herself.'

Before they left, he gave each of his visitors a fat wallet of papers. 'Facts and figures,' he said, 'my observations concerning crime in this area. Perhaps, if you take the information to heart, you may bring collective pressure on your people to do something to help us.'

'He's a charismatic guy,' Lenny said on the way back. 'I meant to ask what made him come here in the first place. I can imagine him being a lot more at home in good ol' gregarious Manhattan.'

'It's a sad story,' Ram said. 'He was in private surgical practice in Massachusetts, quietly going places, and he came out here on a holiday with his wife.'

'When?' Lenny asked.

'Fifteen years ago. It was at the time they advertised the Vale of Kashmir as the Switzerland of India. Mrs Arberry was so in love with the place she persuaded the doc to buy a plot of land, so they could have a house to go to on holidays. But breast cancer killed her before she ever got a chance to come back.'

74

'I wondered about a wife,' Lenny said. 'Men like that don't usually live alone.'

'He told me her death changed him,' Ram said. 'He felt her spirit was where the plot of land was, so he moved here and bought acres around the spot. He built the mansion and since then he's devoted himself to improving the area his wife fell in love with.'

'Reverend Young was afraid the troubles might drive Dr Arberry out,' Mike said. 'The way it sounds to me, he would take some budging.'

'But I bet he knows they could do it,' Lenny said. 'He's civilized, remember. Civilized people don't stand a chance against the bears. He's certainly keen that the UN should find some way to run the bad guys off the territory.'

'I only had a quick skim through this,' Mike said, patting the wallet of papers on his knee, 'but it looks like a better dossier on the killing and the sabotage and the drug-running activities around here than you guys on Drugwatch International ever put together.'

Lenny stared at him in the dim yellow glow of the overhead light. 'You really know how to wound a person.'

'Nothing personal.'

'It's the doc's drive that makes him so capable,' Ram said. 'I've watched him. He won't settle for less than excellence. Everything he does is a masterpiece of its kind.'

'I wouldn't mind a smidgen of that drive,' Lenny said.

'The secret's in his sense of impermanence,' Ram said.

Lenny looked at him. 'You going philosophical on us?'

'I'm talking about the way he's convinced that even the best, the most seemingly everlasting, can be taken from us. It began with his wife. Now he sees something he loves with as much intensity coming under threat. And that makes him want to hang on harder. He lives every day with the pain of the threat, and the pain makes him want to prevail at all costs.'

'He said the whole thing when he was seeing us off just a few minutes ago,' Mike said. 'Remember?'

The other two nodded. Standing with them on the steps in

front of the white porch Dr Arberry had said, 'What hurts me most, what pains me to my soul, is to see mindless thuggery reduce beauty and progress to ashes.'

TEN

Srinagar, the summer capital of Kashmir, is a noisy, colourful, bustling city with its own distinct look and atmosphere. Each time Lenny Trent went there, he could not shake the feeling that he was much further east. The people even looked different, and he had heard businessmen, preparing to return south, say they were going back to India.

Nowadays Srinagar looked like occupied territory. Everywhere there were roadblocks; armed soldiers sat in bunkers on all the major street corners. An after-dark curfew was in operation and most nights there was fighting, most of it in the old city.

'It resembles Beirut over there,' Commissioner Jabar Mantur told Lenny. He pointed from the barred window of his second-storey office towards the craggy skyline of the old quarter. 'So many factions it's hard to keep track. New movements spring up overnight, every weekend old ones get wiped out.'

Commissioner Mantur was the second most senior police officer in Kashmir. He was a short, thickset man with iron grey hair that swept down each cheek in wiry sideburns, almost touching the ends of his moustache. He wore a lightweight grey business suit, a stark white shirt and a red tie. As he spoke he smiled a great deal and shook his head, as if it were necessary to disparage most of his own remarks.

'You will have noticed,' he said, 'that our police station here is more like a fortress. Twice in three months we had a bomb thrown into the reception area, and a grenade which was lobbed through the canteen window wounded ten of my officers. I was under pressure to do something about our security, so I took my lead from Northern Ireland.'

Lenny noted the benevolent eyes and the affable smile, and realized he was in the presence of a born diplomat. This wry, civilized administrator had a reputation for operational toughness that made Norman Schwartzkopf look effete. Confidential records at the HQ of Drugwatch International revealed that less than a month ago, Mantur had personally broken into a drug laboratory, shot the three guards dead and beaten up four chemists who were free-basing cocaine with industrial solvents. A note from a field agent formerly based in Kashmir described Mantur as 'a hands-on police chief who can't keep his hands off criminals'.

'I have a Security Council memo telling me I should co-operate with you, Mr Trent. You must be an important man.'

'I'm a reliable functionary, Commissioner. I'm a good bridge between sources of information and the people who have to act on it. Important is something I'm not.'

'To be reliable is more satisfying, anyway,' Mantur said. He went behind his desk and unlocked a drawer. 'These maps I will give you, they do not officially exist. They contain information which my masters in government would call speculative. They would call it that because nowhere on the maps, or in the accompanying notes, have I indicated how I obtained any of the information, nor do I offer anything else by way of corroboration.'

He put a sheaf of folded maps on the desk. Lenny picked up the top one, unfolded it and stood with his arms spread wide, marvelling at the scale and the detail.

'I can see this is done by hand, Commissioner, but it looks like the work of an artist . . .'

'The work of a jailed cartographer, as a matter of fact. I managed to, um, how do you say – *cut a deal* for him with the Justice Department on condition he would co-operate on the project. He would have co-operated anyway, you understand, but because I made it seem that his eventual early release would depend very much on the quality of the work, he turned out the best stuff he's ever done in his life.'

'The red lines are – what? Drug convoy routes?'

'Correct.'

'And the blue ones?'

'Dead routes. They indicate trails that have gone inactive as a result of police or military action. You could say each blue line represents a dead drug caravan.'

Lenny looked at the Commissioner over the top of the map. 'Dead?'

'Literally. There is no point in arresting bandits and trying to interrogate them. They might as well be a different species for all the help they provide. So they are eliminated as they are encountered. It's tidy.' Mantur smiled delicately. 'It's also confidential.'

Lenny refolded the map. 'You stand by this information, then. The red lines are active drug convoy routes.'

'It cost a lot of time, sweat and called-in favours to make sure the maps are accurate, Mr Trent.'

'Then I have to ask you, sir – why haven't you acted on this intelligence, if it's so reliable?'

'Manpower, that's the first obstacle. I don't have the men. Every time I mount an offensive against drug peddling I have to borrow officers from other regions. I have to justify the expense to my masters. I even have to give one month's notice of my intentions – which, of course, gives the peddlers roughly three weeks' warning that I'm on my way.' Mantur spread his hands. 'All I can do, to be effective in any measure, is to keep my intelligence updated in the hope I can use it from time to time.'

'And in the meantime?'

'I concentrate my main efforts on the kind of local drug manufacturing outfits whose liquidation does not rely on the deployment of large numbers of police officers.'

Lenny started to say something, then realized Mantur had only stopped for breath.

'The other obstacle is disloyalty. Most of my officers are straight and honest men, Mr Trent. But there are a few, an unidentified few, who keep the criminals informed of our planned movements. On balance this would not mean that every assault on drug convoys would be fruitless, but because my masters know there is a problem with disloyalty, they are even less inclined to support my efforts.' Mantur smiled again. 'Can I take it that your people are planning some kind of major assault on the drug people?'

'Nothing's planned,' Lenny said. 'First we're getting acquainted with the situation, as fast as we can. Then when we know the scale of the sickness, we'll try to formulate a remedy.'

'The drug problem is not a new one, Mr Trent. Nor will it ever be stamped out. Sources of supply are remote and beyond our reach, so as long as someone is prepared to pay poor men and hardened criminals to transport the poison, the trade will survive. I hope you don't think you can wipe it out.'

'Our concern is a specific area of trade, Commissioner. There's been an escalation of violence, political agitation and drug running in a previously stable territory, in the west of the Vale of Kashmir . . .'

'Yes, yes,' Mantur said. 'I hoped that would at least figure in your schedule of matters requiring attention. In fact it's my biggest concern. The old drug trade has at least discernible limits and predictable features. To some extent it can be contained. Most importantly, it doesn't carry the threat of all-out chaos.'

'But the troubles in the Vale do?'

'At the centre of those troubles is the traffic in drugs. We are dealing there with a brand new line of supply, and it passes right through that territory. I am aware also that some of the drug couriers are recruited from local communities.'

'And this traffic is well organized?'

'Dishearteningly so. And it is a new style of drug trade. The merchandise includes exceptionally refined cannabis oil, very *very* fine heroin, top grade cocaine and even quantities of crack. It is a more profitable trade area than the others and it is operated more ruthlessly.'

'Who are the main customers?'

'Moneyed intermediaries and end-users in South China and Thailand.'

Even the exhaustive data supplied by Dr Arberry hadn't mentioned a new kind of trade, or what was being peddled. 'I'd

80

appreciate anything you can tell me about this, Commissioner.'

'I have notes, I will give them to you. But briefly, the drug couriers, or mules as they're called, are recruited from peasant areas. They work one time only, and they are paid very highly for their single trip. The drawback is that if they are caught, they must poison themselves. They are supplied with capsules of potassium cyanide for the purpose. If they do not kill themselves, or if they try in any way to renege on the deal, their families will be tortured and killed.'

'Do you have much intelligence on the line of supply?'

'Information is thin, because no one will talk. They would sooner rot in one of our stinking jails than say anything.'

Mantur took three slim school exercise books from the desk drawer and put them on top of the maps. 'My notes on the new trade. There is much speculation in there, Mr Trent. For the present, it can't be any other way.' Mantur spread his hands and shrugged. 'Manpower.'

'Do you happen to know anything about a bandit leader alleged to be active in Kashmir, an American, name of Paul Seaton?'

Mantur rolled his eyes. 'I have heard of him, yes. He has a number of names, but I must say Paul Seaton is one that is used more than most. Again, Mr Trent, it's speculation. Lots of people have *heard* lots of things, others know people who know people, who have seen this and that. Personally, I happen to believe there is never this amount of smoke without there being a fire somewhere. And I suspect Mr Seaton may be an active element of the new trade through the Vale.'

'What makes you think that?'

'He moves around a good deal, or so the story goes, and his brand of savagery, what we know of it, seems to fit the general characteristics of the new trade operators.'

Lenny looked at the maps and the notes. Information wasn't going to be in short supply, he thought. But organizing it would be hard.

'You said you hoped we would be interested in this particular area of drug traffic, Commissioner. Is that because it's likely to

81

cause dangerous instability right at the heart of the state?'

'Certainly, but foremost in my mind is the certainty – the *uninformed* certainty – that for once, there may be a chance of finding the manufacturers. For once, we can look at the possibility of wiping out a line of trade all the way, with nothing left over to grow again.'

'What makes you so certain?'

'A small thing,' Mantur said. 'We have confiscated drugs from maybe ten, eleven peddlers on this new route. All of those peddlers, I may say, are dead.'

'Suicide?'

'Exactly. They died in accordance with their terms of employment. But it was their merchandise that made me sure the stuff is manufactured not far from the western territory of the Vale. It was so fresh-looking, Mr Trent. The packaging, the wrappers and bags and phials and capsules – they simply had not travelled very far when we intercepted them.'

The possibility of drugs actually being manufactured in the Vale of Kashmir put a new light on the project. Lenny looked at the Commissioner. 'Neat observation,' he said.

'Yes, I thought so.' Mantur smiled broadly. 'I would stake my chequered reputation that we made those busts – that's the phrase, yes? – very close to home base.'

Daylight burglary was a very unnatural activity, C. W. Whitlock decided. The whole business of theft from property, all the way from breaking and entering to going through drawers and cupboards and then sneaking out again, was an activity that screamed for the cover of darkness.

Adequate forward planning was something else he should have considered: maintenance plans of the twenty-sixth floor of the UN Secretariat building were comprehensive when it came to showing where everything was, but they didn't reveal – to take the case in point – that the air shaft above the office of the Secretary of Policy Control narrowed to a width of forty-five centimetres at the grille opening.

Whitlock lay with his arms doubled under him, his elbows

82

pressing on the sides of the shaft. He was pretty sure the office below him was empty, because Secretary Crane was a creature of habit, and he always went to lunch at 12:30. It was now 12:38. Nevertheless, having come this far, and at the expense of so much trouble and discomfort, Whitlock wasn't going to take any unnecessary chances.

He eased his hands forward and seized the grille by its two handles. He pushed gently and felt the resistance go as the grille detached smoothly. He turned it sideways, pulled it into the shaft and used his knees to inch himself forward far enough to look down into the room.

A second before he poked his head through the opening he heard Crane's voice and jerked back into the shaft.

Crane was down there! He was in the office using the telephone!

'Issues in that category are always the province of the Director,' Crane said, his voice sounding curiously close in the metal confines of the air duct. 'I'll be happy to pass your concerns along to him on your behalf, but that won't be possible until he gets back from lunch. As a matter of fact it won't be possible until I get back from lunch, and the longer we keep this conversation going, the later that will be.' A pause. 'Not at all. Goodbye.'

Whitlock lay there, listening. Crane had made one break with custom so he could make another. The office door opened, then closed. The key turned. At no point had there been the soft beep of the movement-detector being switched on. Crane probably considered himself thorough but not obsessive: who was going to break into his office in broad daylight?

Whitlock turned over on his back and slowly, painfully inched his arms up on to his chest. Reaching downward with the fingertips of both hands he pulled the coiled nylon ladder from the top of his overalls and let it uncoil out through the end of the duct and dangle down into the office.

Holding the end of the ladder with one hand, he eased out a telescopic brace from his breast pocket and pushed it through the looped end of the ladder. He then placed the brace lengthways at the edge of the duct opening and squeezed the spring release on the brace. It sprang out at both ends, its rubber stops clamping to the sides of the duct.

To get down the ladder he had to slide back along the air duct the way he had come, until he reached a four-way junction. He turned around and inched himself back to the opening, feet first.

He had never before used a ladder made entirely from nylon. His feet skidded uncontrollably on the first two rungs and he had to freeze all movement and wait for the ladder to stop swinging before he eased himself down any further. He began taking the rungs slowly, letting his weight settle on the centre of each one, waiting until the ladder was stable before going down another rung.

When he was finally on the floor he stood by the desk and let his gaze travel around the fastidious tidiness of the place. He could not even be sure the snapshot of Philpott was here. But it was likely to be.

He began with the filing cabinet, a six-drawer unit with a single lock at the top. A U-shaped piece of piano wire had the lock open in three seconds. In six minutes he went through every file in the cabinet. He found no snapshots, but he did come across a folder marked *UNACO Hearing – Notes Towards Structured Argument*.

He laid the folder on the desk, took out his Minox 16mm camera and photographed the four pages in the file, using the desk lamp for illumination. He put back the folder and locked the filing cabinet.

The desk drawers were locked but they were as easy to open as the cabinet. Whitlock found a whole range of unused desk equipment – stapler, paperclips, tape dispenser, paperknife – all in their original packets. There was also a book of personal telephone numbers, a dictation machine, tapes, personalized notepaper and envelopes, a loaded Mauser 7.65mm pistol, a Nikon F501 camera, handsome Pentax binoculars and a plastic wallet marked EVIDENTIAL. It contained ticket stubs, bills of sale and expense sheets relevant to departmental investigations; among the papers at the back of the folder was the photograph of Philpott.

Whitlock put it face down under the desk lamp and centred the pencilled writing carefully in his Minox viewfinder. A moment before he took the picture he detected a bell ringing in some shadowy corner of his memory. He took a second shot, closer this time, then put away the camera and returned the picture to the wallet.

He put everything back where it had been and looked round the room to make sure nothing was out of place. Satisfied, he turned and heard the bell ring again, a tiny irritation, nothing he could pinpoint or even narrow down.

'Time to get back up the ladder,' he whispered.

As he stepped on the first rung and began to sway, the words on the back of the picture came back to him. He could see them, the smudged curves, the way the letters looped and slanted.

It occurred to him suddenly why the bell had rung. He had seen that handwriting before. He didn't know where, but he had definitely seen it.

ELEVEN

'This temple,' Deena said, 'is dedicated to the worship of Ganesh.'

Sabrina smiled in the gloom. The faint light that seeped into the room through a high slit in the wall was growing now. For long hours they had been in darkness and for a while Deena had slept. Their preparations were made and now they simply waited. There was nothing else to do. Sabrina could scarcely see Deena's face, but she knew from the way the girl talked, from her nervousness and her growing animation, that the effects of the marijuana leaves had all but worn off.

'How can you tell, Deena?'

'From the symbols and pictures painted on the walls. Also from the images on the coloured window at the far end.'

'You remembered all that, even though you were so frightened?'

'It is long afterwards that I remember things.'

'And who is Ganesh?'

'The child of Siva and his consort Parvati, the beautiful. Ganesh is the god of prosperity and wisdom. He has an elephant's head.'

'Why is that?'

'The story is that one day, coming back from a long journey, Siva saw Parvati in her private quarters with a young man. Siva forgot that in his absence, his son would have grown. So he mistook Ganesh for Parvati's lover and cut off his head. Parvati was furious, she made Siva understand what he had done and demanded that he bring their son back to life. Siva could only do so by giving Ganesh the head of the first living thing he saw, which happened to be an elephant.'

At another time Sabrina would have been enchanted. Now she was too alert to sounds beyond the room, too focused on the need to be ready. Two hours earlier she had nearly fallen asleep. When she caught herself nodding she stood up, marched up and down for ten minutes to re-oxygenate her blood, then sat down and began declining Latin verbs in her head. It was tough work, but it kept her awake.

'Our companions will be dead by now,' Deena said. Her voice trembled. Her fear was gaining control.

'You mustn't think about that. You have to concentrate on one thought: there is a world of freedom outside. It is only the thickness of a wall away. Think of a straight line between you and the outside world. Think of nothing being able to stop you travelling along that line.'

'I don't think I can.'

'When the time comes, do what I told you,' Sabrina said. 'Do what we've gone over and over. I'll lead the way, all you have to do is follow, and have faith.'

Deena nodded and took a deep shaky breath. 'I am very afraid. I can't help that. I'm sorry.'

'Afraid is better than too confident.' Sabrina squeezed Deena's arm. 'Afraid is cautious and alert.'

Throughout the night there had been sounds in the temple, distant creaks and clicks, the sounds of shrinkage in wood, cooling in glass and in stone. Now there was a different sound, harder, louder. It grew and there was a sudden bump from the direction of the temple door.

'They're back,' Sabrina whispered.

Deena let out a whimper and clamped her hand over her mouth.

'Act drowsy, as if you've chewed up all the bhang.'

The sounds of boots on the tiled floor shuffled and bumped at random. The men muttered and once or twice they laughed. The two women sat side by side on a blanket, scarcely breathing. Their heads were bowed, making them look obsequious and small, the very opposite of a threat.

'They are coming,' Deena whispered.

'Sit tight. Just be ready. Your wits'll do the rest.'

Feet approached along the passage outside and a key clattered in the lock. The door swung open, letting in bright morning light. Sabrina kept her head down on her chest. Deena did the same. From under lowered eyelids Sabrina saw two pairs of boots, standing two metres away. A moment later tin plates were placed on the floor, each with a pile of yellow rice and chopped vegetables. Another dish of marijuana leaves was put beside them.

One of the men clapped his hands. Sabrina pretended to wake up. Her hand slid under the blanket.

The man leaned down and pushed the plate towards her. Sabrina's hand swung out from under the blanket clutching a chair leg. It went up at speed, hitting the man on the jaw, and came down faster, cracking him behind the ear.

As he fell Sabrina sprang to her feet. The second man drew a knife and lunged at her. Deena threw herself at him and wrapped her arms round his legs. He toppled and Sabrina swiped him savagely across the throat with the chair leg, cutting off his voice before he could shout.

Deena rolled away as the man landed on his back. She jumped to her feet. Sabrina stooped over him. She pocketed his knife as she put her index and middle finger on the side of his neck.

'What is it?' Deena was wide-eyed, shaking violently. '*What is it?*'

'He's dead.'

'But he can't be!'

'It's called vagal inhibition. It takes too long to explain.'

Sabrina took the pistol from the waist of the dead man's trousers and shoved it in the baggy pocket of her jacket.

'See if the other one has a gun, Deena. Hurry!'

Deena dropped to her knees and searched the man. 'Nothing. No gun, no knife.'

'Come on.' Sabrina pulled the door wide and saw Deena was staring at the dead man. 'It's them or us, Deena! Now come on! Hurry!'

They ran along the passage on their toes, making no sound,

Sabrina clutching the chair leg, straining her ears, trying to pick up sounds as they approached the door to the temple.

There was a small oval window in the door. Sabrina peered through it. The temple looked empty. She squinted the other way. The main door was half open. Beyond it she saw golden loamy earth and trees. She took the gun from her pocket and elbowed open the door.

'Stick close, Deena.'

They slid into the temple. Five metres in, Sabrina put a finger to her lips and paused. She looked all around her. The place was silent and empty. She pointed at the main door. They made their way steadily towards it, keeping to the wall, Deena panting softly.

Three metres from the door Sabrina saw a rifle leaning against a pillar. She ran across the tiles to get it. Halfway there she froze at a sound behind her. She spun and saw Hafi in the open doorway of an anteroom. He had his arm around Deena's waist. His other hand held a long pointed knife at her throat.

'Put down the gun and I will not kill her.'

Sabrina knew that was nonsense. He would cut Deena's throat whether she put down the gun or not. To avoid a catastrophe Sabrina needed time, a few seconds at least.

'All right,' she said, 'all right, I'm putting the gun down. Don't harm her. I'm putting it down.'

Sabrina crouched slowly, her arm outstretched as she put the gun on the floor. As it touched the tiles she watched Hafi's eyes. She stood up again, still watching him, waiting for the movement in his eyes, the split-second signal.

It came and an instant later the point of the knife moved. Sabrina threw the chair leg. It struck Hafi's wrist with a crack. He howled and dropped the knife. Deena whirled away from him.

A bound and a jump put Sabrina on top of Hafi, shoving him backwards, ruining his balance. She kicked his right foot clear of the floor as her weight carried him down. As he hit the floor he twisted sideways, holding on to Sabrina's arms, putting her under him. She tried to lift herself. Hafi banged her in the mouth with his elbow, stretched out his arm and snatched up his knife from the floor.

'Get off me!'

Sabrina punched him in the neck. She drew back her fist for a second shot and felt the point of the knife against her cheek. She let her arm drop to the floor.

Panting hard, his breath hot on Sabrina's face, Hafi let all his weight settle on her. He shifted the knife from her cheek to the tip of her nose. He inched the pointed end of the blade down the entrance to her nostril. Sabrina tried not to move her head. Her hand slid to her pocket.

'Let me tell you what I will do now, Petrushka,' Hafi grunted. 'I will split your nose to the eyebrows, then I will fillet your face. Have you heard of such a thing? Have you?'

She had. She had seen it, too. Her fingers closed round the handle of the knife in her pocket. She drew it out slowly.

'Please don't do that to me,' she said.

'Aw.' The knife edge touched the margin of her nostril. 'A big tough Russian girl like you is frightened? Surely not. I would have thought –'

Hafi stopped talking. He stiffened and jerked back. His eyes went wide. He sucked air with a rasping noise as the knife in Sabrina's hand sliced upward between his ribs and punctured his heart.

Sabrina pushed him off her and jumped to her feet. Deena was crouched by the wall, whimpering into her cupped hands. Hafi lay in a frozen, buckled spasm. Blood flowed from his mouth. As brain function disintegrated, his body twitched and jerked, the knife sticking hideously from his chest, his boots and belt making scratching noises that echoed through the temple.

Deena yelped. Sabrina turned and saw the man whose knife she had taken. He had snatched up the rifle from against the pillar and was pointing it at her.

She didn't hesitate. She dropped to her knees, forcing him to adjust the angle of the gun. Her left hand found the pistol she had put on the floor. It was in her hand and pointing at the bandit as his finger tightened on the rifle trigger. Sabrina fired three times and put three holes in his face. He jerked backwards and fell across a marble table. The rifle fell from his hand without firing.

Sabrina got up, pocketed the gun and went to Deena. She was trembling so hard she couldn't make herself speak.

'Listen to me,' Sabrina said. 'What has happened here will make a miniature earthquake. It will mean a huge change in the balance of criminal power in these parts. Hafi's followers will be really sore about that. So I have to get well away from here, and so do you.'

Among the bags of money by the altar Sabrina found her own shoulder bag. She checked and was again grateful to find that everything she valued was intact – even her gun, snug below the false bottom. She snatched up a leather folder full of papers and stuffed it into her bag.

'Help me carry the money, Deena.'

They made their way out to the daylight. Deena stumbled as she walked, still shaking and dazed.

'Oh, glory!' Sabrina pointed. At the edge of a stand of trees her car was parked. Branches had been thrown over it in a casual attempt at camouflage.

Sabrina ran to it, pulled off the branches and opened the passenger door. 'Put the money on the back seat, Deena.'

'Will you keep it?'

'I hadn't planned to.' As they put the last bag in the back Sabrina pointed to the writing on the sides. 'What does that say?'

'They are the names of towns. They are not far away.'

'I'll find them on the map, then I'll drop the money outside the police station in each place. First, though, I'm taking you home.'

'Will that not cause you inconvenience? It is two hours away.'

'If you get back to where you came from without being seen around here, and say nothing about being taken away, then no one will connect you with what happened to Hafi.'

Deena understood. She slipped into the front passenger seat. Sabrina got behind the wheel and started the engine. 'The sooner you're home, the sooner I'll do the Robin Hood bit, and the sooner I'll be on track again.' She glanced at Deena. 'You maybe find it hard to believe, but I have a serious job to get back to.'

Philpott was on the telephone. 'Speak to me, Michael,' he said, 'and try to keep it informative. I'm pressed for time, as ever.'

'I wanted to go on record as saying it was a great idea of yours to draw Lenny Trent into our act. He's an ace co-ordinator.'

'I had to weigh his obvious merits against the probability that the two of you would put your friendship before your function as colleagues on a mission.'

'We both have a sense of professional balance, sir. With respect, I think you sometimes over-simplify things.'

'And for my part I think you occasionally evaluate my motives in a childlike way,' Philpott said coolly. 'Which is all beside the point. Tell me how things are shaping.'

'You know about Reverend Young being murdered, and I told you about our visit to Dr Arberry. No headway has been made on the murder and there's not likely to be any. As for Arberry, I've now had time to read his notes. His suspicions about bandit activity, especially the drug-running kind, tend to be supported by several things Commissioner Mantur told Lenny.'

'I gather, from Trent's comments in his last report, that there is suspicion of a new kind of trade in top quality drugs, with rich clients and dealers waiting to collect. Do you go along with that?'

'I do,' Mike said. 'I also find it credible that the source of supply for the new trade is right here in the Vale of Kashmir.'

'In that case,' Philpott said, 'I think you should be formulating a plan to seek and destroy.'

'That's what we'll be doing, as soon as we've some idea of where our target is. First off, I'm setting up a local agent of Drugwatch International to make himself available for mule duty. Then I plan on getting myself up into the hills and sniffing around a convoy or two.'

'With a view to what?'

'Thrashing them at their own game, sir.'

'Splendid.'

'Any news of Sabrina?'

'I spoke to her an hour ago,' Philpott said. 'She's suffered another setback, but she's on the road again, moving up towards you and learning about India the hard way.'

'What happened to her this time?'

'I'll leave her to tell you herself. It'll make colourful after-dinner talk.'

'How's the review of techniques and procedures coming?'

'You mean,' Philpott said icily, 'the bureaucratic plot to bring me to heel? We're trying to mount a counter-attack, *we* being myself and Whitlock.'

'Do they stand a chance of nailing you?'

'I pray not, Michael. I'll know better what I'm up against after lunch tomorrow. I'm meeting an old friend whose ear is tuned to the rumblings of the disturbed creatures who run Policy Control.'

'Best of luck, anyway,' Mike said.

'Luck be damned,' Philpott snapped. 'If I win this one, it'll be on the strength of the combined talents of Whitlock and myself. Luck's for people with no resources of their own.'

TWELVE

'This is Amrit Datta,' Mike told Commissioner Mantur. 'We have high hopes for him.'

Mantur winked at the young Indian. 'They say they have high hopes, Amrit, yet they want you to take a risk similar to marching blindfold across a Delhi street at rush hour.'

'Such is my destiny, Commissioner,' Amrit smiled. 'I was born to be put upon.'

He was twenty-seven, a slim Kashmiri with fine, regular features and a boyish quiff of sleek black hair. He had a look of innocence that suited him for his job. The last thing he resembled was an enforcement officer, but in two years with Drugwatch International he had helped dismantle major trafficking operations in three Indian cities.

'I can't say I have a pleasant morning organized for you,' Commissioner Mantur said. 'Mr Graham here selected the illustrative material, so blame him. Not many laughs, but it will be instructive.'

The Department of Records at Srinagar Police HQ was in the cellar, a green-and-cream painted room with fungus on the walls and a smell like wet livestock. An early model Kodak Carousel slide projector was set up on the table, its lens pointing at an old projection screen on a rusty stand. The Commissioner, Mike and Amrit sat down in canvas chairs and the clerk in charge of records doused the lights.

The first slide on the screen showed a young Indian woman smiling stiffly at the camera. She was ordinary looking, a healthy enough person whose clothes indicated she was quite poor.

'Kadija was recruited as a mule six months ago by a man who stopped to buy a paper at her father's corner news stand in

94

Allahabad. She swore to tell no one about the offer, but of course she told her best friend, since best friends are not other people, they are extensions of ourselves. The best friend told us Kadija thought about the proposition for a week, at which time the man returned for her answer. She said yes.' Mantur shrugged. 'It was an extremely tempting offer. Ten thousand rupees for one job. In English money that would be about two hundred pounds, Mr Graham. A fortune for a peasant girl trying to scrape a living in the city.'

Another picture came on the screen. It was the same girl. This time she was not smiling. Her eyes were half closed and her tongue protruded at one side of her mouth.

'She paid the penalty for being caught,' Mantur said. 'Police on the Chinese border stopped her and found two kilos of heroin. She was put in a detention cell, where she took a capsule of cyanide from her navel and swallowed it.'

The next slide was of a man in a business suit, complete with club tie and a dark yellow silk handkerchief in his breast pocket.

'You're not saying he was a mule?' Amrit said.

Mike nodded. 'That's what we're saying.'

'What tempted a man like that? He looks like he doesn't need money.'

'Come on, Amrit, everybody needs dough. The point the picture demonstrates is that no one knows for sure what he's looking at. Keep it in mind. The trick of selling yourself as something you're not is to conceal by display.'

Amrit pursed his mouth politely. 'I'm not sure I know what you mean.'

'I mean you can best hide something about yourself by covering it with something that says more, or says otherwise. Any seasoned undercover police officer will tell you – when you're pretending to be what you're not, make sure you throw in a percentage of exaggeration, just to hide the fact that you *are* hiding something.'

'So what if I want to look poor?'

'Then lay it on with a trowel. Look poorer than poor, look like poor is what you've always been, like it's what you can't help being.' Mike pointed at the screen. 'Do what he was doing. Exaggerate, submerge yourself in the falsehood.'

'What was he?'

'A street sweeper.'

Amrit stared at the picture. 'Him?'

'Nearly impossible to believe. It's true, though. And he's a success story. That shot was taken as he boarded a plane out of India for ever. He made a stack by taking on three deliveries at one time.'

'The money for that kind of deal isn't triple,' Commissioner Mantur said. 'Because it's possible to move a lot of product at one time, the value of the deal goes way, way up. A hundred thousand rupees, plus a ticket and a work permit to the USA.'

'He was the perfect mule,' Mike said. 'I wouldn't have dreamed of stopping a guy like that.'

'The only reason we found out about him,' Mantur said, 'was because he likes sailing close to the wind – which was probably why he became a mule in the first place, and why he took the risk of carrying such a big load.'

'How did you find out about him?' Amrit said.

'He told us about himself.' Mantur nodded at the screen. 'Sent us that picture. Gave us the whole story.'

'Was he extradited from the States?'

'It wouldn't be likely, even if we could have found him,' Mike said. 'By the time he revealed how the scam had worked – how he had made the big delivery using so many disguises along the way that nobody could keep track of him – he was already somebody else in the USA. Adopting new personas and new appearances to match them appears to be either a vice or a compulsive game with this man. But bear in mind what I said, Amrit. What he did and the way he did it, that's how to pass yourself off to the drug people, or to anyone else you need to impress with a lie.'

They looked at pictures of another thirty mules, mostly before-and-after sets, with Mike supplying some of the commentary and Mantur providing the rest. When it was over the three of them moved out of the police HQ to a sidewalk café a block away.

'The concentration of carbon monoxide in the air at this spot,' Mantur said, 'is marginally less harmful than the mould spores in our basement. I hope you learned something from the exercise, Amrit.'

'I think so, sir.'

'Then tell Mr Graham and me what you learned.'

Amrit frowned. 'I learned what makes a winner and what doesn't. If I want to pass myself off as a candidate for mule work, I need to look helpless but not stupid, poor but hopeful, and worn-down enough by poverty to jump at any chance of decent money that I'm offered.'

Mike took his wallet from his pocket and slipped something from inside. 'I brought this as a clincher. It's to show you how important it is to convince drug people you're who and what you say you are.'

He passed a postcard-size photograph to Amrit. He looked at it and winced. The man in the picture wore a T-shirt with the Nike logo, and his jeans were good-but-ancient Levi's. His hair-cut looked expensive. His face was not recognizable, because someone had fired a gun into it at zero range.

'John Lenehan Patel,' Mike said. 'He was half American, half Indian. Spoke Gujarati like a native. He came over here to work undercover for the UN in 1992. He managed to get himself recruited as a mule, with a six-job commission, doing back and forward flights to New York carrying heroin and prime Indian cocaine.'

'What happened to him?'

'He wasn't a good enough actor,' Mike said. 'He fooled some of the people, but not all of them. Somebody got suspicious of the sophisticated and clearly expensive work he got done on his hair. And there were mannerisms that didn't fit a downtrodden person. And the general glow of health, the kind never seen in a person who has gone hungry more times than not.'

Amrit stared at the picture. 'Did he know they were on to him?'

'I don't think he had a clue. He was a good operator. But that wasn't enough.'

'It's like Mike says,' Mantur said. 'Learn to act, learn to put on a thick coat of who you are not, right on top of who you are.'

'And always remember,' Mike added, 'for someone like you, working undercover on the side of the angels, it's not the rigours of the law you have to worry about. It's the viciousness of the people you try to fool. If they ever catch on to you, you're a goner. Now have you got all that?'

'I hope so,' Amrit said. He sighed. 'I think I could use another coffee.'

'In the end it comes down to whether you want to be sure you survive, or whether you accept a few serious risks with a view to making progress.'

Lenny Trent was lying at the foot of a tree on a sloping hillside ten kilometres south-east of Srinagar. The tree was one of a cluster growing five metres below a narrow road that ran from Parbor, a kilometre north of Srinagar, all the way south-east to the Chinese border.

'Those options apply to any job,' Mike Graham said. He lay at the foot of an adjacent tree, peering up at the road through a night-vision scope.

'Except that when people like you and me use the term "serious risk", it's death we're talking about.'

The road they were watching had been selected from eight probable drug-traffic routes on the maps provided by Commissioner Mantur. Lenny knew the road and had suspected it himself, although surveillance, until now, had never been seriously proposed. For one thing the road was hard to see unless an observer moved dangerously close; it was also impossible to organize a confrontation or an ambush because there was not enough flat ground to deploy men in useful numbers. Tonight Mike and Lenny had decided to go on watch because it was Tuesday, and Tuesday, according to Mantur's notes, was a day when drug convoys passed through the Vale of Kashmir.

'The worrying thing about the risks,' Lenny said, 'is I get to need them.'

'Old story.'

'But I never thought it would apply to me. I visualized work as something I did, not something that would turn into a major part of what I am. When I take a risk and it pays off and I come out without a scratch or with only a couple, I'm up for days. My feet skim the ground. But the time comes round when I'm edgy again, strung out, needing my fix. Do you get that way?'

'I play it differently,' Mike said. 'I take elaborate precautions, I keep myself ready for anything that might turn up –'

'But you don't avoid trouble.'

'Uh-uh.'

'You run at it.'

'Well . . .'

'It's true,' Lenny said. 'You get the machine all oiled and battle-ready, but then you got to test it. No sense leaving it in the garage, all sleek and capable and full of potential it'll never achieve. It's not that kind of machine, is it?'

'I think what we're doing here is, we're dressing up the fact we're both kind of suicidal.'

Lenny raised his hand at a sound from the road. They put their night scopes to their eyes and watched. Above them to the right a horseman had appeared, ghostly green and white in the flickering artificial brightness of the viewfinder image. As he moved nearer, another horse was visible, then another and another. As they passed above Mike and Larry, loose dirt and stones rattled down among the trees.

'A full-blown convoy,' Lenny whispered. 'Twelve or fourteen horses carrying big panniers.'

Mike watched as the last horseman stopped and dismounted. He called something ahead, another voice acknowledged, and he crouched beside the horse. Mike could see that a pannier strap had snapped. The man unwound a length of twine from his pocket and began looping it through holes in the strap above and below the break, drawing the twine tight, uniting the broken ends.

'Do the clothes tell you anything?' Mike whispered.

'Nothing.' The man wore a heavy dark cloak, a turban and a swathe of cloth across the lower half of his face. 'He looks like any other hill bandit. Probably smells the same, too.'

Mike watched the rest of the convoy disappear round the bend. He lowered his scope. 'I know we're only here to watch and digest – but what do you say? Do we go for this?'

'I'd say it fell in our laps.'

They crept up the hill side by side and moved apart as they neared the road. Lenny waited for a signal from Mike, who was crouched two metres behind the horse. When the signal came, Lenny stood up, right on the edge of the road.

'A fine evening for a spot of smuggling!' he said.

The horseman leapt back at the sound. Mike grabbed him by the back of his cloak and swung him face down on the ground.

'Don't go being gentle, now,' Lenny warned. 'There's no point with these characters.'

'As if I would.'

Mike punched the man behind the ear and stood up. The man groaned but didn't move. Lenny had opened one of the panniers and was pulling out the contents. Mike opened the other one and did the same. When they were finished they had piled up twenty-four two-kilo plastic sacks of powder.

'We better move back down the hill,' Lenny said. 'Somebody will be back to look for this guy.'

Mike tied up the horseman, who was still unconscious, while Lenny led the horse up the slope on the far side of the road. At the top of the slope there was a narrow wind-blasted ridge with gnarled remnants of trees sticking up. Lenny tied the horse to one of them and went back to help Mike push the sacks down the hillside.

In less than five minutes they had transferred the sacks and the horseman to the shelter of the cluster of trees. The man was conscious now, sitting against a tree with his hands tied behind his back. In the shielded torchlight he looked profoundly menacing, although so far he hadn't even struggled. He sat staring at

100

the pile of sacks as Lenny split one open and tasted the powder.

'Heroin.'

'Good quality?'

'Incredibly bad,' Lenny said. 'It's already been cut with something, chalk maybe, and there's husks and dirt in it.'

'So this guy doesn't work for the upmarket peddlers.'

The man moved suddenly, lashing out his foot as Mike eased past him.

'Steady, my friend.' Mike held up his pistol and waggled it. The man spat.

'Like I said a while ago,' Lenny murmured. 'No point being subtle. If you want to impress him with the gun, smack him on the nose with it.'

Mike stared at the hillock of sacks. 'We should start getting this down to the wagon.' Their jeep was parked in bushes half a kilometre away. 'We can drop it off at police HQ in Srinagar, together with old grouchy here.'

Lenny stood and held out his arms. Mike began piling on the sacks. 'Six is just fine,' Lenny said, grunting. 'Hernia's a treat I'd like to save for old age.'

Mike bent to pick up the sixth sack and heard the man make a gulping sound. Mike turned and the man was still staring, looking into the torchlight.

'What the hell . . .'

The stare was different. Glazed.

'God almighty.' Lenny put down the sacks and knelt beside the man. 'He's dead.' He felt for a carotid pulse. 'Stone dead.'

'How?'

Lenny was running his fingers along the man's neck. He forced open the mouth and shone the torch inside. 'He swallowed his tongue.'

Mike looked, saw the thick, mauve blob at the back of the man's throat. 'I always thought that was a myth.'

Lenny put down the torch. 'He must have done it a minute ago, when we were distracted. It's a thuggee technique. Death before dishonour.'

101

They stared at the motionless face, the eyes half closed now, drowsy looking.

'Every day I learn something new,' Mike said. 'I only wish, now and then, it would be something nice.'

THIRTEEN

'Malcolm, I picked up an amazing book in Barnes and Noble's annexe a couple of months ago,' Harry Lewis said. 'I should have brought it to let you see. It's called *Scotland Yard, Bastion of Justice*, and there's a picture of you and me in it.'

Philpott stared at him. 'Really? How long ago was it taken?'

'The book was published in 1970, so it was a while ago. But there we are, all young and keen, coming out of a house in Shepherd's Bush where some people had got themselves murdered.'

'You must bring it and let me see. I half hate looking at old pictures of myself, but the other half's fascination, I – ah, here's the waiter.'

They were in Il Mulino in Greenwich Village, a restaurant Philpott favoured for lunch because, quite apart from the excellent food they served, the place had a stylishly spartan air – exposed brick, bentwood chairs – that made him feel he wasn't being too self-indulgent.

'Maybe I should have resisted the *lagniappe*,' Lewis said. 'Fried courgettes are delicious, but they also make me feel I'm halfway through my lunch already.'

He settled on a *scaloppina alla valdostana* and Philpott ordered *osso bucco*. The waiter poured the Chianti and they toasted each other in silence.

Aeons ago, it seemed to Philpott, they had been detectives together at Scotland Yard. They had both followed a rapid-promotion path but Harry Lewis was the one the reporters always latched on to for scene-of-crime statements, because Harry was the one they wanted pictures of; he had been strikingly handsome, a movie-goer's idea of a detective, and he had a good presentational style, firm but always affable, even under the worst kinds of pressure. Philpott, on the other hand, had always been consulted by criminologists, politicians and the more serious, less well-known journalists.

Lewis was still a fine-looking man, Philpott supposed, and his special skills in crime detection and public relations had served him well: for eight years now he had been an Investigative Director with the World Health Organization.

'Before our food comes, Harry, I want you to tell me the worst.'

'You mean the scuttlebutt from Policy Control?'

'That's what I mean, yes. Don't make me have to say it.'

'When there's a back-stabbing afoot,' Lewis said, 'they have a tendency to talk behind hands and with averted heads. Working from that criterion, I'd say they're determined you should face the music.'

'I guessed that anyway.'

'Well, if you want specifics, there's been a memo from the Director of Policy Control, Tom Lubbock, and the Secretary, Desmond Crane – '

'Tweedledum and Tweedledee . . .'

'Quite. The memo was sent to the Director General. It says that in view of procedural irregularities and a general lack of harmony with other elements within the UN organization, the administration of UNACO should be subjected to a policy scrutiny, with a view to tightening rules and guidelines.'

'Well again, Harry, I guessed – '

'Let me finish, Malcolm. They add that if it takes a change of Director to ensure the implementation of more satisfactory working methods, then no one should baulk at taking steps to appoint a replacement.'

Philpott stared at his wine glass for a moment. He looked up at Lewis. 'So they don't just want to put me on a leash. They want to get rid of me.'

'That appears to be the thinking. They're currently planting the notion among heads of departments that whatever is suggested to improve UNACO's, um . . .'

104

'Obedience?'

'. . . whatever is suggested, however liberal, you will reject it out of hand. In the words of Secretary Crane, you are a man with scant respect for discipline and even less for authority.'

Philpott sighed. 'We used to work with people like that, didn't we?'

'Everywhere you go in life you work with or near people like that,' Lewis said. 'They're a law of the workplace, something you have to put up with.'

'Like viruses.'

'And bilious attacks.'

The food came. Philpott attacked his and didn't speak again until he had finished. He sat back and watched Lewis toy with the last triangle of his veal.

'I don't want to talk any more about Policy Control, Harry.'

'Then talk to me about work. What's holding your attention at the moment?'

Philpott outlined a job being handled by Task Force One in Tirana, where criminal elements from former Eastern Bloc countries were taking advantage of the Albanian crisis to set up black market operations and spurious money-for-land deals.

'We also have a team out in Zaire. Rebels have taken hold of the Kinsangani, in the east, and they're posing a threat to the diamond mines there. The economy would go downhill without the diamonds, so we're keeping a watching brief at present, waiting for the usual band of international gem barons to step in and try to rob the country blind. Elsewhere, Task Force Three are investigating a crime-based upheaval in Kashmir that might boil over into big trouble if it's not defused.'

'Have they come across Dr Simon Arberry, by any chance?'

'Graham and Jarwal, an Area Observer, had dinner with him the other evening.'

'Arberry's an incredible chap. Brains and drive in equal measure. He'd be a godsend in our Third World aid programmes.'

'Why so?'

'He's a born organizer, and he's a magnificent persuader.'

'So your foreign aid work's suffering?'

'It's being undermined.'

Philpott looked interested. 'By politicians? Criminals?'

'Today, Malcolm, corruption eats into the heart of every charitable venture. Red Cross aid is stolen and sold in street markets to people with the money to buy luxuries like condensed milk, white sugar and aspirin tablets.'

'What's the scale of the loss?'

'In some areas criminal co-operatives absorb eighty, eighty-five per cent of all material aid from the West.'

'You're the Investigative Director, aren't you?' Philpott said. 'What are you doing about it?'

'I have good, detailed evidence on the worldwide black marketing of charity aid. But I don't have the resources it would take to root it out.'

Philpott was drumming the table now, thinking. 'Send me round some details on this, would you?'

'You mean you've never heard about how rotten everything's gone lately?'

'I didn't realize the scale.'

'I'll send you the full depressing details, then.'

'And maybe I'll find some small way in which I can help.' Philpott smiled tightly. 'That's enough about work. Let's talk about something else.'

'Anything you say. You're buying, after all.'

'I'll tell you something about that,' Philpott said. 'I just worked it out. The ten per cent tip I'll leave here today is about fifteen per cent more than I used to spend on a three-course lunch for the two of us in a Fleet Street pub.'

Sabrina crossed the border into Kashmir at Dalhousie, forty kilometres south-west of Jammu. The guard at the border post, after scowling at her and demanding to see her documentation, became suddenly deferential when he saw the UN symbol on her WHO accreditation. He stamped the appropriate blank page with a flourish and waved her through.

It was late afternoon and she had driven since dawn. Assuming her maps were reliable, she estimated that if she drove till dusk, rested and made an early start, she could be in Srinagar by noon the next day.

On a wide stretch of road to the west of Jammu she pulled over, took half a dozen items from her shoulder bag and laid them out on the seat beside her. They were a mirror in a rigid folding case, a comb, a rectangular powder compact, a dog-eared paperback of *Jane Eyre*, a ballpoint pen and a small pair of opera glasses.

'Begin with the mirror,' she muttered, recalling the training session where she had finally managed to work this conversion without looking. That had been two months ago; there was no one here to impress, so on this occasion she would watch what she was doing.

When the mirror case was held open with the hinge pointing upward, the mirror tipped out of its housing and hung down. Sabrina reached behind it and folded out a thin circuit board; from behind that she folded out another. With the mirror and the two boards in place, she was holding a ten-centimetre cube with one open side.

She put down the cube and opened the paperback. The first eighty pages were real but after that it was a box. She took out a flat ten-centimetre panel with a circular hole in the centre and laid it on one side of the cube. By dismantling the opera glasses she produced a neat zoom lens with a ratio of 60 to 1; she added a manual operating ring by combining the ridged bezels of the binoculars. She screwed the lens into the hole in the square panel, put it down and stared. For a moment she was lost.

'Viewfinder,' she said, remembering.

She opened the compact, carefully removed the powder tray and took out a plastic bag containing a flattened, hinged housing and the four glass viewfinder components. She fitted them together and clipped the unit to the top of the cube. The back of the comb came off and gave access to a slender titanium antenna with a miniature powered booster above its socket plug.

The main power source and electronic storage medium were

in the book; she fitted them into slots inside the cube, tipped six screws and a tiny screwdriver from the barrel of the ballpoint pen and used them to stabilize the instrument. Finally she teased a laminated cover from the pen, unrolled it and fixed it with adhesive tape around the body of the cube.

'*Et voilà.*'

The neat finished instrument she held between her hands was the EVC12A, designed, refined and perfected at a cost of six million dollars. It was a camera capable of taking and electronically storing twenty colour pictures, which it could transmit in digital form to a satellite, via its boosted antenna.

'After all that, let's hope I get a chance to use it.'

Philpott had told her he wanted broad-scale input, which meant he wanted alert observation, creative snooping and, if necessary, selective theft. It also meant pictures. No mission was a failure if it could be reinforced by random intelligence, and although Sabrina had the sheaf of papers she took from Hafi, she didn't know if they would be any help to anyone. Even if they were, even if they turned out to be solid gold, it would still be marvellous, on top of all that, to knock out the old man's eye with some top-rate photographic intelligence.

She put the camera carefully in the glove box. Juan Pereda, chief designer on the camera project, had warned her, again and again, that such an instrument would be prized by any foreign power without the resources to spend on advanced electronic development.

'This is breakthrough technology,' he told her in his thick Mexican accent. 'Cutting-edge kit, you understand? You must not expose the camera to jeopardy, *señorita.*'

Philpott said the best way to safeguard the camera was not to assemble it until she knew she was in relatively safe surroundings.

'Another way to make sure you don't let any harm befall the instrument,' he added, 'is to bear in mind that if it gets damaged or lost, Juan might just get mad enough to insist a replacement be paid for from my budget. If that were to happen, your salary would be the first indirect casualty.'

This place looked safe. Sabrina had not stopped at any communities since crossing the border, but she guessed the bandits had as tight a grip on populations here as they had further south. The big difference was, this was open country. In the spaces between towns and villages she did not find herself on roads with blind corners or ominously close woodland or menacing overhangs. This was territory where she could see who was coming in any direction, and be ready for them.

A sharp rap on the window made her jump. Her first thought was, *Thank God I kept the windows shut.* It was possible to drive around all day with them closed: a concealed feature of the car, operated by a foot switch behind the brake pedal, was its air-conditioning unit, which kept the sealed-up interior at a steady 16 degrees Celsius.

Sabrina took a loose grip on the pistol tucked between the front seats. She turned her heads slowly and looked.

'Jeez . . .'

The man at the window looked horrible. He wore a voluminous yellow turban which emphasized the bony sparseness of his face, like a skull with eyes. His teeth protruded evilly, yellow and crooked, and as Sabrina stared at him his purple tongue snaked out and ran along his lips.

'What do you want?' she shouted, simultaneously thinking, *so much for seeing them coming.*

The man said something. She couldn't hear. She watched his eyes go narrow. Her fingers tightened on the gun, her thumb eased off the safety. She looked to right and left. There was no sign of anybody else, but that went for nothing.

'Speak up!' she shouted.

The man's expression changed. His eyes wrinkled at the corners and he made a helpless gesture with his hand. Now he didn't look so menacing. Sabrina wound down the window a couple of inches, bringing the gun out from between the seats and letting it lie alongside her leg.

The first thing she noticed as the window came down was the scent of jasmine. The man was wearing cologne. She was so conditioned to bandits smelling bad that his scent disconcerted her.

'You are English?' he said. His voice was surprisingly soft, entirely lacking the harsh edge she expected.

'American. How can I help you?'

'First of all let me apologize for disturbing you,' he said. 'I do not make a practice of encroaching on privacy or solitude.'

'Um, that's OK.'

The man sounded like an actor, she thought. His voice was finely modulated; his one-handed gestures rhythmically under-scored his words.

'I thought it a duty, no less, to warn you that the rear left side light of your motor is broken.'

'Oh.' Sabrina felt deflated, and a little charmed. 'Well thank you . . .'

'My name is Aziz,' the man said, making a little bow. 'I am a teacher in the village three kilometres from here.'

'Well, Aziz, I'll have the light fixed first chance I get. Thanks again.'

As he stepped back Sabrina saw he leaned heavily on a walking stick. He nodded and began hobbling away. Sabrina considered her position for a moment, and decided her humanity needed more exercise than her caution.

'Can I offer you a lift, Aziz?'

He stopped and turned. 'That is most generous.'

'Not at all.' Sabrina opened the passenger door and slid the gun back down into its hiding place. 'It won't be the smoothest ride, I'm afraid. The suspension's kind of stiff.'

She was surprised at herself. A minute ago she was reading a life of dissipation and crime into the old man's appearance. Now as he clambered in beside her she saw nothing but frail gentility and kindly warmth in his eyes.

'We'll have you home in no time.' She started up the engine. 'Have you lived here all your life?'

'For seventy-six of my seventy-seven years,' Aziz said. 'I am technically an outsider. My parents moved here to live when I was just over a year old.'

110

'And you still work as a teacher?'

'Oh yes.' He grasped the handle above the door as the car pulled away. 'Teaching children is my purpose, so I will do it until I drop.'

Sabrina looked across the scrubby open land to the east, noticing how it gradually sloped towards the foothills of the mountains.

'Is life pretty quiet around here, Aziz?'

He nodded. 'On the surface. And it is quiet enough for a man if he does not make himself prominent, you understand?'

'What happens if he makes himself prominent?'

'He attracts the attention of the bandits.' Aziz pointed at the mountains. 'There are many bandits up there.'

'Really?' Sabrina sat up in her seat. 'Many of them, you say?'

'Enough to make great trouble, when they choose.'

'That's fascinating. Absolutely fascinating.' Sabrina hoped she looked like the intrigued tourist she was trying to be. 'Do tell me more.'

FOURTEEN

'If you don't mind, Mr Graham, I'd like to get on with it,' Amrit Datta said. 'More rehearsal won't do anything but make me less believable.'

'It's your call,' Mike said. 'But remember, you'll be on your own. You'll have to be good, there's nobody to save you if you're not.'

They were in the Drugwatch International office at Srinagar, a couple of shabby rooms fronting as a motorcycle courier agency; when prospective customers called, which they rarely did, there were never any couriers available. Mike stood by the window, looking out at the smoky traffic churning dust into the air. Amrit Datta sat on the edge of the plywood desk with his arms folded.

'I know you're concerned I'm rushing things,' he said, 'but I don't think I am. In all the time I've been with this outfit, I've never once behaved like myself on the street. It's always an act, I'm permanently behind a fake identity and a counterfeit personality. This is nothing new.'

'The penalties in the mule racket are higher, that's the difference,' Mike said. 'And there are precious few escape routes if things go wrong.'

'I won't forget that.'

Mike opened the package he had brought. 'You're on secondment to UNACO, so you get UNACO issue.' He took a gun from the big brown envelope and handed it to Amrit, together with a box of ammunition. 'SIG Sauer P230, your dearest pal if you get into a corner. Trust it more than the silly little Stenda you carry around.'

He pulled a greasy, worn brown leather wallet from the envelope and opened it flat on the table.

112

'This is your history. They will look at it, whether you know it or not. And if your act's a good one, this will corroborate it. The whole thing was put together by people who specialize in manufacturing identities.'

Inside the wallet was a picture of Amrit taken two days ago. Now it looked as if it had been behind the glassine window for a year at least. He was shown as part of a smiling group – a wife and three children, none of whom he had ever met. In a pocket of the wallet was a crumpled birth certificate identifying the owner as Opu Hikmet. Other documents – letters, a folded picture postcard, more snapshots – bulged the sides of the wallet, which had been sprayed with the authentic odour of artisan sweat.

'Now this,' Mike said, taking a chunky amulet from the bag, 'is a very important piece of gear.' He handed it to Amrit. 'What do you make of it?'

Amrit hefted it, turned it over in his hands, shook it and finally took it to the window to examine it in full light.

'It's an oval disc, wooden, about four centimetres by two-point-five centimetres at its widest point, and maybe fifteen millimetres thick. It has a metal loop at one end with a thin leather cord through it, which I suppose is for hanging the disc around the neck. The disc is smooth on one face, on the other it is carved with a representation of the face of Narsingh, the man-lion incarnation of Vishnu.' Amrit looked at Mike. 'Did I miss anything?'

'I'm pleased to say you did.'

Mike took the amulet and pressed down hard on the metal loop at the top. The centre of the front panel dropped inwards and glided aside. In the gap a small lens could be seen gleaming.

'Oh, boy,' Amrit said, shaking his head. 'It's a camera.'

Mike pressed a high spot on the grooved edge of the disc and the back panel opened. It had a spring-loaded carrier for a flat circular film cartridge.

'It's sixteen mil,' Mike said, 'it takes twenty shots per cartridge, and it works in low light. It's autofocus, so all you have to worry

113

about is getting it pointed the right way so it catches what you happen to be looking at.'

'How does it fire?'

'Press on the point of Narsingh's chin. Like this.'

Amrit watched. 'I didn't hear anything.'

'Right. It's good, isn't it?'

The final item out of the bag was a slim gold finger ring with a single cheap-looking stone set into it.

'It should fit the little finger,' Mike said.

Amrit tried it on. It fitted perfectly. 'Not the kind of thing I would have chosen,' he said.

'Yes, it's pretty tacky. But it'll find you if we ever lose visual contact.'

'A tracer?'

'The stone is the beacon,' Mike said. 'Wear it in health.'

Mike crumpled the empty bag and put it in the trash basket. 'So tell me,' he said, 'what makes you so anxious to get under way?'

'They're recruiting again,' Amrit said. 'It happens in waves. Moving around the city every day, you're aware of a pattern of faces, people you barely look at but you know they're there, working in the markets or running errands or just hanging around street corners. Then all of a sudden two or three of them are gone, and you know they've been pulled into the mule game.'

'So you want to get on to the streets while there's a chance of being spotted.'

'That's it, Mr Graham.'

'Call me Mike. Listen, I'll tell Lenny Trent what you just told me, and we'll line up one last rehearsal session for later today.'

'If you think it's necessary.'

'I know you're impatient, but please give the rehearsal all you've got.'

'Of course I will.' Amrit paused. 'Mike.'

Old Aziz had given Sabrina tea in gratitude for the lift home, and as they sat on his ramshackle veranda and talked, he had turned out to be a gold mine. After several minutes of polite inconsequential chat, he stood up and pointed to all the places on the lower slopes of the mountains where he regularly saw bandit convoys.

'Who knows what they carry,' he said. 'I know it is not always contraband. Often they are moving their dwellings, their entire communities, every stick, from one place to another. That way they avoid conflict with the authorities, and with each other. Much of the time, though, they carry illegal merchandise.'

Then Aziz had fetched an ancient pair of British Army binoculars, which had been given to him by a soldier in 1944. He handed them to Sabrina and showed her how to point them, until she saw an area of mountainside Aziz called the bronze pass.

'A fanciful title,' he said, 'but you will see, in the late sunlight, how the path glows a rich bronze. It is a combination of colours in the rock stratum and the sandy earth at that level.'

Sabrina saw it, like a long, undulating red-brown strand along the side of the mountain.

'That is where the truly bad men travel,' Aziz said. 'Once every week, at dusk, they pass within the reach of my binoculars. They carry heavy loads, and they eliminate whatever is in their path. Twice they have killed men whose curiosity has taken them up there to take a closer look. Twice, also, they have come down to this village and demanded water for their horses and food for themselves. They did not treat people cruelly, as some might, but they were strangers to sympathy and compassion, nevertheless.'

'How often do they appear?' Sabrina said.

'Twice a week. They will pass that way tonight.'

Sabrina tried to blank any sign of excitement. She swallowed what was left in her cup, then got up to go. She thanked Aziz for the tea and for the information. He shook her hand as she left and wished her well on her journey through Kashmir.

Twenty minutes later she was parked in a shadowed cleft in the foothills, elbows braced on the bonnet of the car as she pointed the EVC12A up at the mountainside. Dead in the centre of the viewfinder she had a convoy of twelve heavily-laden horses, moving obliquely towards her, the faces of the riders visible in the late golden sunlight.

She took twelve pictures before the convoy moved along out of sight. Then she got back in the car, pulled up the rubber mat at the driver's side and snapped open a metal flap in the floor. She took out a modified cellular phone, set to call one number only. She went outside again, the phone in one hand, the camera in the other. She pulled up the phone's antenna with her teeth, thumbed the green button and put the phone to her ear.

'Secure Communications,' a woman's voice said.

'I have a P-I-G transmission,' Sabrina said. The initials stood for Peripheral Information Gathering.

'What hardware are you using?'

'The EVC12A. I have twelve shots total.'

'Raise the antenna on the camera and set it to send.'

Sabrina put the camera on the car bonnet, pulled up the titanium antenna, and pushed the SEND button.

'We are homing on the equipment,' the woman said. 'Please confirm when the contact signal shows.'

Sabrina watched the camera, holding her breath. A tiny green lamp winked.

'Contact,' she said.

There was a long pause, then the woman said, 'Twelve pictures received. Closing communication.'

The phone went dead. Sabrina dropped it in her pocket. She pushed down the camera's antenna and put the whole unit into her shoulder bag. As she got back in the car the telephone in her pocket rang.

She shut the door, fished out the phone. 'Yes?'

'Sabrina!' Philpott said. 'What a good girl you are! I was in Secure Comms when your pictures came through. Magnificent quality, my dear. Who are those people, exactly?'

'I don't know, sir, beyond the fact they're bandits with a pretty bad reputation among people who live near the foothills.'

'Can you get the location co-ordinates, at all?'

'Well I'm still there. Will I use the phone?'

'By all means.'

Sabrina wound down the window, held the phone out through the gap and pressed her thumb firmly on a blue button on the side. Ten seconds later the phone beeped and she pulled it in again.

'Got it,' Philpott said. 'I gather from this that you're quite close to Srinagar.'

'I'll be there tomorrow, with luck.'

'And I'm sure that Mike and the others will be glad to see you. In the meantime I'll send them printouts of the pictures, along with the co-ordinates. Good work, Sabrina.'

'Thank you sir.'

'Keep in touch.'

As Philpott came out of the Secure Communications Suite he saw Whitlock, who immediately waved a folder at him.

'And what would that be?'

'My notes on the life and later career of Arno Skuttnik. I just picked up another snippet.'

They went into Philpott's office. Whitlock pointed at the coffee machine. 'May I?'

'Pour me one, too.'

Philpott sat down to wait. Whitlock poured two black coffees and brought them to the desk.

'This whole thing,' he said, opening the folder, 'makes me wonder how much buried history gets overlooked in any investigation.'

'It depends who's digging,' Philpott said.

'And how desperate they are to find *something*, anything. We set out with zilch on Skuttnik. He was a nobody immigrant with a history hardly worth the name. Now his story's fattening into the material of a pretty good mini series.'

'What's the latest?'

'He was married.'

'After he came to the United States?'

'Six years after.'

'How did you pick that up?'

'When I fed his social security number through Public Records it came up blank. No marriage, no criminal record, no unpaid taxes. So then I fed his immigration number through the same channels. Still no criminal record, no civil misdemeanours. But the marriage showed up. It turns out the people who registered the wedding were so keen to get Skuttnik's immigration status right, they completely forgot the social security notation.'

'So now you're following up on the marriage?'

'I've got tracers going right now.'

'I don't want this turning into a saga, C. W. Especially if it isn't going to produce anything we can use as a defence.'

'Or as a counter-attack,' Whitlock said.

Philpott looked at him. 'Do you know something you're not telling?'

'When I know everything, I'll give it to you whole, sir.'

'So you still feel this is worth pursuing?'

'More so than ever.'

Philpott tasted his coffee. He pointed to a typewritten document on the desk in front of him. 'While you're here, I'd like your opinion on something. This is a summary of investigations into the widespread theft of charity aid around the world. It was supplied by my old friend Harry Lewis at the World Health Organization.'

Philpott opened the document to the third page. He held it up for Whitlock to see. A short paragraph had been circled in red and alongside was written, 'What a coincidence.'

'The paragraph covers a piece of intelligence supplied over a year ago, but so far uncorroborated,' Philpott said. 'It's about an alleged black market operation centred on a farm eighty kilometres east of Srinagar.'

'Maybe a coincidence, but it's hardly a surprise. The hill bandits have transportation and supply sewn up. Farms make perfect way-stations.'

'I was thinking of looking into this one myself.'

Whitlock saw that Philpott was waiting for his reaction. 'Why?'

'Because some all-round balance-correction in that area of the world wouldn't go amiss, and this particular piece of suspected villainy suits my sneaky style.'

'Softly, softly.'

'If you want to call it that. Anything I might do would be an adjunct to the work the others are engaged upon, I suppose. But the overall effect would be a comprehensive defusing of villainy in the region, wouldn't you say?'

Whitlock smiled. 'Do you want me to say I think it's a good idea for you to go to Kashmir?'

'Only if you mean it.'

'Well . . .' Whitlock scratched the tip of his nose. 'While you're not here, the people at Policy Control can't pull any fast ones, like getting a review date called before I've built a case.'

'I hadn't thought of that.'

'Are you kidding me, sir?'

'Well . . .' Philpott shrugged. 'It crossed my mind.'

'All things considered,' Whitlock said, 'I guess it'd be a really good thing if you high-tailed it to Kashmir, fast as you can.'

'Thanks, C. W.' Philpott smiled. 'I always value your judgement in these matters.'

FIFTEEN

'I have not seen you here before,' the fat man said. He peered at Amrit Datta's face as he spoke, ready to catch a lie before it could take off. 'You are not from this area, are you?'

'For two years I have worked in there.' Amrit pointed to a warehouse behind the market where he was sweeping up. 'Two years of moving sacks and boxes, emptying drums, filling bottles. For two years I didn't see daylight except in the morning when I came to work.'

'And why did you leave the warehouse?'

'Why are you asking me these things?'

The man frowned. 'Don't you want to do yourself some good?'

'Of course.'

'Then answer me, and something good may come of it.'

Amrit wiped his forehead with the back of his hand. It was hot and he was sweating freely. He wore a drab grey T-shirt and cheap baggy cotton trousers. His feet were bare and he had dark lines of carefully-applied dirt under his fingernails.

'I kept asking the foreman to let me work in the open, or at least do work that brought me outside for a little time each day. Eventually he paid attention to what I asked. He told me that if I wanted to spend my days out in the open air, I was now free to do that.'

'He sacked you?'

'Yes, he did. And when I begged him to let me have my job back, he told me I should have considered just how valuable the job was before I threw it away so carelessly.'

'So now you sweep up in the market.'

'It is hard work and it pays less than one-third of the wage I made in the warehouse.'

The fat man patted his belly thoughtfully. 'I like to help people like yourself whenever I can,' he said.

'I would be grateful for any work,' Amrit said. 'Real work,' he added, 'not anything like this.'

'What family do you have?'

'A wife and three children. The children are still small.'

'So you must provide for them, too.' The fat man sighed, as if he was full of sympathy. 'What would you say to a little job, nothing too difficult, which would earn you enough money to take it easy for a while, or to travel south where the work is more plentiful and the wages are higher?'

Amrit looked suspicious. 'What kind of work would that be?'

'Courier work. Delivery work. You would deliver one consignment of merchandise, and for that one delivery you would be paid in advance –'

'In advance?' Amrit looked astonished. 'You are saying you would give me my wages before I even did the job?'

'That is correct.'

Amrit scowled suddenly. 'It is a joke, isn't it? You are having fun with me.'

'It is no joke, uh, what is your name?'

'I am called Opu Hikmet.'

'Well, it's the truth I tell you, Opu. I offer you the work because you look like a strong and decent young man who deserves a helping hand at this stage in his life.'

'What do I have to do?'

'Simply tell me you accept my offer.'

'Oh I do, I do.'

'Then I will come and see you in a few days' time.'

'I will be here, sir.'

The fat man walked away and was soon lost in the crowd. Amrit patted the amulet hanging on his chest. He had taken three shots. He hoped at least one of them would come out.

Ram Jarwal was alone in the cabin. Mike Graham and Lenny Trent were at police HQ in Srinagar, going through mug shots to try to identify the dead bandit from the drug convoy.

121

Ram enjoyed having his solitude back, however briefly. Mike and Lenny were excellent company, they were diverting and their professionalism was endlessly fascinating; but they had filled the cabin with human sounds and movement, they had upset the gentle daily routines of a man who led a distinctly quiet life.

Tonight was a bonus. Ram sat back with a beer and his feet up on the couch, watching CNN News with the sound barely audible. As he watched he thought he heard the sound of an engine outside, then he decided it was the stereo output from the TV misleading him.

A banging on the door made him jump so hard he spilled his beer. He leapt to his feet, wiping himself. The door was hammered again before he got it open.

'Thank God you're here!' It was Dr Arberry. Ram had never seen him so dishevelled or so upset. 'I was going to call the police, but my lines have been cut – then I remembered your guests . . .'

'What is it? What's wrong?'

'Mr Graham and Mr Trent, are they here?'

'I'm afraid not. They have business in Srinagar.'

'Will you come then, Ram? Something awful has happened. I have to . . .' Arberry put his hands over his face for a moment. 'I have to make contact with someone who can influence outside help. I – I am frankly distraught.'

Ram told him to wait in the car. He went back inside. He called Mike at police HQ and explained.

'I'm going with him now. No, he hasn't said. He's too agitated to give explanations. Maybe you and Lenny should meet up with us at his place. Move fast and you could be there first.'

Mike and Lenny got to the Arberry estate in a police car a full three minutes before Ram and the doctor arrived in Arberry's black Mercedes.

'We didn't see any signs of activity so we sat tight,' Mike said. 'What is it, Doctor?'

'Please follow me.'

Arberry led them along the side of the mansion and around

to the back. There was a sloping floodlit lawn. The butler and the maid stood by a dark bundle lying ten metres from the back of the house.

'I heard a sound like nothing I can describe,' Arberry said, striding ahead, combing the fingers of both hands through his hair. 'It was hideous. Then I came out and found this.'

They stopped where the butler and maid stood with their backs to the bundle. Mike crouched, confused by the shadows, reaching for his torch. He flicked it on and saw that the bundle was a boy, his head protruding from the folds of a dark garment, his tousled hair moving gently in the breeze. He was obviously dead.

'Any idea what happened?' Lenny said. 'Who is he, anyway?'

'What happened was an act of unbelievable savagery,' Arberry said. 'I know nothing more about it than that. The boy worked for me, I employed him as a general servant in the household.' Arberry stared at the waxen face. 'He was a fine young man.'

Mike pulled back the collar of the garment and began to see what had happened. The boy's head was not attached to his body. Neither were his arms or legs. They lay in a loose pile on his abdomen. The head rested on the grass where it had fallen.

'My butler threw the cloak over the remains,' Arberry said.

Mike stood up. 'Whoever did it used a machete,' he told Lenny. He turned to Dr Arberry. 'I don't suppose you've any idea –'

'The bandits!' Arberry said. 'The damned bandits, that's who! They're not content to ply their squalid trade, they have to live up to type. They have to disrupt and terrorize and destroy . . .'

'Would there be any reason in this case?' Lenny said. 'Any specific reason, that is?'

'The same old reason, the one that's behind this escalating campaign that's costing good decent lives!'

Nobody said anything. They waited for the doctor to get control of himself.

'They want me out of the Vale of Kashmir.' Arberry was staring off into the darkness beyond the lower slope of the lawn. 'I'm a unifying influence, you see. People like me give law and order a foothold. The bandits hate that.' He turned and looked at Mike. 'What can be done? Are we simply to give in to the barbarians? Do we move aside and let them have this place for themselves?'

'I think we may be close to effecting a solution,' Lenny said carefully. 'I can't go into details, not yet. But we have hopes.'

'And we're staying on the case,' Mike added.

Ram, feeling as inadequate as the other two, came forward and said he had told the police driver to radio for the detectives.

'They will come and they will go through the motions,' Arberry said wearily. 'Now every minute that passes without something being done, I will be reminded that by just staying here, I'm putting other lives at risk.'

'You're an asset to this place, Dr Arberry,' Mike said. 'It would be a borderline tragedy if you left. I promise you, whatever action is possible, we'll make sure it gets done. And soon.'

Ram, Mike and Lenny travelled back to the cabin in the police car. As the headlights cut over the rim of the final rise, bringing them round on to the flat ground at the front, they saw another car parked by the door. It was a beat-up Peugeot.

As Mike stepped from the police car the Peugeot's door opened and Sabrina got out. For a moment he didn't recognize her in the baggy clothes and straw hat.

'Well, and aren't you a sight,' he said, pecking her cheek. 'What kept you?'

'Devotion to duty. If you don't have it naturally, it's a hard concept to explain.'

Mike wrinkled his nose at her. 'This is Ram, and I think you know Lenny.'

'Nice to meet you, Ram.' Sabrina shook his hand. 'And hello again, Lenny. It was Colombia last time, I think.'

Lenny nodded. 'Barranquilla. It was the only time I ever saw a woman beat up a Caribbean dope pusher and take his gun off him.'

'Memories,' Sabrina sighed, 'memories . . .'

They watched the police car leave, then Ram unlocked the cabin and they went inside.

'You must be hungry after your journey,' he said.

'Hungry and weary,' Sabrina admitted. 'I got lost a couple of times or I'd have been here sooner.'

'I'll rustle you up something.' Ram paused in the kitchen doorway. 'Scrambled eggs, melba toast, coffee?'

'Magnificent,' Sabrina said. 'You've made a dusty, poorly-dressed woman very happy.' She turned to Mike. 'Did you get the pictures?'

'What pictures?'

'They came through after you left,' Ram shouted. He came to the kitchen door again. 'There was a note on the cover sheet. It said you were due for a surprise, so watch out. Signed *Uncle*.'

Mike looked at Sabrina. 'What's he up to now?'

SIXTEEN

Amrit Datta was taken in the back of a small covered truck to a place in the countryside south-east of Srinagar. Two others travelled in the van with him, both young men, both warned like himself to say nothing on the journey.

'You will wait here until someone comes for you,' the fat man told Amrit as he pushed him into a small hut with a wooden bench along one wall. The other two, he noticed, were led to separate little huts.

It was obvious they didn't want the recruits to talk to each other on any account. No comparing of notes, no knowledge of one another. It made sense. In the van, they would have had to shout above the noise of the engine to make themselves heard and any communication between them would have been detected at once. In a hut together they could have whispered; hence, Amrit thought, separate quarters.

He put his face to the side of the hut and was able to see through the slats. Although it was night there was a bright moon. He could see he was on a small farm, one of the dozens that dotted the countryside in that region. Chickens were wandering around and he had heard goats as he was shown into the hut. There was no way to establish his co-ordinates; it would be too risky to carry anything electronic since they were bound to search him. He had seen the town lights briefly as he got out of the truck and he knew he was looking at Srinagar from the south-east. That was something.

He patted the front of his thin shirt and realized he had made a reflex action. Countless times a day, most days, he checked to be sure his gun and his ID were still there. Now he had nothing on him, nothing at all. There were only his habitual reactions to give him away.

He remembered what Mike Graham had said: 'Assume you're being watched at all times, for you won't know when they're *not* watching. You can't carry two amulets, so a freshly loaded camera and a gun will be delivered to you after you've been declared clean. Remember, give no sign that you're anything but what your appearance suggests – a shambling un-touchable.'

Amrit gave himself a sharp reprimand about the body-patting and sat back with his head against the wall, waiting.

Half an hour passed before the fat man came for him.

'Look lively now, hurry up. You mustn't keep people waiting.'

The tone of his approach had changed now, and he no longer smiled the way he had. He was brusque, pushing Amrit ahead of him towards the little house at the centre of the farm, warning him to behave when he was inside and only to speak when he was asked a question.

In the cottage he was shown along a short passage and into a smoky room with a low ceiling. Two men were in there: one was old, stooped and stony-faced, with one eye so watery it appeared to be dissolving; the other man was much younger, broad-shouldered and so tall that his head nearly touched the ceiling. The old one pointed to a chair by a small table in the centre of the room. Amrit sat down.

'What is your name?' the big man said.

'Opu Hikmet, sir.'

'Can you read?'

'Yes, sir.'

'Can you remember things you are told?'

'Yes, sir.'

The old man came forward and handed Amrit a folded sheet of linen paper. 'This is your map,' he said, his voice gravelly. 'You must follow it exactly. You must take no shortcuts, you must not try to change the route in any way. The journey will take you three or maybe four days. At night you will rest where it is safe, because you will be carrying valuable merchandise.'

127

The big man pointed to a burlap sack on the table. 'Pick it up with one hand,' he said.

Amrit reached forward and lifted the sack. It weighed roughly ten kilos. He put it down again.

'Will you have difficulty carrying that? It will be a long journey, remember, and you must travel on foot.'

'No, sir, I will have no difficulty.'

'It must stay with you at all times,' the old man said. He produced another folded piece of linen paper. 'Three men will approach you when you have crossed the border and gone to the place described here and marked with red on the map. Do you understand?'

'Yes, sir.'

'When each man says the phrase that is written, and when you reply with the other phrase that is written, you will give each man one bag from the sack.'

Both men were silent now, looking at Amrit. For a moment he wondered if a reaction was expected. It dawned on him that they were watching for signs of uncertainty.

'Repeat what you have been told,' the big man snapped.

'I have to carry the sack with me at all times and at night I must sleep only where it is safe, for the merchandise is valuable. I must follow the map and must not take any other route. When I cross the border and go to the place marked in red I must wait for three men.'

'And when they make themselves known to you?' the big man said.

'I must reply with the second phrase that is written, and give each of them one bag from the sack.'

The old man nodded curtly. 'Now I will give you two more things.' From a drawer in the table he took a thick bundle of banknotes and a small envelope. He handed the money to Amrit. 'That is yours. It is payment for the one and only delivery you will make for us.'

Amrit tried to imagine it was the most money he had ever seen at one time. He put on a face of restrained rapture.

'You may do with the money as you wish,' the old man said,

without a glimmer of a smile. He held up the small envelope.
'This is something else you must keep with you at all times.'

He opened the end of the envelope and tipped a black capsule
on to his palm. Amrit stared at it, knowing what it was, feigning
bafflement.

'If anything should happen to make the plan go wrong, if you
should lose your merchandise, if you are arrested by the police,
or if for any other reason you do not deliver the merchandise
to the three men named on the second piece of paper, then you
must not hesitate to swallow this. Keep it hidden about your
body, somewhere that it will not be found but somewhere you
can reach it if you need it suddenly.'

Amrit looked at the old man, then at the other one. 'What is
it, please?'

'It will make you die very quickly,' the big man said.

Amrit gulped softly. His fingers tightened around the money.

'That is our bargain, our agreement,' the old man said. 'You
do what we have told you to do, and if you cannot do it you
swallow the potion. You must do it at once, you must do it
without talking to anyone or answering any questions.'

Amrit watched the old man drop the capsule back into the
envelope.

'If anything goes wrong, and yet you do *not* take the potion,'
the big man said, 'then your family will suffer.'

The old man held up a sheet of paper. It was a rural census
sheet, the kind kept in district registries. It had pictures of Amrit
and his fictitious wife and children. These people had been
thorough, Amrit thought; but so had UNACO.

'They will suffer in ways you cannot imagine,' the big man
said. He looked grim now, like a policeman issuing a warning.
'There will be no pity. You may be tempted to think you could
run away with our money *and* our merchandise, but if you do
your wife and your three fine children will be seized at once.
They will be taken to a place where their arms and legs will be
broken, and then while they still scream with pain they will be
put into a pottery furnace and burned to death.'

It took no effort for Amrit to look sick.

'You can change your mind still, if you wish,' the old man said.

Amrit looked at the money, ten centimetres thick in his hand. He looked up at the old man. 'I will make the delivery,' he said.

The old man nodded and handed him the envelope with the capsule.

Sabrina stood under the shower in the neat little bathroom at the cabin. For five whole minutes she had let the hot water sting her and revive her sense of wellbeing. Now as she killed the flow, she felt the throb in her leg start up again.

She pushed back the shower curtain and took a shaving mirror from the window ledge. Twisting round, with the mirror positioned at the back of her thigh, she was able to see the knife wound. In spite of the immediate treatment she had applied, and subsequent fresh dressings, the edges looked raw and angry.

She got out, dried herself, then fumbled in her bag. From the zippered emergency pouch she took a flexible ampoule of penicillin powder. She broke off the top and squirted the contents in a white stream on to the wound, moving the jet of powder up and down until it was exhausted. She put on a fresh dressing, told herself that would fix it, and got on with preparing herself for the day.

Ten minutes later, wearing jeans, sneakers and a OuiSet denim shirt, she joined Mike and Larry in the kitchen. They had pushed the used breakfast things to one end of the table and had her photographs of the hill bandits spread out in two rows.

'Great shots, Sabrina,' Mike said.

'Thanks, but the EVC12A deserves most of the credit.'

'That's no way to get yourself a reputation,' Lenny told her. 'Never praise the equipment – in fact never praise *anything* that can't argue.'

'They're a lot better than I expected,' Sabrina said. She picked up a print and peered at the detail. The pictures had been sent directly to the cabin through the high-definition laserfax, and they looked like lab-printed glossies. 'You can see all the faces,' she said. 'Pretty grim faces, at that.' She looked at Mike. 'Have you gained anything from them?'

'The man at the front, the leader, is definitely Paul Seaton,' he said.

'Who's he?'

Mike gave her a summary of Seaton's career.

'And what's your special interest in him?'

Mike blinked. 'Did I say I had a special interest?'

'You didn't have to. When I came in just now you were staring at this picture with your teeth gritted. You do that when something you're chasing turns up in your sights.'

'You're imagining things,' Mike said.

'Am I imagining things, Lenny?' Sabrina said.

Lenny grinned and looked away. Ram came in through the back door wearing a tracksuit and trainers. He was panting.

'Ram, I've something I want you to look at,' Sabrina said. She went to her room and dug out the papers she had taken from Hafi. She brought them to Ram. 'I wondered if anything here might be relevant. I majored in languages, but this is beyond me.'

Ram went through the papers, reading a little of each. 'It's mostly correspondence to this Hafi character from other men who call themselves Unit Commanders.'

'Hafi was a bandit,' Sabrina explained. 'I understand he had a lot of satellite outfits.'

'*Was* a bandit?'

'I'll tell you about it some time.' Sabrina nodded at the letters. 'What do you think?'

'It looks mostly like bragging and gossip,' Ram said. 'I'll go through them in more detail once I've made you breakfast.'

'You'll spoil me.'

'That's my brief.'

While Ram grilled bacon and fried eggs Sabrina sat down and studied the pictures with Mike and Lenny. 'So what is it?' she said. 'A private vendetta?'

Mike looked at her. 'Why does it have to be anything like that?'

'Vendettas and grudges bring out that atavistic glint you get now and then. What happened?'

'God, you're persistent.'

'So tell me and I'll stop being such an aggravation.'

He told her about the wrecking of a sportsman's career, and the casual savagery that had been the stock in trade of Seaton back in the days before he took to the Indian hills.

'In that case I believe you've every right to catch him and do your worst,' Sabrina said. 'Just remember he's not likely to be a sitting duck.'

'Breakfast,' Ram announced, putting a plateful of eggs, bacon and toast in front of Sabrina. 'Eat.'

She was starving and she ploughed through the food with a minimum of decorum. As she dropped her knife and fork and grabbed her mug of coffee, Ram came over from the window, where he had been reading Hafi's papers.

'This is interesting, in a grim kind of way.' He held up a sheet of yellow paper with tiny writing on it. 'It's from a Unit Commander called Sadjit. He reports that on a scouting mission in the Vale of Kashmir, one of the men in the unit caught a recruiting officer . . .'

'What kind of recruiting officer?' Mike said.

'A man who recruited mules. This Sadjit and one of his lieutenants tortured the man to get information from him. They were too zealous, and the man died before they were able to learn very much, but before he expired they were able to learn that the upmarket drugs are manufactured in the Grotto of Moksha.'

'Never heard of it,' Lenny said.

Sabrina asked what moksha was.

'A Hindu concept,' Ram said. 'It is taught that all people go through a series of reincarnations that eventually lead to moksha. Moksha is the spiritual salvation that frees a person from the cycle of rebirths.'

'That's when a person's karma gets all straightened out, is it?' Mike said.

'That's right.'

'In that case it'll be a few centuries before Mike gets a glimpse of moksha,' Sabrina said. She saw Mike scowl. 'Same goes for me,' she added quickly.

SEVENTEEN

Amrit set off before first light. By the time the sun was up and he could feel its warmth on his face he had gone fifteen kilometres. The dirty, nondescript sack swung from his shoulder and his sandals kicked up dust as he strode along at a marching pace.

Eventually he would travel without surveillance, but for probably the first third of his journey, there was no way to tell if he was being watched. Mike had told him to presume someone was watching all the time. Amrit sensibly mistrusted everyone he saw along the way. A large percentage of the surveillance provided to criminal institutions came from casual informers and paid hangers-on, the slurry of society who could whisper to lethal effect. Every tramp and low-life was a potential seeing-eye that led all the way back to the men with the power.

Amrit had been walking for three hours when he spotted a beggar he had been watching for. The man was tall and stooping, with a small red patch on his filthy grey turban. He stood by the roadside coughing against the palm of one hand while he held out the other to passers-by.

Amrit fished in his pocket as he approached the beggar and pulled out a crumpled banknote. He tossed it to the man, who caught it, brought his hands together with the fingertips touching his chin and bowed, muttering elaborate thanks.

When Amrit had gone past the beggar stood there a while longer, still coughing fitfully, still putting out his hand to everyone who passed. Finally he glanced up at the sun, mopped his forehead with his arm and began walking in the direction of Srinagar.

Hours later he reached the town and made his way through

a network of back streets, several times doubling back and stopping to cough. Finally, when he had spent twenty minutes threading through variations of a route around the same seven little streets, he slipped suddenly into a darkened doorway with a sign above it advertising a motorbike courier service. He pushed open the door beyond and threw himself into a chair in front of a desk.

'The things I do for authenticity,' he groaned. 'Tea, for the love of God . . .'

There was a rattle of cups in the tiny kitchen off the main office. A moment later Mike Graham brought in a steaming mug. He put it in front of the beggar, who pulled off his turban and revealed himself to be Ram Jarwal.

'Mission accomplished, I hope.' He took a gulp of tea. 'Lord, that's just in time. Another minute and I'd have expired.' He fumbled in the pocket of his pantaloons and threw the crumpled banknote on the desk.

Mike opened it and spread it out flat. 'That's great. Hey, Lenny!'

Lenny Trent was in a small room at the back, viewing videotape of a suspected heroin peddler operating in one of the town markets. He switched off the VCR and went through to the office.

'Your boy has done us proud,' Mike said.

He pointed at the smoothed banknote. Stuck to its surface was a white label on which Amrit had scrawled a summary of his route to the Chinese border, with details of a rendezvous at a town called Boyding.

'I hope nobody saw him do that,' Ram said.

'They wouldn't,' Lenny said. 'We rehearsed that one till he had it oil smooth. The drill is first, he memorizes the details of where, what, and when, then when he's off and walking, he slides his hand into his pocket and flattens the banknote against his leg. He pauses for a minute to get something out of his eye with one hand and uses the other hand to scribble out the message with an old stub of pencil he has in his pocket.' Lenny winked. 'He's a talented fellow.'

Later, back at the cabin, Mike, Sabrina and Lenny sat round the big table in the sitting room, mapping out a plan of assault against Paul Seaton and his bandits. Ram snored quietly on the couch.

Lenny asked if they were agreed on their objective.

'If we can be sure Mike keeps his personal feelings under control,' Sabrina said.

'Don't worry about me,' Mike snapped. 'The objective is direct and uncomplicated. We grab Seaton and bring him in for questioning.'

'You definitely believe he's involved in the upmarket drug trade?' Sabrina said.

'It's practically tailor-made for a man like him. High-risk, high-profit. The elements of disruption and sedition running alongside – they're his mark, too.' Mike nodded firmly. 'I'd put money on it. Seaton's our guy. Or he's one of them. Catch him and we're halfway to getting a handle on the big-bucks trade and wrecking it.'

A number of ideas had been formulated, talked over and discarded. One that kept coming up without really being rejected was that they use a team of police marksmen for cover and fire-power while they separate Seaton from his men. The plan had two areas of difficulty that tended to make it look like a non-starter: for one thing, police marksmen were in critically short supply in Srinagar; for another, it would take a helicopter to transport the team to the target area, and the local UN machine would not be available for three days at the earliest.

'We could always try asking Commissioner Mantur,' Mike said. 'When he refuses we'll at least know that road is completely shut off and we can stop considering it.'

On the third attempt Mike got through to the Commissioner. He explained the plan and the predicament, as he saw it.

'Then let me tell it to you as *I* see it, Mr Graham,' Mantur said. 'It is not only numbers of men that I lack, but numbers of bullets for them to fire, on those rare occasions when they can put up a concerted show of belligerence against the villainy which envelopes us in these parts. As for transport, well you are right, you couldn't expect us to provide that. However, perhaps there is another way of looking at all this.'

'Tell me about it.'

'The various departments of the UN have provision in their budgeting for *ad hoc* ventures, am I not correct?'

'Well yes, I believe so.'

'Well why don't you get in touch with your people and suggest an *ad hoc* assault on these bandits you are so keen to intercept, and talk over with them the matter of *ad hoc* finance.'

Mike thought about it.

'OK, I'll do that,' he said. 'What kind of figure should I mention?'

Mantur was silent for a moment. 'In US dollars,' he said finally, 'if we are talking about the hire for half a day of ten marksmen, plus the hire, fuel and pilot fee for a helicopter, I think we would be talking in the region of fifteen thousand US dollars.'

Mike thought about it. 'I can try,' he said.

Philpott was not available. Mike spoke to C. W. Whitlock, who seemed preoccupied. 'I need authorization to hire the marksmen and the helicopter,' Mike pressed him. 'Can you get it for me? This is just a tiny bit urgent.'

UNACO did not have a Deputy Director. All major decisions were taken by the Director; in his absence, decisions waited.

'I don't see what I can do, Mike,' Whitlock said. 'Anything over five thou has to be given the all-clear by Philpott.'

'Try to get him, then.'

'I can't just –'

'C. W., this is my chance to get my hands round the neck of Paul Seaton. Think about it. Call Philpott.'

Whitlock was silent for a moment. 'Give me ten minutes.'

Mike went back to the planning table. 'Just in case Uncle says no,' he said, 'can we bolt a decent alternative together?'

All the alternatives were hazardous and carried such a high possibility of disaster that they could scarcely be considered alternatives at all. Any way they angled it, they would be outnumbered and easily outflanked.

'There's still a probable gain in being outnumbered if the guys doing the outnumbering are everyday mercenaries,' Mike said. 'But I'm not going to be stupid enough to let a horde of hill bandits with a psychopath at their head outnumber *me*.'

'Then you might lose Seaton,' Lenny pointed out.

'Don't rub it in. Think of something else.'

The phone rang. It was Whitlock. 'Go ahead,' he told Mike.

'What?'

'You heard me.'

'Are you serious?'

'No, I'm making it up because I secretly want to see you foul up and get blown out of the service.'

'How come the old man agreed?'

'He's like me,' Whitlock said. 'He has other priorities right now. Be grateful for that. The confirmation will be faxed to you within the hour.'

Mike put down the phone and turned to the others. 'We're in business,' he said, and couldn't resist rubbing his hands together.

By late afternoon Amrit was beginning to understand how tough a man had to be in order to walk all over Kashmir wearing nothing on his feet but flimsy sandals. He was once or twice tempted to stop at a market and buy himself sports socks and a good pair of trainers. But he resisted. An impoverished mule, after all, would be used to going everywhere in sandals or bare feet, and when it came to spending any of his sudden fortune, he certainly wouldn't lay it out on flippant non-essentials like decent footwear.

At a town called Muraka, Amrit decided he could stop and eat his evening meal. He thought of the food at his favourite Srinagar restaurant: plump grilled chicken, properly steamed vegetables and fluffy rice, washed down with a German beer. In Muraka he would have to settle for a good deal less, so he was grateful to be hungry enough, right then, to eat just about anything.

He found a dingy little café called The John Boy. All over India, there were these bars and hostelries named after characters from long-defunct American TV series. The bar two doors away from The John Boy was called Starsky's Hutch.

At the counter he ordered an omelette and strong tea. He sat down at a table near the door and put the sack at his feet. He knew he mustn't fall asleep, but in spite of himself he began to drowse.

He woke with a jump when he felt the sack move. A youth had sat down opposite. He was staring at Amrit, openly hostile, waiting to be asked why he was steadily kicking the sack.

Amrit sat up in his chair, seeing another youth just beyond his left shoulder. He leaned forward and put his arms on the table. He said nothing.

'What's in the bag?' the youth opposite said.

'Nothing that concerns you.'

'I'll ask you again.' The foot stopped kicking the sack and kicked Amrit's foot instead. 'What's in it?'

'Same answer.'

'I'll have a look for myself, then.'

The youth put his head down to duck under the table. Amrit bunched his toes, brought up his foot and kicked him in the mouth. The youth roared and jerked back, banging his head on the metal table.

Amrit grabbed the pepper pot and was on his feet before the other one had a chance to react. He spun off the cap and threw a wad of pepper in the youth's eyes. The youth screamed and dropped to the floor, clutching his face.

As the first one came up from under the table Amrit saw he had the sack in his hand. He ran for the door and by the time Amrit got there he had vanished.

Amrit leaned on the wall, thinking. He quashed an impulse to run around unfamiliar streets while his quarry simply disappeared.

He pushed himself away from the wall, went back into the café and grabbed the youth on the floor. He hoisted him to his feet by the hair, picked up a water carafe and threw the contents in his eyes.

'There. Medicine. Now you're all better. Tell me where your

139

friend is or this time I'll really blind you. And that'll be for starters.'

The youth was hyperventilating, overwhelmed by pain, shock and fright. Amrit slapped him hard on both cheeks. When the youth tried to retaliate, Amrit tightened his grip on his hair, gathering it into his fingers, putting agonizing stress on the roots. The youth screamed once, loud and sharp.

'One more time before I do you terrible harm. Where is your friend?'

The youth jerked his thumb at the door. They walked four metres along the pavement outside, then he stopped and pointed to a stairway.

Amrit frowned at him. 'Are you sure?'

'I swear it . . .'

Amrit let go his grip on the youth. He climbed the stairs two at a time, silently, tensed for trouble.

On the first landing he found the sack. He picked it up and looked inside. Nothing had been taken. He heard a sound and looked in the corner. The youth he had kicked was lying in a heap. Amrit turned him over. His face was torn and bloody.

'What did you do to yourself, you idiot?'

The youth whimpered and slid to the floor again when Amrit released him.

'He did nothing to himself,' a voice said. 'I did it.' A man stepped forward. He was short and stocky. He held up a baseball bat with blood on the thick end. 'They are thieves. They stole from you, yes?'

Amrit nodded.

'For weeks now they have used this place as a getaway, you understand? They rob down on the street, then run here to hide until the commotion is over. Well not any longer. This is where I live. I do not want this.'

Amrit nodded again. He took his sack and went back downstairs. He told the youth waiting at the bottom that he'd better clear off, or he would be in line for more pain before the day was over.

Walking back to the café, Amrit wondered at the tiny shifts

of circumstance that could make such gigantic changes in a life. If he had been an ordinary mule, the loss of the sack would have been a disaster. He would have been doomed.

If he had been an ordinary mule and the stocky little man had intervened, as he just did, could that man have imagined how with one blow of a stick, he had saved another human being from sudden and painful death – or a whole family from brutal murder?

'Forget the omelette,' Amrit told the man in the café. 'I'll just have the tea.'

EIGHTEEN

Sabrina left the cabin before dawn, driving a super-tuned green Range-Rover supplied by Commissioner Mantur. He had put the vehicle at the disposal of Lenny Trent with the added promise of a driver and limited additional manpower should the need arise.

'A small act of thanks,' he told Lenny. 'It is not often we are done the honour of being paid in dollars for an assignment.'

The plan was that, by mid-afternoon, Sabrina should be back in the region where she photographed the bandits. She would conceal the Land-Rover in dense hill forest a kilometre west of the spot where she hid to take her shots, and she would keep Mike and Lenny informed of the situation in the region right up to the time they were due to fly south.

'Any snags,' Mike reminded her before she left, 'any sign at all that our arrival could be monitored, let us know and we'll abort.'

With decent maps and a solid all-terrain vehicle to drive, Sabrina made good time. She took a direct route to the northern perimeter of the village where Aziz lived, then drove the Range-Rover up into the foothills. She kept to the rough, following ravines and rock fissures until she reached the twisting mountain road used by Seaton and his bandits.

Staying on the rocky terrain below the road, she travelled north until she came to the forest. It was high and dense, the foliage so thick that only a dim green light penetrated. It looked, Sabrina thought, like a damp, faintly steamy film set with overdone mood lighting.

She drove into the forest for a distance of twenty metres and parked the Range-Rover in a thicket of smaller trees. She switched off the engine, undid her lap strap and opened the door. She stood to get out and her leg gave way. She fell through the open door and landed on her back among dead leaves and debris.

For a moment she did not move, a habit of the job, checking all was well before she risked getting up. As she lay there she felt the throb in the back of her leg. The wound was not responding to treatment, and now it was infected enough to interfere with the interaction of nerve and muscle. She knew she should have seen a doctor by now, but what with one thing and another . . .

She sat up and pressed the dressing through the thickness of her camouflage trousers. The moment she removed the pressure of her fingers there was a rebound throb. Not a good sign. Toxins from the infected site would be entering her bloodstream.

Carefully she stood up and leaned on the side of the vehicle. The agitation caused by the fall was definitely affecting her chemistry. Her hands shook and she felt a sensation of clamminess on her skin that had nothing to do with the atmosphere in the forest.

'Mild septicaemia,' she diagnosed aloud, feeling the density around her absorb the sound, muffling it. 'All I need.'

Something rustled and moved across her boot. She jumped aside and saw a snake, over a metre long, yellow-and-black-banded. It slithered away under the back wheels.

'God . . .'

She had never seen the species before but she knew what it was: a krait, relative of the cobra and highly venomous, capable of killing half the people it bit, whether they had antivenin or not.

'You're supposed to be nocturnal,' she told the retreating reptile. 'You're supposed to live in open country, too.'

Her heart was thumping and now she was aware of darkness at the edges of her vision.

'Not-so-mild septicaemia,' she muttered.

She sat on the step of the vehicle and put her head between her knees. The blood pounded harder and her temples began to ache, but the shadowing on the perimeter of her sight disappeared.

Slowly she stood up, reached under the driving seat for her rucksack and pulled out the scrambler radio. She pressed the button and waited until a green light showed she had an encoded line.

'Sabrina to Mike or Lenny, come in.'

A couple of whistles and Mike was on the line. 'Where are you, Sabrina?'

'More or less on top of map reference B.'

'You're in the forest.'

'Just far enough in to still see daylight. It's extremely eerie and a krait just slithered across my foot.'

'They're supposed to live in the open.'

'I told it that.'

'Is everything as expected?'

'Tomb-like,' Sabrina said. 'I only called to make sure the radio's working.'

'What are you going to do now?'

'Recce north of here, then south. After that, if it's all clear, I think I'll get myself nested into the rocks above the stretch Seaton and his gang were on when I took the pictures. I'll buzz through every hour until you leave.'

'Sounds OK to me,' Mike said. 'I'll see you.'

The helicopter took off from a field twenty kilometres north of Srinagar at 3:10 p.m. local time. On board were Mike Graham, Lenny Trent, and ten weapons-and-tactics marksmen drawn from police forces in Srinagar, Anantnāg and Nunkum.

As they flew south across the border, passing over the sprawl of Delhi, Lenny pointed out six or seven areas where he had worked, or had helped co-ordinate offensives against dope peddlers.

'I look down at them all,' he said, 'and I realize that now we've moved on, the trade is probably as strong as ever.'

'You have to keep trying,' Mike said, shouting above the noise of the rotor.

144

'I know, I know. My only regret about the job is that there's no place for a sense of achievement. Not ever.'

As they drew within a hundred kilometres of the target zone the pilot took a sweeping route south-east. He continued in a wide sweep and came back north-west, avoiding passing over the mountain track. He finally landed in an area south-west of the forest where the Range-Rover was hidden.

From the rounded cleft of two craggy rocks Sabrina watched through binoculars as the police marksmen, led by Mike and Lenny, made their way up the mountainside, heading for the eastern perimeter of the forest.

It was cool up there in the rocks, but Sabrina was sweating. She lowered the binoculars and saw the sheen of perspiration on her arms and on the backs of her hands. A couple of times as she climbed to this eyrie, she had slipped and bumped the injured leg; now the wound was too tender to touch.

She could hear her breathing, shallow and tremulous, and when she shifted her position between the rocks a dull pain seized her stomach, like a cramp. In the space of five seconds the pain went from dull to sharp, and became so intense she had to grit her teeth to keep from crying out.

'Gastric involvement,' she whispered, past caring now whether she talked to herself or not. 'Take counter-measures.'

The rucksack was at her feet. She opened it and unzipped the medical pouch. Among the foil-sealed packets she located six tablets of activated dimethicone with aluminium hydroxide. After some fumbling she managed to break the foil around two tablets and push them into her mouth. She sat chewing them, promising herself she would never again delay seeing a doctor when she knew she needed one.

The stomach pain subsided. Sabrina began to feel calm again, though not entirely in control of herself. She looked to the right suddenly as a scarlet bird landed on the rock less than two metres away. It was an amazing creature, long-legged like a wader, with a similar hooked beak, but it was all in miniature, the entire bird standing no higher than a pigeon.

'Look at all that *red* . . .'

The feathers resembled scarlet velvet, and the eyes were like pale amethysts.

'What are you, birdie?' she whispered, trying not to disturb it. 'I never saw anything like you before.'

There was a sound down near the edge of the forest, a faraway click like one stone shifting against another. Sabrina picked up the binoculars and looked. One of the marksmen had lost his footing and had slid a little way down the mountainside. Two others were helping him back up. Sabrina moved the binoculars to look at Mike. Even at that distance she could see how annoyed he was.

She looked at the bird again. Her heart thumped. It was still there, but now it was green. Bright emerald green with orange eyes. Sabrina touched her forehead and felt the wetness. It was as if someone had doused her with warm water. She was aware that she was having selective hallucinations, the kind that inserted themselves into reality. The pain in her stomach was coming back.

'More dimethi-whatsit,' she muttered.

She reached for the tablets, noticing the bird had gone, if it was ever there. She took the packet between both hands and shakily tried to burst the foil blister covering one of the tablets. She pressed too hard and the tablet shot out over the edge of the rock. She tried again. This time the pressure was just right. She slipped the tablet into her mouth and began chewing.

'One more,' she panted.

As the plastic bubble split, a hand landed on Sabrina's shoulder. The tablet fell at her feet. She turned her head and looked at the strong brown fingers pressed into the material of her shirt.

This was real, she decided. She was not imagining it.

The operation to get the marksmen in position along the mountain track took more time than Mike had expected; it was already late in the afternoon by the time they were all tucked down out of sight. They were deployed in two groups of four, with a pair of men wielding long-range rifles stationed to the rear of the others in case of a retreat. Mike and Lenny, armed with

146

revolvers, lay in a natural rain trough facing north, a metre down the mountainside from the road and twenty metres from the nearest marksmen.

'They've all been warned not to put a mark on Seaton,' Mike said.

'So you can mark him yourself.'

'So I get to interrogate him straight away. Men lying in hospital get time to set up their defences. I want him picked up off the road and bundled straight into that helicopter, no delay. I want to keep him off balance all the way back to Srinagar and then I want to grill him until he tells me everything. My customary compassion,' he added, 'will not be activated on this occasion.'

Lenny was watching the sun. It had sunk visibly in the ten minutes they had lain there. 'I'm getting a leery feeling they're on to us,' he said.

'What makes you say that?' Mike snapped irritably. 'Is that you playing opposites? Say it ain't going to be so, which is sure to make it happen? Is that what you're doing?'

Lenny sighed. 'Ease up, will you? I know you're anxious to get your hands on Seaton. I'm just saying I have a feeling –'

'From where?' Mike was glaring, unwilling to face the possibility that the bandits wouldn't show. 'Have you got some special sixth sense? Or a seventh one to back up the sixth? Huh?'

'I'm going by the time of day,' Lenny said.

'What does that mean?'

'It'll be dark in an hour. Hill bandits are timetable creatures. It's part superstition, part sticking to what they know works. They're late. That's what I'm saying, and on that fact I'm basing my suspicion that they're not coming.'

'Let's just wait and see.'

'Sure,' Lenny said. 'Nothing much else we can do, really.'

Twenty minutes later there was still no sign of bandits. Mike decided to raise Sabrina on the radio. He got no response.

'It's not turning out such a swell day,' Lenny observed.

Mike said nothing.

*   *   *

147

An hour before dusk, on a hot stretch of road fifteen kilometres from the Kashmir border with China, a man riding a noisy moped jumped off his machine as it stalled and began shouting at it. There were few people around to see him, but those who did were amused. He was a comic-looking figure, white-bearded, dressed in an eccentrically large turban, flowing yellow shirt and blue pantaloons. He was furious, calling his bike an ingrate, a traitor, a worthless assemblage of junk held together with rust.

Then he stopped shouting and wheeled the moped to a patch of rough ground by the roadside. He put the machine on its stand, crouched by the side of it and started pulling off pieces of the engine.

Even at close quarters, nobody would have been able to tell that this was Ram Jarwal, steeped in his latest role, thoroughly enjoying himself as he tore off excess parts of bike engine and peered crazily at each one before he dropped it on the ground.

Several of the bits hitting the ground actually came from a pocket in the folds of Ram's vast shirt. When he had finally reversed the procedure and put back all the pieces he had pulled off his machine, there was one visible item on the ground that had not been there when he arrived. It was an oval flat stone, like thousands of other littered about the roadside.

At his third attempt to restart the engine it fired and he jumped on. The bike tore off and in less than a minute Ram was out of sight.

It was nearly dark when Amrit Datta came striding along the same stretch of road, his sack dangling from his shoulder. At roughly the spot on the corner where the moped had stopped Amrit began limping.

He stopped and bent down beside an oval stone with a notch chipped cleanly out of its edge. In the gathering darkness he appeared to remove a pebble from his sandal and adjust the strap; in fact he lifted one side of the stone, uncovering a hole in the ground. The hole had been put there by Ram as he fussed with his engine parts and deftly used their natural digging edges – each one time only – to prepare a receptacle in the earth.

It was too dark for Amrit to see what he was taking out of

148

the hole, but he could identify the items easily by touch. There was a replacement amulet for the one he would leave under the stone, and under that was his gun.

As he began walking again a few moments later, he patted the gun where it now lay, in the waistband of his baggy trousers, the metal cool against his skin.

He began to smile, and after a few more minutes he started to whistle. It took so little, he thought, to make him feel really sure of himself again.

NINETEEN

The bandits didn't show.

'You're entitled to say you knew this would happen,' Mike told Lenny.

'You know I don't do stuff like that.'

'Yeah. Ignore me, I'm just sore. *Very* sore.'

A call had come through from Srinagar to the helicopter pilot five minutes earlier. The assistant to Commissioner Mantur told the pilot that he and the marksmen, who were now running into overtime, had to return to base without delay.

As the men began filing silently down the mountainside to the tiny plateau where the helicopter sat, Mike grabbed Lenny's arm. 'I'm staying,' he said.

'What for?'

'I don't feel like I've tried. Going now is just defeatist.'

'Staying can't help that. They won't be along tonight. It's getting dark, they've obviously changed their schedule. We can come another time.'

'Now what are the real chances of that happening? Who's going to give us the leeway after this bummer?'

'Mike, what are you hoping to do?' Lenny peered at his face in the dusk, trying to get a pinch of reason past the impulsiveness. 'It's going to get very dark soon. You're all alone up here . . .'

'Sabrina's around somewhere.'

'You don't know that. Her radio was out. She probably took off when she realized she couldn't make contact. That would be the drill, right?'

'Yeah,' Mike sighed, 'that's the drill.' He shrugged. 'I don't care. I'm staying. I've no idea what I'll do, but I know I don't

150

want to go away from here empty-handed – not without really trying.'

'You've no resources.'

'I'm good at commandeering. And stealing.'

'OK,' Lenny said. 'I'll stay, too.'

'You don't have to.'

'When you're back in New York bragging about how you hauled in Paul Seaton single-handed, I don't want to have to skulk out of the room in case somebody asks me where I was at that moment.'

'We'll have to rough it,' Mike said.

'That won't put me off. I bet I've roughed it more times, and worse, than you ever did.'

They caught up with the others and explained what they were doing. The pilot, a tall bearded Sikh, told them they were crazy. 'But I wish you luck, nevertheless. If by some miracle you ever get back to Srinagar, look me up and I'll buy you a beer. Your story should be worth hearing.'

Mike and Lenny took their padded windcheaters from the helicopter and stepped back, watching the others get on board. They stood and waved as the craft rose vertically for fifty metres and then swung away towards the north.

'It's going to be quiet around here with the boys gone,' Lenny quipped.

Mike was gazing up at the ridge of rocks above the mountain path. 'I hope Sabrina's OK,' he said.

They moved up the incline along the eastern side of the forest and sat down on the edge of the road, facing west.

'Might as well catch the sunset,' Lenny said.

They watched orange light fan out across the western horizon. By swift stages it turned to gold, red and purple as the sun dropped halfway below the dark margin of rock and mountain.

'It never disappoints,' Mike said.

They both turned at a sound to their right. Coming from the perimeter of the forest were six men, their faces dark amber in the fading blaze of sun. They all carried rifles, all of them pointing at Mike and Lenny.

151

'One of us has to run for it,' Mike said, lips scarcely moving, his voice no more than a whisper.

'You go,' Lenny grunted.

It was the rule. If two agents were cornered, and the prospects for survival looked slight, then one agent must try to escape.

'No. You go.'

'You're a top UNACO man, for God's sake . . .'

As they stood up, their hands in the air, Mike shoved Lenny violently with his shoulder, knocking him over the edge of the road. Lenny could do nothing but run.

'Go like the wind!' Mike yelled.

Lenny ploughed down the mountainside, arms flailing as he galloped over stones, leapt boulders and ran headlong through thickets and under overhanging trees.

Five of the bandits formed a circle around Mike. The sixth man went to the edge of the road and got down on one knee. He steadied his elbow and took aim with his rifle.

'No!' Mike yelled at him. 'No, you bastard!'

A single shot rang out. Mike saw Lenny stumble and fall. The gunman stood up, walked down the mountainside a distance, then fired again. When he came back he gave his companions a thumbs-up.

Mike threw himself at the gunman but didn't get past the two in front of him. They each hit him once, on the ears with clenched fists, deafening him, making his skull hurt so badly he had to clamp his hands over his head.

He was pushed and pulled towards the forest and marched through the trees in almost total darkness. After five or six minutes he began to see light, and as they marched forward, threading their way, he could hear the hum of a generator.

All at once they were on the edge of a clearing and he could see bright electric lights, mounted high on tubular metal stands. There were tents, cooking fires with spits mounted over them, and horses tethered in a long line by a wooden trough.

As Mike was shoved forward into the wide circle of light he saw a woman tied to a pole near one of the guttering fires. Her head was bowed and he saw blood caked on the front of her shirt. Drawing nearer he realized it was Sabrina. He jerked forward, making the men holding his arms stumble.

'Sabrina! Sabrina honey! Are you OK?'

Somebody slapped him on the neck. Mike's head jerked round, 'You goddamned scum!'

He pulled an arm free and punched the nearest bandit on the chin. As the man fell Mike spun and kicked the one on the other side.

'Vermin! Woman-beaters! You're filth! *Filth!* I'll kill every last one of you!'

For a moment he was out of their control, free, moving to his own rhythm while they bumped into each other trying to block him. He put his hands on the shoulders of a barrel-shaped man and head-butted him on the nose. The sound of cracking bone gave Mike fresh energy.

'Get out of my way!' He slipped his hand under his jacket and pulled out his gun. 'Back! Get back!' He thumbed the hammer as men scattered. 'Sabrina! Wake up!'

He turned to the pole where Sabrina was tied. A bandit behind him waited with his rifle raised until Mike lined himself up. In that split second the rifle butt came down with flashing speed and struck Mike's head. He stopped moving for a moment, staring at the pole and Sabrina's sagging body. Then he fell over on his face.

TWENTY

His first recollection when he came round was that Lenny Trent was dead. Through his pain and immobility he felt a terrible distress. There was a kaleidoscope of tumbling images, all of Lenny, all the pictures bright, full of energy and laughter.

The images were an assertion: *He isn't dead!* The vehemence was a voice inside Mike, his own, chanting over and over to a banging fist, reinforcing his refusal to believe.

The pain in his head intruded but he hung on to the images, knowing they were going to fade, wanting them to stay and wipe out the reality.

'Stay, buddy, stay . . .'

How could it be that Lenny Trent no longer existed? In a buzzing, sickening haze, surfacing quickly to full consciousness, Mike saw Lenny's mobile face again, the eyes so alive behind their lenses. And then he faded away, and Mike accepted the hollow certainty.

Dead and gone.

He opened his eyes and more pain scythed across his skull. He was aware that he was sitting, and that his arms were tied. Another face moved in close to his, hairy and belligerent. It was familiar.

'Paul Seaton,' Mike said.

'Nowadays I am called Memet-Muhammad.'

'Crap by any other name . . .'

Seaton stiffened. *Not used to people talking back*, Mike thought.

'I have plans for your poisonous tongue,' Seaton said, 'once you've told me what I want to know.'

The American accent was overlaid with the clipped syllabic

delivery of Indian speech. Seaton probably hadn't spoken English for years.

'I'm telling you nothing.' Mike turned his head to one side. There were maybe fifty people moving about in the clearing, a third of them women. 'So this is where you live.'

'Astute of you to work that out.' Seaton grinned. He still had the hard and dangerous manner, but now it had a reckless edge, the bravura of a man who won every fight. 'It amused me the way you all kept clinging to this forest for cover, hiding from me right under my nose.'

A woman brought a plate with food on it. Seaton took it and began eating with his fingers.

'Tell me who you are.'

'No.'

'Shall I ask the woman instead?'

Sabrina! Mike suddenly remembered. He looked anxiously around and finally saw her. She was still where he had seen her last, still sagging against the pole in the middle of the clearing.

'If my hands were free,' Mike said, 'I'd kill you with them.'

'Aw, sorry – I have to frustrate you by denying you the chance.'

Seaton reached out with greasy fingers and twisted Mike's nose. He kept twisting until the pain made Mike cry out.

'I've guessed a thing or two about you and your friends, mostly from the equipment the woman was carrying. But I need to fill in the gaps.'

'Didn't she tell you, then?'

Seaton shook his head and popped more food into his mouth. 'She's very well trained. Not a word, in spite of everything.'

'How did it feel, putting your grubby paws on a civilized person?'

'Civilized! Ha!' Particles of food flew from Seaton's mouth. 'You have no idea what civilization is. You think you are cultured, enlightened, a citizen of an advanced society. What you are, Mister Interloper, what you lamentably are is the feeble instrument of a corrupt western fixation with territory and material wealth.'

155

'You reckon?'

'You and your kind will be swallowed by the wilderness created by your own greed.'

'Fine ideological words,' Mike said. 'They don't sound so good coming from a crummy bandit who started his career as a lump of mouth-breathing hired muscle.'

'That tongue of yours,' Seaton said, wagging a finger.

'I remember how you once destroyed a good man, Seaton. A man you didn't even know. You did it without a qualm. You did your harm the way an insect would. And today you killed my friend just as brutally, with as little feeling. You're not entitled to an opinion or to justice. You're a barbarian.'

That appeared to sting Seaton. He blinked at Mike a couple of times, then he said, 'People can be misunderstood.'

'Not people like you.'

'Yes. People change, remember.'

'Oh sure. Time and circumstance, the great changers. Now you're an Islamic separatist honcho. You're into laudable pursuits like scaring pathetic drug mules into killing themselves sooner than face your notion of punishment –'

'Hold on!' Seaton shouted. 'I won't have that!'

'Too late. I just gave it to you.'

'No! *No!* You won't hang that on me!'

Seaton jumped to his feet. He went to the centre of the clearing, shouting and gesticulating. Mike felt the bonds on his wrists being cut. He dropped his hands in his lap and flexed his fingers. The blood came tingling back. He watched as Sabrina's ropes were cut and three women put her on a pallet and carried her away to a tent.

Seaton came back, still agitated, waiting while two women put food and water in front of Mike. Mike tasted the meat and found it was succulent chicken. He took a mouthful of water and stared at Seaton.

'What's going on?'

Seaton got down on his hunkers. He pointed at the plate. 'Eat.'

Mike put a chunk of chicken breast in his mouth and chewed. It was as good as anything he had ever tasted.

'What you said about the mules, being forced to kill themselves, that is what happens to people in the new trade.'

'New trade? You mean the traffic in highly refined drugs?'

Seaton nodded. 'Superfine heroin, MDA, pure coke, concentrated cannabis oil, crack – all that stuff is down to somebody else. I'm no part of the trade and I'm no part of the practices. Do you understand that? It's got nothing to do with us.'

Mike pointed to his plate. 'Why the sudden generosity?'

'We're obviously not so totally on opposite sides as I thought. Or as you thought. For all I knew before, you were an outcrop of the DEA.'

'I could be. My friend that one of your goons shot for sport – he used to be DEA.'

'Listen, about your dead friend – he had a gun, he would have shot me or mine given a chance, so let's not get mired down in recrimination here. Just tell me one thing. Is it any part of your brief to stop the new trade?'

'It certainly is.'

'Well now let me tell you about my operation. It's nothing angelic, but there's a big difference between what we are and what they are, believe me. First off, we have no part in terrorizing peasant people or poor people of any kind.'

'What do you do, then?'

'Fundamentally, we look after ourselves.' Seaton smiled briefly, showing surprisingly white teeth. 'That's what it's about, survival. To survive we have to do some unpopular things, hard and damaging things, just to keep our status. If we ever softened we would be swamped.'

'You haven't really told me what you do.'

'I operate drug convoys. That's where the revenue comes from. The life-blood. But in my operation there are no hapless couriers, no victims within the trade. There's only me, my men and their women and children. The merchandise we transport is traditional low-quality hashish and heroin destined for the usual outlets in the West. Any garbage will do for them.'

'What's your exact stance on the new trade?'

'For months I've watched and I've searched. I caught one of

157

their mules but he executed himself before he could be questioned. I'll keep on watching and searching.'

'And if you get lucky?' Mike said. 'What'll you do?'

'When I find the people who run the market in refined drugs, I'll kill them. I don't care how many there are. They will all die.'

'That's one way to deal with the competition, I suppose.'

'They won't be eradicated because they are competitors,' Seaton said. 'They are the worst kind of parasites, they devour our society. *That* is why they will die.'

'You're not exactly a credit to your society.'

'We make waves and we make trouble but we do not destroy the fabric of community,' Seaton insisted. 'Call me what you like, but nobody can say I ever exploited or harmed the poor or the vulnerable.'

They stared at each other for a tense moment. 'I made a mistake about you,' Mike said. 'I jumped to the conclusion that suited my prejudice. I was wrong.' He swallowed the last of the chicken and took more water. 'You're still a rotten man, though,' he added. 'Your principles don't save you from that.'

Seaton shrugged. He stood up and walked away. A minute later Sabrina was led out of the tent where the women had taken her. She had been bathed and her hair was combed. She looked pale but unharmed.

Two women helped her on to a horse. Mike was nudged and when he turned a man pointed to a horse standing saddled and ready at the edge of the clearing. Mike climbed stiffly into the saddle and coaxed the horse to where Sabrina's stood.

'Are you OK?'

'Better than I expected,' Sabrina said.

Seaton appeared and pointed to three of his men mounted on horses. 'They will take you to a main road, and from there you will be able to make your way back to wherever you came from.'

'What about the Range-Rover?' Sabrina said.

'A bonus we can really use,' Seaton said, 'for which we're grateful.' He looked at Mike. 'Your friend's body has been taken to the railway station at the town of Jerrida. Given your obvious

158

resources, I'm sure you'll be able to arrange its removal to wherever you want.'

Without another word Seaton turned and walked into one of
the tents. The three horsemen moved off. Mike and Sabrina
followed them.

By the time they reached the main road it was bright daylight.
Mike and Sabrina sat on their horses and watched the bandits
disappear into the rocks of the mountainside.

'So here we are,' Mike said, 'wherever here is.'

A fresh morning breeze blew Sabrina's hair out behind her.
Mike told her she looked like an ad for shampoo.

'Death warmed-over is what I feel like.'

'They treated you pretty badly?'

'Well, no . . .' Sabrina shrugged. 'It wasn't like I was tortured
or anything. The blood that was on me, I got that falling over
a couple of rocks on the way to the forest. What they did was
threaten, mostly.'

'So what's wrong?'

'I developed septicaemia over the last few days –'

'Septicaemia? How –'

'Knife wound in my leg, it's a long story. Anyway, I hit the
crisis while I was up in the rocks, keeping watch. I can't help
feeling it was my fault it all went the way it did.'

'You couldn't have prevented what happened.'

'I could have been more alert, and if I'd been more alert I
might have spotted something going on in the forest.'

'Forget it,' Mike said. 'The hills are Seaton's territory. We
didn't stand a chance.'

'I'm sorry about Lenny,' Sabrina said, stroking her horse's
neck.

'He was a good, dear friend,' Mike said. 'If I talk about him
I'll get maudlin. There'll be time for that later. First things first.
How's the leg now? Should we try to get medical help?'

'No need,' Sabrina said. 'Back there in the tent the ladies gave
me the hill-bandit version of a blanket bath, and when they saw
the dressing they had to have a look. Well I don't know what

159

they did, but they did it with squashed leaves and powder from a leather bag. It stung like hell for maybe three minutes, then they washed it off, bound the wound again and now it feels like it's healing. The rotten way I feel, that's just aftermath. The fact is I'm mending fast.'

Mike looked at the sun and pointed along the long dusty stretch of the road. 'That way's north. For now, that's all we need to know.'

Sabrina brought her horse around, getting it to stand beside Mike's. 'This has been a terrible setback, hasn't it?' she said.

'You could put it that way. We're God knows how many miles from where we should be, we've wasted time and huge resources on chasing the wrong people, and a fine operator and good friend has been wiped out. It's all loss, there's been no gain at all.'

'So it's a time for taking one of Philpott's axioms to heart.'

'Which one would that be?'

Sabrina recited from memory. '"Defeat in a venture should be regarded as a challenge, just as an obstacle should be seen as a disguised opportunity. Adversity should make us even more determined to succeed."'

'Hear, hear.' Mike smiled wearily. 'Good old Uncle Malcolm. I'll definitely do that one in cross-stitch when I get a minute.'

They began travelling north, the horses keeping in step, treading the road as if they regularly made that journey.

'It's odd,' Mike said after a while, 'but we haven't started fighting yet.'

'I noticed that.'

'By now we should have been full of recrimination and blaming each other for all this catastrophe.'

'Could we be maturing?' Sabrina said.

'Nah.'

'What, then?'

'I reckon we're just too low to take the trouble to bicker. Give it time. We'll revert to type.'

Sabrina was shielding her eyes from the sun, gazing at the winding stretch of road ahead. 'I've no idea where we are,' she said, 'but it would be great if we came to the village where old Aziz lives – you know, the man who put me on to the convoy route?'

'He could help us now, could he?'

'I don't think so,' Sabrina said. 'But he makes a terrific cup of tea.'

TWENTY-ONE

Malcolm Philpott's arrival in India was precisely as low-key as he wanted, and his transfer from Delhi to Jammu was just as discreet. He arrived at the area office of Charity Distribution International in mid-afternoon and was shown into the office of the Senior Co-ordinator for northern India, Sarj Deerpaul.

'Mr Philpott, your reputation comes before you!'

Deerpaul came around his desk with arms wide and for a second Philpott though he was going to be hugged. But the rotund little man brought his arms down again, executed a short bow, and reached out his hand. They shook and Deerpaul showed Philpott to a chair.

'Harry Lewis speaks so highly of you.' Deerpaul got behind the desk again. 'I gather you were once colleagues.'

'Many years ago. But we've remained friends. I suppose he told you why I'm here?'

'Indeed.' Deerpaul patted the square knot of his yellow silk tie. 'He tells me you hope to direct your expertise towards a solution, or at least a partial solution, of our biggest problem, the black market in charity aid.'

'I hope to arrive at an evaluation, at any rate.' Philpott was reluctant to make extravagant promises before he knew anything. 'A plan of attack is the first essential.'

'From our experience, I would say you will find yourself up against some very unpleasant characters, Mr Philpott. In our own probing of the problem we have lost investigators, and not just a handful. Good skilled men and women have died for doing no more than asking casual questions in the wrong quarter.'

Philpott explained he was particularly interested in a farm near Srinagar where aid consignments had appeared to be taken regularly for redistribution.

'I know of that place,' Deerpaul said. 'It looks so vulnerable, so wide open to inspection and so entirely above board. We have not been able to do more than harbour suspicions, however. Two investigations have drawn blanks. Officers conducting a third investigation of the place never came back.' Deerpaul smiled wincingly. 'Melodramatic, no? But that is exactly what happened. Two seasoned investigators decided to tackle the owner of the farm – it is really no more than a smallholding – and those officers were never seen again.'

Part of Deerpaul's trouble, Philpott knew, was that he and his investigators had to respect the laws of any region where they worked. UNACO had to do that too, officially. Unofficially there were agreements, and codicils to agreements, that made sure the law of a territory did not obstruct the work of a Task Force or anyone else connected with UNACO.

'I would like to visit that farm tonight, if that's possible, Mr Deerpaul.'

'Why, yes . . .'

'Is there a problem?'

'Well . . . ahem . . . I had not expected you to be so *avid* in your need to get started. Consequently I have no agents available at present who can be assigned to go with you. The day after tomorrow, perhaps –'

'Don't worry about it,' Philpott said. 'Give me a map, provide me with a car, and I'll take care of the rest myself.'

Deerpaul looked shocked. 'You would go there alone?'

'Oh yes,' Philpott said brightly. 'I do find that I function better in the field if I don't have to take anyone else's presence into account.'

'But I was thinking of the potential for danger.'

'Oh, I'm still potentially dangerous, all right.'

Deerpaul laughed dutifully, but he still looked worried. 'There is the most awful risk attached to visiting such a place as that farm on your own, Mr Philpott. I strongly advise you to wait

163

until someone familiar with the territory can go with you.'

'I simply don't have the time.'

Deerpaul began to look very uneasy. 'This is not right,' he said. 'Here you are, prepared to put yourself at hazard on behalf of this organization, and I can be of no help to you at all. Frankly, Mr Philpott, I feel terrible about this.'

'Then try not to.'

'Is there anything at all that I can do? After all, you have taken the trouble to come here –'

'If you could let me have a summary of how much stuff, and what kind, goes through the farm in an average month . . .'

'I have those figures to hand,' Deerpaul beamed.

'Then that would be a great help.'

'Thank heavens.'

Deerpaul touched a button on an intercom and asked his secretary to bring in the latest estimates of black market dealing in the Vale of Kashmir.

'Now you are sure this will help you, Mr Philpott? You are not simply humouring me in order to save my feelings?'

Philpott assured him the figures would be of great assistance. They would help, for a start, in putting Philpott to sleep later on. Nothing worked better on his insomnia than rows and columns of dry official figures.

The car supplied by Deerpaul's office was mechanically sound and it handled very well on the rough half-formed roads between Jammu and the southern territory of the Vale of Kashmir. The suspension, on the other hand, was the hardest Philpott had ever withstood. At ten minutes to nine in the evening he drew up fifty metres from the perimeter fence of the farm, with an ache in his back that would take his New York chiropractor a month to put right.

He left the car locked up at the roadside and walked across wooded land in the direction of the farm. Deerpaul had provided a powerful MagLite torch but Philpott chose not to use it. Instead, he walked along in almost total darkness, making himself see. When he came out of the woods and was approaching the fence, he could make out the dull sheen of the wire against the surrounding blackness.

He stood by the fence for a while just listening. There were the sounds of animals, the rustle of leaves and grass in the soft breeze, an occasional small sound – bumps, the scraping of a chair on a stone floor – from the cottage at the centre of the farm. Nothing special, no indication of bustle or business. Everything he heard was consistent with a quiet, sleepy farm.

He walked along the fence, feeling for a gate, and eventually found one. It was a high double gate with two heavy padlocks. Philpott paused to consider if it would be worth his while to go over the fence. He decided to do it.

Back where he had first stood listening, there was a broken plastic bottle crate lying in the grass. He went back and found it and stood it on end close to the wire. When he climbed on it the crate dipped under his weight and creaked ominously, but it held.

He paused, licked the tip of his right forefinger and touched it to the top wire of the fence. The shock was severe enough to throw his hand away from the wire. He wet his finger again and touched the next wire. Nothing.

His leather gloves, as always, lay flat in his right inside jacket pocket. He put them on and gripped the top wire of the fence. The manoeuvre he was about to use was not one he would let any of his agents see him employ; it was ungainly and ergonomically unsound, and it would certainly make someone like Mike Graham laugh like a drain. It would make his doctor despair, because ever since Philpott's heart attack a few years earlier, the old physician regularly complained that he didn't take his health seriously enough. But the manoeuvre usually worked for Philpott, and for the moment that was all that counted.

He got up on his toes on the crate, then bent his knees sharply, keeping hold of the wire.

'One.'

He breathed in, flexing his legs, pushing his shoulders as high as they would go,

'Two.'

He repeated the move, stretching his back as far as he could, getting right up on his toes. He came down again and this time he crouched. He took a deep breath.

'Three!'

He shot up, aiming himself into the air, pushing with his toes and pulling with his forearms. His body went up in an arc and sailed over the fence. He landed on his feet on the other side and sank to a squatting position.

When he was sure he had raised no alarms, he stood up. He brushed his jacket and began walking towards the dim lights of the cottage.

Halfway across the compound he heard a noise behind him. He turned and saw lights approaching. It was a truck, bumping over the stony ground between the perimeter fence and the road. Philpott dropped to the ground and flattened himself in the grass.

The truck stopped, someone got out to open the gates, then it rumbled through and stopped in front of the cottage. Philpott waited, listening for the sound of the gates being locked again. But no sound came from that direction. He noted that a clear escape route was now available should he need it.

As he lay there he saw someone being helped out of the back of the truck and led into the cottage. It looked as if there were two other people as well.

The cottage door opened, spilling out a fan of yellow light, then closed again. Philpott ran across the grass at a crouch.

He stood to one side of the largest of the three lit windows and peered in at the side. At a table, below an oil lamp dangling from the ceiling, a nervous-looking young man sat with a thick wad of money in front of him. On the other side of the table an old man stood, wagging a finger as he addressed the young man. Lurking back in the shadows were two men with the kind of faces Philpott generally described as being born for the gibbet. On a side table was a bulging sack and on another table beside it, a pile of unmistakable merchandise in telltale plastic bags: heroin, nearly fluorescent in its stark whiteness.

Philpott pulled back from the window. This was an odd happenstance. He had come looking for evidence of a black market in charity goods and stumbled on a drug-running operation.

He stood a moment longer, wondering about a course of action. Finally he decided the best thing was to leave and evaluate the evidence over a large brandy, preferably somewhere quiet and comfortable.

As Philpott made his way through the darkness towards his car, back in New York it was close to noon. C. W. Whitlock was in the Sculpture Garden on top of the twentieth-century wing of the Museum of Modern Art. It was a bright and reasonably warm day, but very few people had ventured out to the garden.

Whitlock pretended to give most of his attention to a bronze head of a girl, while his companion feigned interest in a pencil-slim Giacometti figure beside it.

'Did it never occur to you, Bridget,' Whitlock said quietly, 'that you were bound to get caught in the end?'

The woman shrugged. She was approaching middle age, a small and tidy woman with attractive dark hair streaked with grey. She wore oval glasses with tortoise-shell frames which she kept pushing nervously along her nose.

'The work, the cause, was everything, you know? Getting caught was a hazard but it was hardly worth considering, since the work had to be done anyway, risk or no risk.'

'So you never feared for your own future? You never thought about the possibility of being shut away for the rest of your life?'

'I thought about it late at night. Sometimes. The same way I occasionally think about death, or getting mugged, or finding myself walking down Fifth Avenue with no clothes on – all that insecure stuff was there, but it didn't hinder me, it didn't make me draw back from what I had to do.'

'None of it came to anything,' Whitlock said. 'Don't you find that disheartening?'

'No. What mattered was my, my . . .'

'Subversion?'

'Sure. Right.' She pushed the specs back along her nose. 'I was doing what was right. I thought that then and I think it

167

now. So I admit it was kind of absurd, it was a wrong tack in just about every respect, but it was something carried out in the right spirit.'

'I think I understand.' Whitlock moved on to the next sculpture. The woman moved too.

'You think I'm a real dope, don't you?'

'No,' Whitlock said. 'I don't agree with a thing you did, but I don't condemn you for it, and I don't think you're anywhere near being a dope. A starry-eyed idealist, maybe . . .'

'So where do I stand?'

'Looking at the situation one way, it's kind of grave,' Whitlock said. 'Looking at it another – well, no harm's done . . .'

'But there are consequences at law,' the woman said.

'If you ever found yourself having to face them.' Whitlock turned to her. 'That's why I suggested we meet up here. Away from people keeping tabs. I'm prepared to let you vanish.'

She stared at him. 'For real?'

'Absolutely.'

She went on staring. 'There's a price, right?'

He nodded.

'How much?'

'Oh, for Pete's sake.' Whitlock looked affronted. 'I don't mean money.'

'What, then?'

'A free and detailed confession.'

'How detailed?'

'I've written it out already.' Whitlock took two folded sheets of paper from his pocket and handed them to the woman. 'Why don't you go over there, sit down and read it. If you feel you can sign it, then I've got a pen with me, too. We can have this whole thing sewn up before we get back to street level.'

'And what happens then, assuming I sign it?'

'Well, I happen to know you're not strapped for money, and you've got fast foreign transfer facilities set up already . . .'

'You're thorough, Mr Whitlock.'

'Frankly, Bridget, there's nobody to touch me in that department. As I see it, you can take off for anywhere you want. I'm sure you've somewhere in mind, a hinterland.'

'She nodded. 'How long have I got?'

'Forty-eight hours, tops.'

She opened the papers, glanced at them a moment, then said, 'Give me the pen. I'll sign now.'

'Without reading your statement?'

'You're an honourable man, right?'

'I hope so.'

'Well then. There's no problem, you won't have stuck me with anything I didn't do, and I'm sure my darkest deeds will be presented in the kindest possible light.'

She put the statement on the plinth of the Giacometti and signed and dated both sheets.

'There.' She handed it back to Whitlock. 'Will this do any practical good, do you think? Or is it just an exercise in detection and tidying up?'

'I hope it'll do some good,' Whitlock said.

'Fine.' She smiled and turned away. 'If you'll excuse me, I should be getting along. I've a lot of packing to do.'

TWENTY-TWO

The first thing Philpott did when he got into his room at the Hotel Jammu Ashok was pour himself a large brandy from a bottle of Remy VSOP he had brought with him. He then settled down to think over the situation. When he reached a decision, he had another large brandy.

Before turning in for the night he put through a call on a scrambler circuit to C. W. Whitlock. There was a delay while the decoder at the US end connected, then Whitlock came on the line.

'I believe I've stumbled on something that will be more than a simple addition to what TF3 are doing out here,' Philpott told him. 'But I'll let you know more later. Has anything important turned up?'

'Well, yes,' Whitlock said. 'It cancels part of your reason for going to Kashmir. Policy Control have sent us a memo.'

'Yes?'

'They've fixed a date for a techniques-and-procedures review. Two days from now.'

'What, even though they know I'm not there?'

'That's it.'

'But how can I defend myself if I'm not there?'

'Strictly speaking,' Whitlock said, 'you don't need to put up a defence, or put in an appearance, since technically you're not under attack.'

'In other words they can bulldoze whether I'm there or not.'

'I'll be here, sir. And I fully intend to speak up on behalf of our freedom to swing to our own rhythm.'

'Do we have much of a case?'

'I'm working on it.'

170

Philpott paused and swallowed more brandy. 'What do you really think, C. W.? Can my skin be saved here?'

'Anything's possible. And I'll be trying my hardest.'

Meanwhile, in open country one hundred and sixty kilometres north-west of Philpott's hotel, Mike and Sabrina, still on horseback, were making their way north with the guidance of the stars. As an exercise in root-level self-sufficiency Mike would have enjoyed it; as a necessity he found it frustratingly limited. He would have felt better about everything, Sabrina told him, if he'd had something to eat.

'The horses have done a lot better than us,' she said, her voice echoing eerily in the dark. 'All that good fresh water, and the fodder – those were nice people.'

Under other circumstances Mike would have found them delightful. But he had been hungry for many hours now, and entering the village he had entertained the hope of a meal, anything at all to cancel his hunger. It was not to be. The people were transients. It was a ghost village, and although there was a good well, and the people carried fodder for their animals, there was no spare food for human beings.

'It could only happen to us,' Sabrina said now.

'What could?'

'Coming on a band of travelling acrobats and jugglers.'

'*Starving* acrobats and jugglers,' Mike corrected. 'Who seemed to value their animals' health above their own, I might add.'

'They were just honest and kind, Mike. You still find that in India. Decent people who don't think about themselves all the time.'

'Whatever. I'm still hungry. I thought it would have passed off by now. It's supposed to, isn't it?'

'Let's just concentrate on making headway. Maybe when we hit a decent-sized town we can sell the horses and get ourselves some food.'

'Ssh!' Mike stopped his horse.

'What is it?'

'Ssh!'

171

They sat in silence. The horses were motionless. There was scarcely a breeze.

'What did you think you heard?'

'It was like somebody choking back a cough,' Mike said.

They listened again.

'I guess it must have been your turn to hallucinate,' Sabrina said.

'Don't make jokes about it. I'm being cautious, I'm staying alert. It's part of the job.'

'Oh, sorry. I forgot myself. I should have been concentrating on learning all I can from you.'

Sabrina couldn't see Mike's face but she could imagine his expression.

'Any little thing, any implied criticism, and you go all defensive,' he said.

His horse snorted. Sabrina couldn't help imagining it was a response to what had he said. She laughed.

'Go ahead,' Mike said. 'Laugh. Mock. Mockery's the gusto of tiny spirits. You know that?'

'I bet you're glad you opened that fortune cookie.'

Mike began to say something else but Sabrina never heard it. A hand grabbed the back of her shirt and pulled her off the horse. As she hit the ground she was punched on the ear.

There was sudden light. On both sides of the road kerosene flares were lit and Sabrina saw the turbaned men who held them.

More bandits, she thought. *This country is all bandits . . .*

She saw Mike. He was rolling away from two men who tried to hold on to him. Sabrina was already into the same manoeuvre. As her shoulders were grabbed she ducked her head and somersaulted, making the hands lose their grip.

Men shouted. Sabrina rolled twice and jumped to her feet. At a sound behind her she shot out her arm and swung left, chopped a man on the upper lip and felt the bone crack.

'Eight!' Mike shouted. 'Eight of them!'

That was something she could learn from him, the ability to calculate while he was defending himself.

'Check!' she shouted back.

A man howled as Mike leapt in the air and kicked him in the belly. Another man screamed as the torch he was swinging was pushed in his own face.

'Two down!' Mike yelled.

Sabrina ran ten paces, braked and turned, arms extended and fists clenched. She hit two men. One of them dropped to his knees and she chopped him on the throat.

'Three!' she shouted.

The other man came at her, waving a knife. She ducked, heard the knife whistle past her ear, clenched one hand around the other and slammed them into his face. He dropped without a sound.

'Four!'

Mike had commandeered the fallen torch and was swinging it like a fiery claymore. The flames roared in the faces of the remaining four bandits as they tried to consolidate into a phalanx. Sabrina paused to kick a man in the chest as he tried to rise, then threw herself at the four trying to surround Mike.

'Geronimo!'

She caught one by the ear and ran sideways, pulling him off balance, making him scream and flail his arms. The other three scattered, confused. Mike grabbed one by the arm and twisted it. The shoulder cracked and the man fell, howling.

'Two left!' Sabrina shouted.

'And running!' Mike yelled.

He picked up a fallen torch and held it above his head. Two bandits were running off into the scrub land. The other six, in various stages of injury and semi-consciousness, were strewn along the road.

Mike looked at Sabrina and grinned. 'Geronimo?' he said.

'It just came out.'

Mike wiped his brow. 'We showed 'em. They've got a lot to learn about dirty fighting.'

Sabrina threw back her hair and pointed as something glinted in the flickering torchlight. 'They have transport.'

Mike picked up another torch and handed it to Sabrina. They walked across the scrub and took a look. Parked behind a clump of bushes was a battered Ford truck.

'Hallelujah,' Mike said quietly. 'I can hardly believe it.'

He got behind the wheel, located the key and turned it. The engine started and turned over with a powerful hum. He revved and the note rose to a whine.

'Hallelujah again. It's been souped.'

'It's vibrating kind of wildly,' Sabrina said.

'It's been abused,' Mike shouted. 'What can you expect from bandits? It should hold up for us, if we take it easy.'

Sabrina went back and surveyed the damage. Three men were on their feet. They backed away as she approached. The three on the ground were not moving. Sabrina pointed to the horses. 'They're yours,' she said. The three men backed off some more. 'Ride them in good fortune.'

From the road she picked up an old Webley.38, a knife and a leather pouch, then went back to the truck. As she got in beside Mike she shook the pouch in his face. It jingled.

'Currency,' she said. 'Breakfast.'

Philpott met Ram Jarwal for lunch in the sunny, fragrant garden of the Tao Café in Srinagar. The food on the menu was mainly Chinese. Both men ordered chow mein, with spring rolls for starters. Ram's manner seemed subdued; Philpott, who had never met him before, assumed that was how he was.

'Coming here was something of a snap decision for me,' Philpott said. He explained that his original intention had been to investigate the black market in charity aid. 'Then I found myself side-tracked. I had planned to talk it over with Mike, Sabrina and Lenny.'

When they talked on the telephone earlier, Ram had explained that the ambush had failed and that Mike, Lenny and Sabrina had stayed behind after the team of police marksmen had left.

'I have to bring you up to date,' Ram said now. 'I spoke on the phone to Mike less than an hour ago. He and Sabrina are making their way back in a truck they took from a gang of rural bandits . . .'

'Life's an endless adventure for those two.'

'The sad bit is, Lenny Trent's dead.'

'Oh, God . . .'

'He was shot. I don't know any more than that.'

Philpott shook his head. 'That's terrible. Terrible. He was such a fine, lively chap . . .' He drummed his fingers absently for a moment. 'What about his remains? Surely we need to make arrangements?'

'Mike told me the body's at the railway station in Jerrida,' Ram said. 'I've already made arrangements through UN Information and Services. They'll contact Drugwatch International and the body should be flown back to the States within twenty-four hours.'

'Well.' Philpott sat back and clasped his hands in his lap. 'That's taken the shine off the day.'

'The whole thing was a fiasco,' Ram said. 'The ambush failed, then Mike and Sabrina were taken prisoner by the very bandits they were hoping to ambush, and to top it all, it turns out the American bandit leader isn't what Mike thought he was.'

'Even so, Mike had good reason for following the lead,' Philpott said. 'I've no doubt about that. An agent can't pass up a possibility just because there's a chance of it leading nowhere.'

'That's like something Lenny Trent said, the night before they left. In his business, he said, failure is part of the motif of success.'

'Wise words,' Philpott said. 'Take a close look at our successes, especially our big ones, and you'll see they're bedded in flops and wrong turnings.'

'So.' Ram, anxious to lift the gloom, made himself sound brighter. 'Do you want to talk about your unexpected side-tracking?'

'Indeed I do.'

Philpott told Ram about the smallholding and how he had gone there looking for signs of black market trading; instead, he appeared to have uncovered part of a drug-trafficking organization.

'It has to be worth following up,' he said. 'It could be a factor in the trade Mike and Sabrina are trying to uncover.'

Ram cleared his throat delicately. 'We know about the farm, Mr Philpott.'

'What – the drug-trafficking side of it?'

'That's the only part we do know about. If there's a black market link, we don't have any intelligence so far to back that up.'

'So what goes on at the farm?'

'It's a place where mules are kitted out and sent on their way. We've already sent an agent through there. What he gathers in the way of intelligence could form the basis of a case against the traffickers. It might even help us find out where the trade originates. The problem with the farm is, if we show a heavy-handed interest in that quarter, they'll simply move the operation somewhere else.'

Philpott was staring at his plate. 'Well don't *I* feel the idiot. I really thought I'd stumbled on to something nobody knew about.'

'I know a little bit about the black market trade in these parts,' Ram said. 'They move their centres of operation whether they're being investigated or not. They are a different animal. Nothing gets established with them, they don't believe in laying down patterns.'

'So if there was a black market operation at the farm a month ago –'

'It's highly likely it's moved on. Black marketeers rent places on very short leases, Mr Philpott.'

'Please don't tell me any more,' Philpott said. 'If you do, I'm likely to get too depressed to finish my lunch.'

Later that afternoon Philpott called C. W. Whitlock in New York. Whitlock already knew about Lenny Trent and confirmed that the body was being returned to the United States. Philpott told him about the misunderstanding over the farm.

'I have a feeling the whole black market trade over here needs a thorough, detailed analysis before any offensive is even considered.'

176

'Don't let it get you down,' Whitlock said. 'It wasn't your only reason for going out there anyway, was it?'

'I suppose not. But I've been thinking, I could come back now and defend myself at that damned hearing.'

'No, don't do that.' Whitlock spoke a little too quickly. 'I'd rather do the defending.'

'But surely, if I'm there in person –'

'Take my word for it, sir, it would be better if you stay right where you are. The presentation of our case calls for a dispassionate approach . . .'

'And you don't think I have that?'

'I just think you should leave it to me.'

TWENTY-THREE

Eighty kilometres south of Srinagar the Ford began to cough. Mike gunned the engine, hoping to clear an obstruction in the fuel line, but that made the plugs misfire and finally the engine stopped.

'Terrific.'

He got out, opened the bonnet and stared. Sabrina came round beside him. 'What do you think?'

'I think I don't know a thing about these engines.'

He slammed down the bonnet.

'It sounded to me like it was dying,' Sabrina said.

'You're really into hi-tech talk, aren't you?'

'Seriously, I mean. I was in a cab in Beirut once when it made that noise. The driver couldn't revive it. The engine had been repaired and patched so many times, it was some kind of miracle of spare-part surgery. But that was the end of the line, there was no saving it. And it sounded just like our engine did a couple of minutes ago.'

Mike tried to start it again, but now the starter motor wouldn't turn over.

'So we walk,' he said.

Where the truck stalled the road had begun to rise. As they walked they found it rose in a gentle gradient for another five kilometres.

'It's levelling out,' Sabrina panted, trudging behind Mike, taking advantage of his shadow.

'I don't feel any difference.'

'I do.' Sabrina stopped and wiped the dust from her lips. 'And hey, look at that.'

She pointed down to their right. Since they had begun walking there had been only trees and bushes on the lower ground. Now they were looking at a road. Fifty metres ahead it veered away to the right.

'There's a signpost where it turns.' Mike shielded his eyes and narrowed them. 'I think it says Srinagar.'

They scrambled down the slope and on to the road. Sabrina took a closer look at the sign.

'Ten kilometres. We're nearly there.'

'If the truck hadn't broken down,' Mike said, 'we'd have missed this road completely.'

'That's the way to talk. Keep making us look lucky.'

Mike made to grab Sabrina. She skipped ahead of him and ran along the road. He ran after her, then they both stopped as a station wagon came round a corner sixty metres ahead and roared towards them.

Mike and Sabrina went to the side of the road. They could see the driver was an Indian, big and broad. Behind him sat an Indian woman, her lower face obscured by a veil. She was surrounded by piles of cardboard boxes.

'That guy doesn't look pleased to see us,' Mike said.

The driver was glaring at them, his mouth moving. He braked the car and it slid to a crunching stop in a cloud of dust. He got out, still looking angry, muttering to himself.

'Hi there,' Mike said, then jerked back as the driver pulled a gun.

'Down!' Sabrina yelled. Mike was flat on the ground already. She landed beside him as the man fired twice, hitting the road inches in front of them.

'What the hell's wrong with you?' Mike shouted. 'Put away the gun, you idiot!'

The man fired again. Mike pulled the Webley .38 from his belt, aiming the gun as it moved. He fired two shots. The first bullet entered the man's head, the second penetrated his chest. He spluttered and coughed, clutching his chest as blood streamed into his eyes. He dropped to his knees, then fell over on his back.

179

As Mike and Sabrina stood up, the woman in the back of the car dived into the driver's seat. She put the big wagon into a screeching turn and roared off.

Mike looked down at the dead man. 'Why do you suppose he fired at us?'

'Maybe he didn't want us to see him and live to talk about it.'

Mike went on staring. 'I've seen him before,' he said.

'Where?'

'No idea.' Mike stooped and felt in the man's pockets. They were empty. He stood up again. 'I've seen the woman before, too.'

'You could only see her eyes.'

'Sure. But they're unforgettable eyes.' Mike shrugged. 'It'll come to me.'

'If this works,' Philpott said to Ram Jarwal, 'I'll feel measurably redeemed.'

They sat in Ram's jeep, watching the little cottage at the centre of the farm. They had been there fifteen minutes and there had been no sign of activity. They were sure someone was inside, because they had been careful to arrive before dusk, and when it began to turn dark, lights went on in the cottage.

Ram looked at his watch. 'Shall we do it now?'

'I'm ready if you are.'

They got out of the vehicle and walked to the gate. There was a bell-push suspended at the end of a heavy electric cable. Ram jabbed it three times.

'Was that imperious enough?' he said.

'Perfect.'

The cottage door opened and an old man came out. Philpott recognized the stoop and the jerky movements; it was the man he had seen the night before, talking to the younger man at the table. The man came to the gate, moving carefully, shining a torch ahead of him. At the gate he stopped and shone the torch first on Philpott, then on Ram. He said something in Kashmiri, then in Urdu.

'Do you speak English?' Ram said.

'Well of course.' The linguistic switch from East to West also produced a lightening of the voice. The old man sounded like a different person. 'What can I do for you, please?'

'We are from the Central Government office in Jammu,' Ram said, keeping his voice smooth, with a firm authoritarian edge. 'May we come inside?'

The man appeared to consider it. 'Very well.'

He unpadlocked a smaller gate within one of the main gates and they stepped through.

'I am Dr Vyas, by the way.'

Ram looked quickly at Philpott. The last thing they had expected was a doctor, even a fake one.

'I am Annat Dishu,' Ram said, his delivery calm and plausible, 'and this is Mr Pilkington of our Bombay liaison office.'

When they were inside, Ram declined a chair and so did Philpott.

'You will excuse me if I sit,' Vyas said. 'My legs are no longer what they were.' He eased himself down into an old armchair, dabbing at one eye which seemed to be permanently watering. 'Now, gentlemen, how can I help you?'

'Perhaps you would care to tell us about yourself first,' Ram said. His manner was more aggressive now. 'I would advise you to leave out nothing that you consider to be important.'

'My name as I told you is Vyas, Jabar Vyas. I hold a PhD degree from the University of New Delhi. My speciality is botany.'

'And this is your farm?'

'Yes, although I do not really farm in the accepted sense. What I produce here – eggs, milk, a few vegetables – is solely for my own use. I am self-sufficient. The farm and its flora are my recreation, do you understand? Botany is my life. This is not a profitable venture, if that is what you thought. I don't believe there is any profit to be made from this land.'

'That is an interesting story,' Ram said, unsmiling, his voice a shade harder still. 'It is well told and indeed almost convincing.'

The old man frowned. 'I beg your pardon?'

181

'Is it not true, Dr Vyas – if that is your name – that this farm, these very premises, are used for the briefing of drug couriers before they set out to make their deliveries?'

'I don't understand . . .'

'I said it plainly enough, didn't I?'

'Please,' the old man said, 'there is no need to raise your voice, I am happy to co-operate with you, but your accusations are so wild, so fantastic –'

'Don't play the innocent with me!'

Now the old man looked frightened. Philpott came forward, slipping into his role. He muttered something to Ram, who instantly looked huffy and stepped aside.

'I apologize for my colleague's manner,' Philpott said, laying a hand gently on the old man's shoulder, 'and for his crass misapprehension. We will go now without troubling you further, and we will make our report strictly on the basis of what you have told us.'

They hurried outside and across to the gate. Philpott paused, watching for a sign of movement in the cottage.

'Back to the wagon fast,' he said. 'I don't fancy we'll have to wait long.'

In the jeep Ram switched on the VHF scanner mounted in the radio slot. He began slowly turning the sensor knob from side to side. After a minute the speaker clicked and there was the sound of pulsed dialling. Ram pressed the LOCK button.

'He's using a mobile, and it's calling another mobile.'

'How far away?'

'No way of telling. We can only hope it's not in another country.'

The old man's voice came on. He sounded squeaky and agitated. An answering voice kept cutting in, making the old man's voice go higher each time until he was practically screaming into the phone.

'What are they saying?'

'He said that two government snoopers have been to see him, and they're on to the operation. The other one is telling him all the time to stay calm, it will be fixed, but he says he's scared and if the government men come back and do a search the whole deal will be in the fire.'

Ram listened again. 'They're telling the old man he should have shot us. He says he didn't get a chance.'

The squabbling continued, then the sound suddenly cut off.

'The destination phone hung up,' Ram said. 'The old man kept saying he didn't want to be questioned again, they had to get him out, he was scared he would say the wrong thing. The other man said he would fix it, then he cut off communication.'

'I thought the old boy was rather convincing,' Philpott said. 'Apart from the telltale eye.'

'The running one?'

'No, its neighbour. If they'd both been watering he would have been entirely convincing, I think, but the good eye kept jerking to the corner of the shelf behind you.'

'What was on it?'

'A pistol. Looked like an old Walther P38 from where I was standing.'

'So what do we do now?' Ram said. 'Wait?'

'Oh yes. This is drug business, remember. Every aspect, every feature of the drug trade is amplified to many times beyond the normal. These men have a problem, and they will fix it, and they will do their fixing with ridiculous-seeming haste and, no doubt, the most extreme means.'

They waited eight minutes before anything happened. Then a heavy black van came pounding along the road and drove straight through the farm gates, sending them flying and uprooting a row of fence posts.

'Enter the extreme means,' Philpott said.

The van stopped in front of the cottage and two men in dark suits got out and went inside. Almost at once they came out again, carrying what looked like file boxes, and put them in the back of the van. They went inside again. When they came out next time they each carried a full sack in one hand and one gigantic sack between them. These were loaded into the van, then one of the men got into the driving seat.

'They don't waste any time,' Philpott said.

183

'That other one's taking out a gun.'

They watched the second man march into the cottage. A moment later a shot rang out. The man left the cottage and jumped into the van. It drove off in the direction it had come.

Ram and Philpott waited three minutes, then ran back to the cottage. Inside, the old man lay on the floor. He was dead. He had been shot between the eyes with a dumdum shell; part of his brain was smeared across the wall.

'I suppose I better call the police,' Ram said.

'No, hang on.' Philpott produced his own mobile and tapped in a number. He waited. 'Is that Andrew Hamilton?' He listened and smiled. 'Yes, right first time, it's Philpott. Long time no see. Look, it's all a bit of a rush, but can I ask a favour?'

Philpott gave the man on the other end the farm's map references, and asked if the full team could drop in and do a comprehensive sweep. Ram stood by, mystified.

When the call was over Philpott put the phone back in his pocket.

'Commander Andrew Hamilton,' he said. 'Ex-Yard, now a senior Interpol forensic chap. Now and then, so long as we don't abuse things, we can call on him and ask to use one of his local teams. They do a lovely job, and so quickly.'

'Where are they based?'

'New Delhi's the nearest, at present.' Philpott winked. 'Don't fret, they'll be here before the deceased starts to ripen.'

The helicopter landed one hour and twenty minutes later. A seven-man, white-suited forensic team moved through the little house from one end to the other. They covered every inch, sifting, taking photographs and collecting samples of hair, fibre, dust and debris. Before they were finished, interim search results were being computed on an analytical bench inside the helicopter. The forensic officer in charge updated Philpott on what they had found, and Philpott passed it along to Ram Jarwal.

'The tentative verdict is that vast quantities of various high-grade drugs have passed through the house, but there is no evidence of long-term storage.'

'Then the farm is nothing but a waystage?' Ram said.

'Correct. But if there is anything here to provide a link with the source of supply, then these are the men to find it.'

'And do you believe they will?'

'No, I don't,' Philpott said. 'Drug people are as devious as we are, they bury their tracks deep. But we've agitated them, and they won't have missed this classy show of intent. They know that we're trouble, and the worst kind.'

TWENTY-FOUR

The techniques-and-procedures review was called for ten o'clock in the Dag Hammarskjöld room on the third floor of the UN Secretariat building. The Secretary General was in Switzerland; a deputy, Sarah Lawrence, a quietly-dressed young specialist in international law, sat in for him. Also at the long table at the far end of the room was Thomas Lubbock, Director of Policy Control, and beside him Secretary Crane. Three lawyers sat at a smaller table on the right of the room and C. W. Whitlock sat opposite, under the tall window, the sunlight on his back.

'Every person having business with this review is now present,' a clerk announced.

Without rising, Thomas Lubbock put the case for the Department of Policy Control.

'In February this year, a search of a deceased hotel porter's apartment in Greenwich Village uncovered a photograph of Malcolm Philpott, the Director of the United Nations Anti-Crime Organization.'

The clerk passed the picture to Sarah Lawrence.

'Written on the back of the picture is Philpott's name and his title within the UN.'

Lubbock was a pink-faced man with tiny jowls that trembled when he spoke. He turned now to look at Ms Lawrence.

'To anyone concerned about security standards within the UN,' he said, 'it is troubling that such a picture should be found among the property of a humble working man. Humble is an adjective that sits well on the dead man, whose name was Arno Skuttnik. He was an immigrant with no criminal record, a man who kept to himself and roused no special curiosity in all the years he lived in New York. We have no way of knowing how

186

he came by the photograph of Mr Philpott, or what use he intended to make of it, if any. The whole point is, the man was *able to get that picture*, which underlines the point, made several times in the past by my department, that UNACO has become so loosely controlled that everyday security has broken down.'

Sarah Lawrence nodded. 'And what does the Department of Policy Control suggest?'

'Immediate corrective measures,' Lubbock said.

Ms Lawrence nodded again. 'Would you specify?'

Lubbock glanced at Whitlock, who was listening attentively. 'Since its inception, UNACO has enjoyed a measure of autocracy. The Director is answerable only to the Head of the Security Council, and to the Secretary General. UNACO's various task forces, covert surveillance units, intelligence gathering bodies and its international liaison networks are administered without reference to any other bodies within the tightly unified structure of the UN.'

'We know that much already,' Ms Lawrence said.

'It is our proposal,' Lubbock continued, 'that UNACO be brought under the UN's conventional umbrella of set procedures and accountability. The Director should be answerable in the first instance to myself and should have no direct access to the Head of the Security Council or the Secretary General. Furthermore, UNACO's activities should be open to scrutiny by my own officers and representatives of departments directly involved in funding, strategy and personnel deployment.'

Sarah Lawrence glanced at her notepad. 'So let's get it in a nutshell, Mr Lubbock. You propose that in view of certain evidence of laxity in the running of UNACO, the organization be pulled into line and forfeit its special status as a semi-autonomous body. Does that cover it?'

'That's more or less it,' Lubbock said.

Ms Lawrence looked at the lawyers. They nodded.

'Well now, Mr Whitlock.' Sarah Lawrence smiled coolly. 'I understand you're appearing here on behalf of Mr Philpott, who is detained in foreign parts.'

'That's correct, ma'am.'

187

'Your purpose here, as I see it, is to try to dissuade the Secretary General's Office of the United Nations from actioning the restrictive measures proposed by the Director and Secretary of Policy Control against the organization for which you work, namely UNACO. Is that how you view it?'

'Indeed it is.' Whitlock stood up.

Ms Lawrence pointed to the lectern standing three metres from the table where she and the others sat. 'If you'd like to come forward, I'm all ears.'

Whitlock brought his notes and stood for a moment with his hands on either side of the lectern, looking at each of the people before him in turn.

'First of all, I want to say that the administration of UNACO does not deny that the photograph of Director Philpott was found in the property of a deceased hotel porter. It is not denied, either, that the finding of the picture could be seen to indicate slackness in UNACO's security arrangements.'

Secretary Crane looked down with a tight smile. Whitlock did not miss that.

'UNACO does, however, refute any allegations of laxness or irresponsibility on the part of its administration or its operatives.'

Now it was Lubbock who looked down, shaking his head.

'We are aware,' Whitlock went on, 'that a simple denial is hardly a defence. It will be my purpose, therefore, as briefly as possible, to show that not only is UNACO the world's premier crime-fighting body, but that its integrity and efficiency far surpass those of lesser outfits who cover their own shortcomings by pointing the finger – in this case, a sadly mistaken finger – at others.'

Lubbock looked as if he had been personally attacked. Crane had turned red.

'Mr Lubbock has told us something about the dead man who was harbouring the picture of Director Philpott. In fact, Mr Lubbock has told us *everything* that he and his department could find out about the dead man, which isn't much. The deceased's name was Arno Skuttnik, he came to this country in the sixties, he led a quiet, law-abiding life. That's it.'

188

'If I might point out, Ms Lawrence,' Lubbock cut in, 'there is nothing else on the record that is of any significance.' He shot a glance at Whitlock. 'It isn't our habit, as it may be with certain others, to pad out our case with inconsequential detail.'

Ms Lawrence waited to see if Lubbock had more to say, but he had withdrawn into tight-lipped staring. She nodded for Whitlock to continue.

'When Secretary Crane brought the picture and the scanty story surrounding it to the attention of Director Philpott,' Whitlock said, 'it was decided that a thorough investigation should be mounted.'

He could see this was news to Lubbock and Crane. They glanced at each other and looked quickly back at their folded hands.

'In spite of what Mr Lubbock just said, there is a lot of fascinating and significant detail in the history of Arno Skuttnik. With your indulgence, I would like to tell his story.'

Lubbock sighed noisily. 'Ms Lawrence, is this really necessary?'

'Mr Whitlock is essaying a rebuttal of what you told us,' Ms Lawrence said. 'On the face of it, I'd say it's important.' She nodded at C. W. 'Please go on.'

Whitlock looked at his notes for a moment, then he said, 'Arno Skuttnik was a spy.'

Ms Lawrence looked at Lubbock, who looked at Crane, who was gaping at Whitlock.

'He was brought up and educated in Moscow, where his father, a Pole, was an inspector of factories. At the age of nineteen Arno was already a Kremlin discipline officer, which means he beat up political dissidents for a living, and by the time he was twenty-two he was a member of Stalin's private staff.'

'Can you prove any of this?' Crane snapped.

'Sure,' Whitlock said.

Lubbock said, 'How did you come by this information?'

'I used means that go beyond your need-to-know status. But I can easily demonstrate the authenticity of the data to the Secretary General and his staff.'

Lubbock's neck was turning purple.

'And so,' Whitlock said, 'we are already in a position where it's clear that no ordinary – or to use Mr Lubbock's description, *humble* – individual, was in possession of Director Philpott's picture. The man in question was a highly-trained Soviet agent, a ranking member of the People's Commissariat for Internal Affairs, who eventually came to America to spy for the Soviets in 1966.'

'I don't believe any of this!' Crane said. 'It's a ridiculous smokescreen!'

Whitlock picked up a folder with a clipped wad of papers inside. 'Maybe we can dispose of further doubts on the point, Ms Lawrence. These are printout versions of all this information, together with details of sources. Perhaps you'd like to peruse it as I go along.'

'Thank you, Mr Whitlock.' The clerk handed the papers across. Ms Lawrence looked along the table. 'Try to keep your contributions positive, Mr Crane. Petulant outbursts use up time and they're entirely counter-productive.' She nodded for Whitlock to continue.

'Skuttnik's in-place handler in New York was Adam Korwin, whose standing as a Soviet spymaster is well known among members of our own intelligence community. What is less well known is something I only recently learned: in the mid-seventies Korwin suffered a stroke. At that time Arno Skuttnik was a sleeper, working a six-day week on a garbage disposal truck in Brooklyn.

'After the stroke Korwin believed he could still control agents and deploy espionage talent, but apparently Russia had by then accepted the obvious. Korwin was a nice old man, good at keeping out of trouble, but as far as spying went, he had lost it. Skuttnik and a few others remained sleepers without guidance, much less motivation. What's more, Skuttnik began to enjoy the American way of life, although at the same time he longed, in a passive kind of way, to be of some service to the USSR. Korwin kept in touch with him but no assignments were floated.

'I will summarize the other significant details of Skuttnik's life as tightly as I can. In 1970 he married a woman who knew

190

nothing of his double life. They had a daughter the following year. The wife died tragically young in 1972; the daughter was brought up by Skuttnik with the active assistance of Korwin, to whom the child became very attached. She was raised on good wholesome food and an ideological diet of Marx and Engels. She grew up a dedicated communist.

'In time she married a schoolteacher, another communist, who three years into the marriage was fired from his post for spreading communist propaganda among school children. He was hounded by the press and by his neighbours and eventually lost his reason and killed himself. This made his wife regard him as a martyr for the cause, and it toughened her own resolve to fight for the survival of a dying regime.'

Whitlock went on to explain that Skuttnik's daughter had been identified from a recent photograph taken with her father on the occasion of his birthday. Her face was only partially visible on the picture, but careful blowing up of the image made it possible to identify a jacket she wore; the retailer was also the manufacturer, and he had kept a copy of the bill of sale. The design of one of the rings she wore was also used to identify her. It was her engagement ring, which was tracked down to the Armenian jeweller who had made it. Whitlock made no mention of the clinching handwriting on the photograph, since he'd had no official access to the print.

'I really must interrupt,' Lubbock said testily. 'Does this tale of domestic tragedy and tenacious political conviction lead us anywhere?'

'Oh, indeed it does,' Whitlock said. 'And I may say it only exists as a story because unlike Policy Control, who took the word of the police that Arno Skuttnik was of no consequence, we at UNACO took the entire matter seriously. Instead of firing off accusatory remarks or instigating back-stabbing campaigns, we investigated. In depth.'

Whitlock paused. As if she were taking a cue, Sarah Lawrence said, 'And what did you find, in the end?'

'We found that a dossier of photographs and basic job descriptions had been assembled from the entire New York base of the

United Nations. It was carefully guarded by Arno Skuttnik, even though by now there was no Soviet Union to make use of such an archive.'

'Hang on!' Crane shouted. 'Are you saying there was more than one photograph? If that's what you're saying, I hope you can produce the others, and I hope you can prove they were in the possession of Arno Skuttnik.'

'There was indeed more than one photograph,' Whitlock said. 'The single picture found by the police had somehow escaped from the main batch of several hundred. I can produce them.' Whitlock held up a concertina file. 'Here they are. They're all in here. And yes, they were in Skuttnik's possession. I have the corroboration of three senior NYPD officers, who stood by while I dug up the floor in his room and retrieved them.'

'How did you know they were there?' Ms Lawrence said.

'The person who put together the archive told me. The same person told me all about Arno Skuttnik's fallow years as a spy, and his gradual absorption into the American way of life. I'm talking about Arno Skuttnik's daughter, Bridget. Married name Bridget Jones.'

Crane sat back sharply in his chair. Lubbock gave him a puzzled look.

'Bridget Jones is a clerical officer here at the UN,' Whitlock said. 'She works in personnel records, which as you're aware, Ms Lawrence, is just *packed* with photographs of UN employees, including all the members of Policy Control, whose pictures are in the illicit archive along with everybody else's.'

Ms Lawrence was already mumbling into her mobile phone. She put it down after a moment and looked pointedly at Lubbock. 'Bridget Jones didn't show up for work yesterday or today,' she said coldly. 'There's no response from her home number, apparently.'

Whitlock squared his notes. 'I don't think I have anything to add, except to point out that Mrs Jones's appointment to the UN was endorsed by, among others, Mr Crane of Policy Control.'

Whitlock turned away from the lectern, then stopped. He faced the long table again.

'In defence of UNACO's present administrative and operational arrangements,' he said, 'I would add only this. Our freedom from restriction produces a special quality of planning and of procedure, unhampered by the dulling effects of communal policy-making. The record speaks for the success of the regime. Our system nurtures and develops the flowering of individuality – true individuality, capable of seeing the wood in spite of the trees.'

TWENTY-FIVE

Amrit Datta was less than ten kilometres from the Chinese border when a motorcycle policeman stopped him. The bike had freewheeled from the top of a sloping hillside road and was beside Amrit before he realized anything was happening.

'Papers.' The policeman got off the bike.

Amrit nodded several times, too quickly, playing the anxious peasant, examining the man's uniform as he dug in his pocket for his ID documents. As with a number of border police units, there was a strong American influence here: the officer wore a short-sleeved pale green shirt, darker green riding breeches with knee-high shiny boots, a white helmet with a green stripe, and very dark Ray-Bans.

'You are Opu Hikmet, is that correct?' The officer flipped through the papers, frowning as if they offended him.

'Opu Hikmet, sir. That is correct, sir.'

'Where are you travelling to?'

Amrit took back the papers. 'I am looking for work, sir. I am not going anywhere special. As soon as I find work I stop until the work is done, then I move on again.'

The officer pointed at the sack on Amrit's shoulder. 'What's in there?'

'My few belongings, sir.'

'Show me.'

Amrit didn't move. 'I would rather not.'

The officer took off the Ray-Bans. He had red-rimmed eyes. They were wide and staring. 'What did you say?'

'My things are private, sir. I would rather not show them to you.'

The officer kicked Amrit on the shin. The sound of it was like something being snapped. Amrit dropped to one knee, rubbing his shin.

'Open the bag.'

Amrit stood up slowly. 'I do not think you have the right to treat me in such a way, officer.'

'It is not your place to *think*, guttersnipe!'

The officer kicked him again, on the other leg. This time it was harder and he broke the skin. Blood seeped through the leg of Amrit's baggy trousers. He set his teeth against the pain and unslung the bag from his shoulder. He handed it to the policeman.

'Perhaps you have learned that in future, when an officer of the law tells you to do something, you do it at once.'

The policeman opened the sack and looked inside. The plastic bags were unmistakable. His mouth dropped open. He looked up and found himself staring into the barrel of Amrit's gun.

'Put down the bag, officer.' Amrit's voice was firm now, controlled. The policeman dropped the sack beside the motorbike. 'Now take off your clothes.'

'You can't do this.'

'I wouldn't normally do it,' Amrit said. 'In the case of a rattlesnake like you, however, I'm prepared to be creative.'

'You'll be caught before you get to the next town.'

'No, I won't.'

The officer brought up his knee sharply. Amrit moved aside and tapped the end of the gun barrel on the officer's lip, splitting it. He yelped and staggered back. Blood poured down his chin.

'Don't get blood on the shirt,' Amrit warned as the officer staunched the flow with his handkerchief. 'Get a move on.'

In five minutes Amrit was dressed in the policeman's clothes. He took time in the procedure to use the bike's first-aid kit to patch his leg and put an adhesive dressing on the policeman's mouth. He put his own clothes in the sack on top of the drugs and put the sack in one of the motorbike's panniers.

'In other circumstances I would have done an exchange of clothes with you,' Amrit said, getting on the bike and positioning the Ray-Bans on the bridge of his nose. 'But I'll need my shabby

195

wardrobe later. Besides . . .' He stared at the officer in his striped jockey shorts. 'You could use a lesson in humility.'

Amrit kick-started the machine and drove away.

'I suppose you could say the Security Council is redoubling its efforts,' Philpott told Dr Arberry. 'We never do anything precipitate. Flying off the handle can be spectacular, but it's seldom ever right. So forgive us if we appear to move slowly, but we like to have all the facts marshalled and verified before we embark on serious action.'

They were in the drawing room at Arberry's mansion with glasses of sherry in their hands, gazing out at the sunset across the gardens. Philpott had arrived unannounced and introduced himself as yet another Security Council fact-finder. A senior one. He was in the region, he said, to evaluate the findings of Mr Graham and Mr Trent, and thought he would call on the doctor, having heard so much about him.

'I stand here many an evening,' Arberry said, 'and I look out over a scene that doesn't, I'm sure, fall very short of perfection. And along with the joy that is generated by such beauty, I get the deepest pain.' He looked at Philpott. 'All this is being eroded and pulled apart by nothing more than people's envy.'

'Envy?'

'Envy and the need that some of them feel to dominate their environment.'

'Envy of what, though?'

'Of me. I'm convinced that's the root of most of the trouble in this area. Or most of the trouble that's been visited on me and those who work for me. There are people who envy and lust after what I possess. Their perspective doesn't let them see that I'm driven by my enthusiasms, they don't see that what I have, I have made. I didn't walk in here and take anything for nothing. I built it all. For everything this divine place gives me, I strive to give back ten times, twenty times.'

'Yet people see you as a menace – would you say that's accurate? You are perceived as a threat to something?'

'Yes, I am,' Arberry said. 'I'm an undesirable, because what I

196

do, what I achieve, stands in the way of some people's ambitions.'

'You mean you're the equivalent of civilization, yes? And what they need, the others, is the opposite, they need chaos in order to control events and to thrive.'

'That is exactly right, Mr Philpott.'

Philpott had compared notes with Mike and had simply handed Arberry back his own point of view, dressed as a fact-finder's assessment.

'So I take your point about envy,' Philpott said. 'But it's incurable, wouldn't you say? Envy is ingrained in humanity. There's a French proverb that says, "People only throw stones at the tree loaded with fruit."'

Philpott glanced at the clock and decided he should move the talk in the planned direction. He was there on a genuine fact-finding mission: he believed Dr Arberry had probably received personal threats. Two of his people had been killed in an effort to discourage him, so it wasn't hard to imagine that the man himself had been the focus of some aggression. Philpott believed that careful questioning could turn up a useful line of enquiry.

'Can I ask you, Doctor, if you've been attacked yourself, or have been threatened with violence?'

Arberry frowned. Philpott waited. After a few seconds it seemed the doctor wasn't planning to say anything.

'Did I speak out of turn?' Philpott said.

'No.' Arberry hesitated. 'I don't like having to be secretive, but I was warned that if I said anything to anyone . . .'

'Surely they can't know what you say in the privacy of your home?'

'They have breached these secure grounds, Mr Philpott. In spite of elaborate security they have been able to walk in and kill my people. Who knows what they are capable of doing or finding out?' Arberry shrugged. 'I'm probably infected with a touch of the superstition of the region. Or I'm just too conscious that people's lives can hang on what I do or don't do.'

'So you have been attacked?'

'I have been threatened.' Arberry emptied his glass and looked at Philpott's. 'Another?'

'No, thank you.'

'Then forgive me if I have one.'

Arberry filled his glass at the drinks cabinet and came back to stand by the window. It was almost completely dark now, with only a dim trace of light along the horizon.

'I was told that if I extend my territorial rapacity – those were the words used on the telephone, territorial rapacity – I would lose the eyes with which I take such pleasure in my works. If I remained after that, I would lose, in addition, the legs with which I walk upon my stolen territory.'

'And have you any idea at all who made these threats?'

'A hill bandit,' Arberry said. 'Which one I've no idea, but they're the only ones who oppose what I do here. It doesn't really matter which one made the calls, anyway. They have an alliance. Whatever one of them does, they all do. What one hates, they all hate.'

'Do you feel different for having told me this?'

'I'm not sure. It's always good to unburden oneself, but I can't say I'm any less anxious than before.'

Philpott was studying the array of recording and communications equipment along one side of the room. 'I suppose you record all your telephone calls?' he said.

'Ordinarily I do. But on both occasions I received telephone threats, the wavelength used to transmit the calls was obscured by noise. When I played back the recordings I got only static.'

'Perhaps there's something there, though,' Philpott said. 'We have resources nowadays that can pick out slender threads of voice signal from whole skeins of noise.'

'Oh, I destroyed the tapes in frustration.' Arberry looked at Philpott rather sheepishly. 'Which I suppose I shouldn't have done.'

'Well . . .' Philpott shrugged. 'No use wasting energy on regrets.'

'So what is the position now, Mr Philpott? Does the UN hope to mount an offensive against the crime wave in our valley? I had the impression from Mr Graham and Mr Trent that a fight-back of serious proportions was being planned.'

'That is still the intention.'

'Good. The sooner the better.' Arberry made a wan smile. 'Apart from any other consideration, I want to go on enjoying the sight of the sunset, and being able to walk in my gardens when I feel like it.'

Mike and Sabrina returned to the cabin an hour after Philpott had gone to see Arberry. Ram greeted them like long-lost family. He told them to sit down and do nothing. Drinks first, he insisted, then he would prepare them a meal.

'It was bad, what happened to Lenny,' Ram said as he dropped the lemon into Sabrina's gin and tonic. He brought the glasses to the couch where they were flopped out side by side. 'Dare I ask if you got the ones who did it? When we spoke on the phone, the details were rather sketchy.'

Sabrina looked at Mike. 'I think you understand what happened better than I do.'

'It was one of Seaton's men that shot Lenny,' Mike said. 'But no, we didn't retaliate. And for a while it looked like we would never be in a position to do that.'

Mike recounted his meeting with Seaton, and the turnaround in events when Mike accused him of being involved in the new trade.

'He let us go,' Mike said, 'because he had to underline that he's not like the new people. Not anywhere near as savage or murderous as they are. He overstated the difference, of course. He's just another kind of savage, the traditional kind. But he didn't want me or Sabrina thinking of him in the same terms as the new guys.'

'And that was all?' Ram said. 'He let you go because he didn't want you to think too badly of him?'

'There was something else,' Mike said. 'Or I should say, I *sensed* something else. But I don't know what it was.'

'That whole episode was doomed,' Sabrina told Ram. 'Apart from Lenny's death, I mean. The ambush flopped, I got

199

septicaemia and even had hallucinations, and after one bad deal and another we came out with what we stood up in. I even managed to lose a police Range-Rover.'

'I know about that.' Ram did an eye-roll. 'Mr Philpott will have something to say, I believe. On top of the cost of the ambush operation, he's had to sanction a payment for replacement of the vehicle.'

'We have to put it all behind us,' Mike said. 'The answer or answers to our problems are here, right here in the Vale of Kashmir. We have to knuckle down, decipher the answers and take appropriate action.'

'You make it sound like a straight matter of spit and elbow grease,' Sabrina said. 'We don't even know where to start.'

'We will, don't worry.' Mike tasted his Jim Beam and smacked his lips. 'Ram, tell us, what's the boss doing here?'

'I think he made an error of judgement, too. But he's working hard to make up for it.'

'Has there been word from Amrit?'

'Nothing. But you wouldn't expect anything, would you? He must be due at the Chinese border any time now.'

'If he's made it.'

The fax machine in the corner rang twice, then began to gurgle. A second later the red URGENT light came on and paper rolled from the front of the machine.

Mike got up and looked at the cover sheet. He read it aloud as it fed out on to the tray.

'"Urgent facsimile message from H. Lewis, World Health Organization, for the attention of M. Philpott."'

'What's it say?' Sabrina said.

'You want me to read the boss's confidential fax?'

Sabrina tilted her head. 'Is there any way I could stop you?'

Mike was already reading, his eye racing across the type as fast as it came out of the machine. 'Oh, my,' he said, and looked up at Sabrina and Ram.

'What?' Sabrina demanded. 'What does it say?'

Mike stared at the fax again. 'My,' he said. 'My oh my . . .'

TWENTY-SIX

Amrit Datta stood by a cracked stucco pillar behind a grain store that occupied half the length of the street. It was a pillar marked with a dab of brown paint near its foot. This was where he had been told to stand. Or he believed it was. The store was in the dirtiest part of the border town of Boyding. It was an area where only beggars, burned-out opium zombies and superannuated street prostitutes gathered at this hour of night.

Amrit had taken a while to convince himself this was the spot. The daub of paint was so casual, so accidental-looking, and it was faded, too; it was difficult to believe anyone would designate a mark like that as an identifying characteristic.

But there were other markers, also part of the specified rendezvous point. Opposite the rear of the grain store was a coal brazier that the derelicts gathered round to warm their hands; it was exactly where he had been told it would be. And there was the boarded-up coffee stall, the Chinese laundry – also boarded up – the half-hearted painting of Siva on a wall by a little candle shop. This was the place, all right. Amrit just couldn't believe he was expected to transfer ownership of 200,000 dollars'-worth of highly refined drugs in such a dump.

After a time he was aware a man was watching him. He was dressed as shabbily as Amrit, which meant nothing, since Amrit was certainly not what he appeared to be. He waited, and after a few minutes the man came across.

'You want to buy kif?' he whispered.

Amrit stared at him. That was not the magic phrase. He thought he should give the man another chance; maybe he was nervous, or just forgetful.

'What did you say?'

'Kif,' the man said, producing a waxy brown wad. 'Very cheap, very best stuff. All the way from Egypt.'

'Go away,' Amrit said.

The man looked offended. 'You can't afford it, right?'

'I said go away. Do it now. Go.'

The man waggled his head. 'Go away. Do it now,' he mimicked. 'What are you, beggar boy, some kind of big-shot in disguise?'

Amrit saw that this could get awkward. It could even ruin the set-up. He looked around. No one was paying any attention to them. It had started to rain and people were huddling in doorways and bunching around the coal brazier.

'Listen . . .' Amrit drew his gun from the folds of his shirt. 'I'm not a big-shot in disguise. I'm a man who's come out to kill someone, I don't care who. Do you want to be the one? I don't mind, I promise.'

He cocked the gun. The man stared at it, his mouth working soundlessly.

'Disappear, or stay here and check out the afterlife.'

The man turned and ran.

Amrit used his foot to edge his sack into the cover of the overhang and stepped back a pace to keep the worst of the rain off himself. He looked at the Pepsi-Cola clock on the side of the old coffee stall. It was still working, he could see the sweep hand moving. It said ten to midnight. He was supposed to wait between 11:30 and midnight. What happened if nobody showed? What did he do then?

'Wares from the vale of beauty?' a sing-song voice said.

Amrit spun, saw nobody for a moment, then realized the man was on the other side of the pillar. He was Chinese in appearance, half turned away from Amrit. He looked, in fact, as if he didn't even know Amrit was there. But he had used the right phrase.

'Precisely the wares you desire,' Amrit said, supplying the other half of the transaction code.

The man turned, came round the pillar and held out an open

linen bag. Amrit pulled the first consignment from his sack and dropped it in the bag.

Nothing is happening, he thought, glancing quickly around. There was nothing. Nobody. Another second and this man would be gone. So would the batch of drugs.

The man tucked the bag under his flowing coat and moved away. Amrit felt his heart sink. He watched the man reach the end of the street and turn the corner. He was gone. Amrit stared at the empty street, shiny with rain.

Things had gone badly wrong. He realized that in this situation, he had no idea what he should do. It wasn't his show, after all. He was the bait, not the angler . . .

His heart thumped as a police officer appeared at the corner for one fleeting moment, holding up his thumb. He winked at Amrit and vanished again. Amrit swallowed back a grin.

It's working! God, it's working!

He realized that in his anxiety and distraction he had wandered out into the full downpour, and now he was soaked. He didn't care. His heart thrummed in him now. *It was working!* He was a crucial part of a big-time operation and it was ticking over like clockwork.

Suddenly, in that instant, standing there with rain pouring down over him, he knew that he never wanted to do any other job. The work had its rotten times, its rotten hours and days, but when the brilliant, winning moments came, they wiped the slate clean and he knew there was nothing else in the world he would ever want to do.

'Wares from the vale of beauty?' a voice said from the other side of the pillar.

Amrit turned, getting his sack ready. 'Precisely the wares you desire,' he replied, and allowed himself one swift, secret, gleeful grin.

When Philpott returned to his car, which was parked a few metres outside the gates of Arberry's mansion, he found a reception party waiting. Mike and Ram were in the back; Sabrina was in the front passenger seat.

'Well, well . . .' Philpott nodded to them each in turn as he climbed in. He was pliant on sherry and a couple of stiff brandies. He smiled with less restraint than usual. 'What were you trying to do? Frighten me to death, perhaps? Where's your transport?'

Sabrina pointed to the jeep on the other side of the avenue.

'Oh.' Philpott shut the door. 'I thought you might have come by Range-Rover.'

'We came because your buddy Harry Lewis sent you a fax,' Mike said. 'We couldn't be sure where you'd go after seeing Dr Arberry, and since you're not carrying a mobile . . .'

'Sorry,' Philpott mumbled. 'A change of climate and scene and my memory deserts me.'

'Well, since the message was something you should know about straight away, we decided to come and wait for you.'

'And what is the message?'

'Harry Lewis carried out a curiosity check on who's been funding the Arberry Foundation,' Mike said. 'And guess what?'

'What?'

'Nobody has.'

Philpott took a deep careful breath. 'What do you mean?'

'No corporation anywhere in the civilized world has donated money to Dr Arberry, or claimed relief on donations to any such foundation.'

'But surely –'

'Lewis has been thorough,' Mike said. 'He's checked with international banks, charitable trusts, finance foundations and the IRS.'

'The bottom line is this,' Sabrina said. 'Dr Arberry runs an ambitious, expensive, multi-faceted medical foundation, but nobody finances it.'

'One other thing,' Mike said. 'The for-your-eyes-only message from Mr Lewis, which we naturally took the liberty of reading in full, points out that Simon Arberry is a doctor all right, but he's a doctor of pharmacology. He's a drug designer.'

Philpott peered at Mike in the gloom. 'What turn are your thoughts taking?'

'I've had time to reflect, sitting here waiting for you,' Mike

204

said. 'Now I'm thinking Arberry could be the source and sub-stance of the whole refined drug trade.'

Philpott groaned softly.

'I'm thinking,' Mike continued, 'that he could easily fund his conspicuous good works out of the small change from a trade in top-line drugs. It would be a brilliant cover and terrific PR rolled into one.'

'His only worry,' Philpott said, caught up in the unfurling logic, 'is that other villains, the traditional traffickers of the terri-tory, are getting close to uncovering his game. So he handles that by bumping off an employee or two and appealing – or getting a friend to do the appealing – to the UN to fight off those terrible bandits.'

'Beautifully devious,' Sabrina said. She looked at Mike. 'How do you prove it?'

'The same way I prove anything. First of all I convince myself. That gives me the thrust to get proof that'll stand up to scrutiny.'

'And have you convinced yourself Dr Arberry is our baddie?'

'You could say so. The driver I shot –'

'The one we left for the vultures,' Sabrina said.

'Yeah, him. Remember I said I'd seen him some place before?'

'Sure.'

'Well it came back to me. He answered the door and served at table the night Ram and Lenny and I had dinner at Arberry's house. The butler. And the woman with the memorable eyes who drove the car away?'

'Surrounded by all those boxes,' Sabrina said, 'just like the kind that high-grade amphetamines are supplied in . . .'

'Right. Well she served at table, too. She's Arberry's maid.'

'All this speculation,' Philpott sighed.

'No, sir,' Mike said. 'Something harder than that.'

'Where are the drugs manufactured, then?' Ram said.

'Arberry has acres of farm and forest land,' Sabrina said. 'Growing the necessary crops wouldn't be a problem. Could he maybe be making the stuff in his clinics and labs and teaching units?'

'Nah.' Mike shook his head. 'I can always spot a man who

enjoys a risk. When the doc showed Lenny and Ram and me the gilded cavern, he was really showing off, and maybe at the same time he was showing his skin to the wind – you know, taking a delicious risk. I'd bet anything that cave's the spot. There, or somewhere damn near there.'

'What do we do?' Sabrina said. 'Go take a look?'

'Right now,' Mike said.

Sabrina started to open the door, then turned back to Philpott. 'Sir, why did you say you thought we might have come by Range-Rover?'

'I presumed you'd got it back.'

'Sorry?'

'The police vehicle you managed to lose. I saw it a few minutes ago, on my way back to the car.'

'Where?'

'Parked at the gates there, by the trees.'

'Must be another one,' Mike said.

'What, with police code plate A1? I'm hardly likely to forget that, am I? Especially since I had to write it out on the triplicated cash transfer forms I signed to pay for the ruddy thing.' Philpott sniffed. 'Good job I haven't processed the forms yet.'

'But sir,' Sabrina said, 'we didn't find the Range-Rover again.'

'Eh?'

'We didn't –'

'Hell's teeth!' Mike threw open the door. 'Sabrina! Come on!'

TWENTY-SEVEN

The Golden Cavern smelled like a slaughterhouse.

The last time Mike had seen it there had been lights shining from every angle, making the pyrite rocks sparkle so brightly that they hurt his eyes. Now a solitary floodlamp threw dark shadows into the craggy lower reaches and highlighted the spreadeagled, mutilated bodies scattered across the rocks.

'God almighty . . .'

It took seconds to register. Mike stood with Sabrina at his shoulder, automatically counting the dead: seven, maybe eight. All of them men, all wearing white coats splashed and smeared with their blood. It had only just happened: the fresh warm smell was unmistakable.

'Look,' Sabrina breathed.

In a deep, hollowed-out corner of the cave Dr Arberry crouched, hugging himself, staring at a point behind a huge glittering rock. As Mike and Sabrina watched, Paul Seaton stepped into the light. He brandished a long curved sword, its blade clotted with blood and tissue. He turned and nodded slowly to Mike.

'My timing's a tad out.' Seaton pointed the sword at Dr Arberry, who went on staring at him as if he was frozen that way. 'I had to wait for the doctor's visitor to leave. Then I brought him along to witness the cancelling of his empire. I was going to add him to the pile. You, or whoever, were supposed to find nothing here but dead people and a wrecked factory.'

'Who are those men?' Mike said.

'The chemists. Some of the cleverest, the brightest and the most cunning. Drawn from around the world, lured by money and attractive working conditions.' Seaton grinned. 'It would break some people's hearts to see all this talent spilt and spattered, lying around like so much chopped liver. But it's neat. The axe was laid to the root and Arberry's operation is finished. It took about five minutes, if you're interested.' Seaton tilted his head, smiling at Sabrina, raising the sword in a little greeting. 'Hi,' he said. 'How do you feel now? That leg healing up nicely?'

'I'm fine,' Sabrina said. 'How . . . What put you on to Arberry?'

'You did.'

'Me?'

'Your papers. They were in the buggy you left us, in a bag in the back.' Seaton watched her frown as she tried to remember. 'It was a confused and delirious time for you, wasn't it? I guess you didn't know what you were doing with half your stuff. But I was glad you kept ol' Hafi's correspondence.' The smile dropped away. 'Tell me something, was it you that killed him?'

Sabrina nodded.

'You did the world a service.'

'My reasons were more selfish than that.'

'He had ambitions to kill me, you know,' Seaton said. 'He reckoned I had no right to be here, me being from the USA and all. That's stupid, of course. A man belongs wherever he can hang on.'

'How did the papers help you settle on Arberry?' Mike said.

'The mention of the Grotto of Moksha being the centre of the new trade in drugs.' Seaton waved the sword in an arc above his head. 'This is it. This is the Grotto of Moksha. Ten days ago we picked up a big Indian frightener called Iqbal. He was chasing a runaway. On principle we hate people like that – he made a living out of terrorizing and probably killing his own kind. Anyway, there was something about Iqbal told me we should hang on to him. We did, and after I'd read Hafi's letters I asked him if he knew anything about the Grotto of Moksha, and he told me. He told me *everything*.'

'Why did he do that?' Mike said.

'Because he thought I was going to kill him. I did kill him, afterwards. He was a big eater, expensive to run. But before the end he told me all about the work he did, and about his boss, who was none other than Simon Arberry, the saviour of Kashmir.'

Seaton turned and looked at Arberry, who still cringed in the hollow, staring up at him.

'He doesn't look anything special now, does he? To hear old Iqbal talk, you'd have thought this was a god. He certainly tried to live like one. The Grotto was the first piece of real estate he bought, and later he built his house and his grounds around it.'

'Why did he want the Grotto?' Sabrina said.

'It came with a built-in trick compartment. Behold . . .'

Seaton leaned on the big rock beside him. Grunting, he levered its side with his knee and it moved suddenly, jerking over by degrees until it was horizontal. A moment later the wall of glimmering rock behind Seaton folded inward, dividing in two. Behind it was a high rectangular space, a windowless room, fitted with benches, cabinets and laboratory equipment. All the equipment appeared to have been smashed.

'I made the chemists wreck it before I wrecked them,' Seaton said. He smiled. 'I have to tell you something. One of the reasons I let you two go was because I realized you were on the trail of this parasite. You told me that catching these people was part of your brief. So I was going to have you watched and followed. The way it turned out, I didn't have to take that trouble.' He jerked his head at Arberry. 'Will you stay for the final touch?'

'I can't let you kill him,' Mike said.

Seaton seemed to consider that. 'Let? *Let?* I think there's a semantic problem here. You're in no position to let me or not let me do anything.'

'He's got to be taken into custody. The law will deal with him.'

'You talk like a machine, you know that? No feeling, just a tin heart pumping out procedure.'

'I'd say you're the inhuman one,' Mike said.

'Semantics again, brother. Let's cut the crap. Arberry's history. You can stay and witness his transfer or you can go. Please yourselves.'

Mike nudged Sabrina. She threw herself forward and ran

across the uneven floor of the cave, dislodging a couple of bodies as she clambered down to where Arberry lay. She grabbed him by the arm and pulled him up.

'Come on!' she yelled. 'Run!'

Seaton was off balance, as Mike guessed he would be. All the time he was talking he had moved nearer the narrow end of the ledge he stood on. Now he hadn't the manoeuvring space to turn quickly and get between Sabrina and the stairs. She ran past Mike, dragging the dazed Arberry behind her.

'Get him outside,' Mike yelled. He turned to face Seaton.

At the foot of the stairs Sabrina stopped, turned to Arberry and smacked him hard on the face. He jumped back, astonished. She grabbed him again.

'Now run!' she shouted. 'Run or you'll die!'

It got through. Arberry looked over his shoulder, his eyes wide and terrified. He saw Seaton move towards him and he began running, clinging tight to Sabrina's hand as he took the stairs two and three at a time.

'I'm not letting you past,' Mike told Seaton. He moved until they were facing each other over a five-metre gap.

'Get out of my way!' Seaton was panting with the effort of jumping off the ledge and scrambling across the rocky floor. He waved the bloody sword in front of him. 'One side, or I'll slice you with this.'

He looked past Mike at the stairs. Arberry and Sabrina were a third of the way to the top.

'You should never have tangled with me,' Seaton grunted.

His free hand flashed to his belt and as it came away again something glinted in the air ahead of him. A split second later Mike felt a searing pain in his arm and cried out. A knife was buried for half its length in his shoulder.

The pain was like electricity, raging and disruptive. He couldn't steady his shuddering. He couldn't get his fingers round the knife handle.

He heard his own howl of pain and remembered the selfsame noise coming out of Lou Kelly's throat as they put him on a stretcher in the parking lot behind the ball ground.

He saw Seaton start to run. He was going for the stairs and to do that he had to pass Mike. Mike shut his eyes tight, still hearing that echoing cry, himself and Kelly, both of them victims . . .

'*Aah!*'

Mike roared with agony as he gripped the knife and dragged it out of his shoulder. He brought it up and round, tightening his hold on it, seeing his own blood fly in the air before him. Seaton's bulk loomed, his feet pounded the rock as he rushed for the stairs.

Mike kept the knife swinging, bringing it down and round, throwing the weight of his body behind it. The blade pointed outward again and met the impact of Seaton's belly.

He roared and fell sideways, his head striking the rock. Mike stood swaying, watching, the pain like fire in his shoulder. He watched Seaton try to pull the knife out of his stomach, scrabbling at the handle, unable to grip it for the rush of slippery blood.

As Mike watched, the movements became weaker and finally Seaton's fingers dropped away from the knife. He looked up at Mike as if he might say something, but by the time his mouth opened he was already dead.

TWENTY-EIGHT

The following afternoon Philpott called an informal meeting in the living room at the cabin. Mike, Sabrina and Ram were present. Business was on the agenda but the atmosphere was informal. There were platefuls of Indian finger-food and a jug of chilled white wine.

'Much sifting, sorting and tidying has taken place,' Philpott announced from his armchair. 'I have spent the better part of a sleepless night and all of this morning collating the data that's come to hand. If there are gaps or omissions I'm sorry. I must plead weariness.' He made a little smile. 'I'm weary but content. I have to say I'm pleased.'

'There'll be a blue moon tonight,' Mike muttered.

Philpott asked him how his shoulder felt. Mike had been bandaged and stitched at the general hospital in Srinagar.

'It's sore, but it's a wound I'll wear with a touch of pride.'

'Well said.' Philpott sipped his wine and squared the notes on his knees. 'Information time. First, Dr Arberry is at police HQ in Srinagar. Commissioner Mantur tells me he is still uncommunicative. The shock of seeing his employees and his business empire wiped out in the space of minutes has unhinged certain of his brain's moving parts, I fear. But I'm sure he'll recover in time to face the charges against him.

'Meanwhile, the response to our transmission of Dr Arberry's fingerprints has produced a voluminous history. He turns out to be a misanthropic, hugely materialistic scoundrel with a well-cloaked history of pharmaceutical villainy.'

'Is he a real pharmacologist?' Sabrina said.

'Yes, he is. With more aliases than some people have teeth. He has great skill at playing the likeable benefactor, usually a

212

wistfully brave widower, although he never married. That talent rises from the same pit of ingenuity which told him Kashmir would grow lucrative drug-producing plants, as well as providing access to a well-heeled customer base.'

'And there was even a ready-made supply of peasant mules,' Mike said, 'with a heart-warming capacity for fear.'

'This was Arberry's biggest scam to date,' Philpott said. 'I think we can assume it was his last. The important thing is, it's all over.' Philpott took another sip of wine and held up a fax sheet. 'From Harry Lewis at WHO. A note to tell me that the late Reverend Alex Young's sister is now in New York City to sort out his affairs with his diocesan administrators. She has told Harry that she recalls she was here in Kashmir when Arberry asked her brother to send an appeal to the UN. Arberry said it might appear like some kind of elitist pleading if a man in his position were to send the letter himself.'

Ram asked if Young's sister knew that Arberry was being charged with her brother's murder.

'She will,' Philpott said. 'And now, there is one final piece of excellent news. Agent Amrit Datta of Drugwatch International yesterday kept a rendezvous on the Chinese border. He supplied high-grade drugs to three bulk purchasers from Thailand.'

'I knew that guy was the right stuff,' Mike said.

'The buyers were each arrested as they took possession of their consignment. Agent Datta has been slated for a commendation, and he should be back amongst us tonight in time for a celebratory noggin before we leave for the States.'

'So have we managed to make the authorities happy, too?' Sabrina said.

'With Amrit Datta's help,' Philpott said. 'The revelation that an American interloper was behind the new trade in drugs has soothed the Pakistani authorities, who are delighted to learn that no blame attaches to them or their people. India is relieved to have something so ghastly uprooted from the Vale of Kashmir, and the Thai police are delighted that three big-time drug peddlers have been delivered to them on a plate.'

Philpott put aside his glass and his notes. He rose, went to the kitchen, and returned with a tray of filled champagne glasses. He distributed them and took one himself.

'A toast,' he said. 'To the triumph of style and cool common sense over old-maidish philistinism.'

Mike, Ram and Sabrina looked at each other.

'You're going to have to explain that one, chief,' Mike said.

'I managed to score a triumph in New York without even being there,' Philpott said. 'Whitlock reports that our battle with Policy Control ended in victory for UNACO. There will be no changes in the way our show is run.'

'Brilliant!' Sabrina said.

'Isn't it, though? Secretary Crane of Policy Control has offered his resignation and Director Lubbock is asking to be reassigned. Full details when we get back.' Philpott raised his glass. 'To success – and to C. W. Whitlock, who scored this particular goal.'

'Success and C. W.!'

They emptied their glasses. Sabrina looked enquiringly at Philpott. He nodded towards the kitchen. She went through and came back with a fresh chilled bottle.

'Quite a catalogue of wins for you,' she said, pouring the boss more champagne. 'Has it something to do with the way you surround yourself with reliable people?'

Philpott looked at her resentfully. But he couldn't hold the look. He gave way and smiled. 'I suppose it has everything to do with that,' he said, 'although I'll never admit it when I'm sober.'